Advance Praise for *The Burden of Sparrows*

The Burden of Sparrows will pull you in and keep you turning pages. You'll feel a range of emotions and care deeply about the characters. If you loved *Where the Crawdads Sing*, this book is for you!"
— Mandy Remai, Seasons of Life Therapy

As someone who is rooted in the natural world, I really enjoyed reading about Buddy's adventures and quiet observations of the garden and woods. Despite all the distractions and craziness that life can throw at us, nature remains a constant source of comfort and inspiration. It provides a space to celebrate the joys of spring and the awakening of the garden, as well as a place to seek solitude and process the day's events. This book reminded me to be kind to myself and to stay open to change and healing, no matter how challenging it may be. Finding a community of loved ones and friends to share that journey with will only add to the beauty of life.
— Renee Penny, conservation specialist, Kalkaska Conservation District

The Burden of Sparrows is simultaneously literary and homespun. Buddy's humble journey is that of the classic Hero; how he confronts his past and his own fears gives readers an opportunity to realize that growth is possible at any stage of life. Healing comes in unexpected ways and forms; lovers can be young or old; a man can be good despite a broken childhood. This is a book about love, both its presence and the effects of its absence. I encourage you to open up your heart when you open these pages.
— Scott J. Couturier, author of *The Box* and *I Awaken In October: Poems of Folk Horror and Halloween*

The Burden of Sparrows

Readers are encouraged to go to www.MissionPointPress.com to contact the author or to find information on how to buy this book in bulk at a discounted rate.

Published by Mission Point Press
2554 Chandler Rd.
Traverse City, MI 49696
(231) 421-9513
www.MissionPointPress.com

Design by Sarah Meiers

ISBN: 978-1-961302-42-6
Library of Congress Control Number: 2024904066

Printed in the United States of America

the Burden
of Sparrows

DEBRA PAYNE

MISSION POINT PRESS

Chapter 1

A Boy Named Ben

Snow crunched under his feet. It was still winter, but he could see glimpses of spring in the way sunrise occurred a tad earlier each day, peeking over the horizon through the forest. He could sense the thawing, but welcomed the crisp air as he performed his annual ritual.

A chickadee scolded him as a plane flew overhead in the distance, on its way to the airport in Traverse City. His knuckles were a little sore from setting the taps, but he was otherwise comfortable in his coveralls. In fact, he was starting to work up a little perspiration from his hat. He took it off and stuffed it into a back pocket. He was trying to get the taps set before work. He pulled a sled loaded with a drill, hammer, buckets, lids, and spiles (or taps), inspecting each sugar maple for the best spots to draw sap. The weather was finally starting to cooperate, inching above freezing during the day and staying cold at night. Timing was everything in maple syrup production.

He followed the tree line methodically and purposefully, so focused on his task that he wasn't sure he realized the first time Mags called him. Her raspy voice finally drew him from his reverie, and he looked toward the house. She was on the front porch, gesturing for him to head that way. He raised his arm in acknowledgment and began walking toward her, though he couldn't resist a backward glance at the perfect sight — aluminum buckets attached to his prized trees. He heard sap dripping into those buckets, the same containers he'd used since he could remember.

Mags was always impatient. She stood on the porch in her bathrobe, her long hair streaked with gray. Her robe didn't quite close around her girth; her face was ruddy, but her eyes were the same clear blue he remembered from the first time they met. As he started up the steps, he smelled the bacon she was frying. He was hungry.

"Mac, she just called your phone and wanted to know if you'd pick her up on your way to school."

"You mean Jenna?" he asked, though he knew.

"Yeah." Mags shrugged. "Their car is probably not workin' again." How yellow her teeth were in the morning light.

"If you leave me out some of that bacon, I'll clean up and head into town."

She nodded, and he followed her past the clutter on the porch. Once they were inside, she said, "Mac, you have to do something about that bathroom one of these days."

He felt the old, familiar mix of regret and resentment at her reminder. "But not today," he replied.

"Yeah, not today and not tomorrow, neither," she muttered.

Mags and he were about as close as two people could be, but she got on his nerves at times. Buddy (or Mac, as she called him) and Mags had been together for over three decades. They met while working at one of the cherry production facilities near Elk Rapids, he noticing her the first week of that season. She walked around like she owned the place, but she had a friendly nature and people seemed to like her. Her hair was long then, too, though she kept it up in a net. He walked outside one day to find her sitting at the workers' picnic table, and sat down himself to eat lunch. He wasn't in the mood for small talk, but he warmed to it as he ate his hard-boiled eggs. The big topic at the table was how to make perfect no-bake cookies. An elderly woman named Eleanor promised everyone her recipe was no-fail, and that she'd bring both a batch and the recipe to prove it. One of the kids at the table said he didn't know what no-bake cookies were, and the older folks groaned. As the group thinned out, Buddy and Mags ended up being the only ones left. It seemed like the thing to do to introduce himself.

"I'm Buddy," he'd said. "But you can call me Mac."

He liked her deep chuckle; that was the first time he heard it. She'd tried unsuccessfully to wave her cigarette smoke away as she said, "Think I will!"

By the end of that summer, she and her kids were living with him. Long time ago now. He wasn't drawn to Mags because of her looks; it was more the way they understood each other. He didn't have a lot to offer in the looks department himself. His shoulders were rounded, and an unfortunate cowlick grew from the top of his head to the back of his skull, which he'd long forsaken trying to cover up. His teeth plagued him. He wasn't looking for a companion when he met Mags, but he sensed she wouldn't ask much of him. Her kids, Lukas and Lennie, were good boys, aged four and two when they moved in. Luke now had three kids, and Lennie lived alone. Buddy still considered them kids, but they were now nearer to 40 than he'd ever be again.

He grabbed the wrench they used to urge a trickle of water from the bathroom sink faucet. Buddy gave himself a sponge bath, then put on his work clothes from the day before. He usually threw them over a hanger and left them dangling on the shower curtain bar. He had five work uniforms, provided annually by the school. They didn't own a washer or dryer, and Mags didn't like to drive, so trips to the laundromat were infrequent at best. Sometimes he washed clothes in the kitchen sink.

The wrench clattered to the floor as one of the cats, Caesar, heard the water trickling and made his presence known at Buddy's elbow.

"Damn animals," he muttered, but he really didn't mind them. They kept Mags company while he was working or outside. He allowed the cat to lap at the spigot, then retrieved the wrench to stop the water. He really did need to buy a new faucet, but that wasn't what Mags meant when she nagged him about the bathroom. The tub hadn't worked for a few years, and he had started to rip it out when he'd noticed mold behind the surround. The plaster was rotten. Now they used the tub as a hamper for dirty clothes; it was never empty. He told himself they couldn't afford to get it fixed, and he wasn't going to expose the mold any more than he already had, so he put particleboard along the wall until he could take care of it. There was always something else that needed attention. It made him tired every time he thought of the constant deterioration of the house. *Much more peaceful in the woods. There, nature takes care of itself.*

Ready to go, he found the bacon laid out flat on a paper towel in the kitchen, so he made himself a toasted sandwich and stood at the counter to eat it. He'd swing by Jenna's on the way to work and still be a half hour early, so he would have time to pick up his paycheck and get it cashed. He sat on the stack of boxes by the front door to get his work boots on, then let himself out without saying goodbye. Mags was absorbed in her morning shows anyway.

As he put his keys into the truck's ignition, he listened for the familiar whine and let it register that one more thing needed adding to his list of things to fix, but not today.

Buddy found Jenna waiting outside the door of her trailer,

smoking. He hated to see that, but she knew he disapproved and did it anyway. Her mom didn't care, and her mom's boyfriend was probably not going to be around for long, as none of those guys were. So who was Buddy to say anything? At least Mags gave it up years ago.

Jenna stomped her cigarette into the snow and threw her backpack between them in the seat. He could smell her soap brand alongside the tobacco. Jenna was a tiny girl, only 17, but she had enough attitude to make up for her slight build. Buddy watched her grow up while working with her mother June, whom diabetes eventually forced to go on disability.

"Car on the fritz again?" he asked, and she nodded.

"How's the syrup gonna be this year?"

"If the weather cooperates, it should be alright," he said. "I tapped quite a few trees this morning."

"Yeah, Mags mentioned you were out there. I was going to stay home today because I worked late last night, but I really can't miss any more days if I want to graduate, and I want to get out of that hell hole," Jenna said. It was no secret she hated school.

"You're getting close," he said. "And if you don't want to work at Big Boy the rest of your life, you need a diploma and college."

"I'm gonna marry a rich guy," Jenna said, laughing. As she did, she put her hands on the dashboard vent. "And he's gonna have a heater that works."

"Dream on."

They rode in companionable silence until Buddy swung into the high school parking lot. Then Jenna sighed.

"You got a way home?"

"Yeah, I'll be okay. Thanks. I'll walk to the restaurant and one of the girls from work can get me home."

"Alright," he said as she slammed the truck door and took off, giving him a slight wave. *The girl needs a warmer jacket,* he thought, but here it was the end of winter and she'd made it this far.

Buddy headed to the maintenance barn behind the high school, intending to pick up his bi-weekly check. He still preferred a real check over direct deposit. The payroll gal in central office had given up on him changing his ways. He owned a cell phone only because he didn't have a land line at the house and needed a phone for work. He and Mags each had one, but he was always leaving his in the house when he went outside, or leaving it home when he was at work. He detested the thing.

Buddy's day started after the kids were already at school, since he stayed afterward to clean up. The other custodial and maintenance staff opened the buildings and did any necessary shoveling of walks before school. Buddy worked in the upper elementary building, and his first task was to set up for lunch. Tables needed to be pulled down from the walls, and he always helped the cafeteria ladies move the salad cart to the center of the room that also served as the school gym. The room always smelled weird, a strange mixture of chicken nuggets and sweat. His custodial room was right next door, and this was where he kept his mop bucket, supplies, vacuum, and cart. Once he got the lunch room ready for another day, he headed to the adjacent administrative office to empty trash, clean the bathrooms, mop, and vacuum if needed.

Since Buddy had more than 27 years with the schools, he had witnessed the arrivals and departures of several school superintendents. They rarely acknowledged Buddy, and the new guy was no exception. The only time he addressed Buddy was to complain. Once he'd advised Buddy to come into his office. He closed the door behind them and pointed out a cobweb at the bottom interior of the door, between the casing and the wall. "You really need to pay more attention to things like this," he'd said. Buddy used his foot to wipe away the cobweb. It wasn't worth saying that he would never look behind the door because that would mean he'd have to close it behind him, and he didn't want to be accused of snooping.

Today the boss's door was shut. This meant Buddy had to ask his secretary if she thought he should skip the trash or if he should retrieve it.

"I emptied his into mine already," she said before he could ask. She was on the phone, so he just nodded.

Buddy used a tennis ball, which he'd punctured and forced onto the end of his broom, to erase scuff marks from the hallway floor tiles. The office was fairly clean today, so he'd get out of there in plenty of time to check a few classrooms while the kids were still having lunch. He liked days where he wasn't hurried. He had time to joke with the kids a little in the hallway. Every year he found a few who were friendly to him. He liked this age of kids — old enough to take care of themselves but still young enough to be conscientious. Middle school kids were a whole different animal.

"Hey, Mr. Robertson," Adam Rodriguez said as Buddy shoved his cart down the east wing. "How's it going?"

"Pretty good," Buddy said. "Another beautiful day in paradise."

"Oh, that's what we call it?" Macy Pierce asked. She was a young teacher who stayed at work late most of the time. Adam was walking with her, helping carry art supplies to her room; the class was working on a project, the kids painting on poster boards. Buddy was going to ask if they needed some help, but a sudden noise caused him to turn his head.

Muffled crying in the boys' bathroom. Macy looked toward the sound, then toward him, and he left his cart to see what was happening. He knew to knock first and prop the door open, so he wouldn't be in the closed kids' bathroom alone with a student. The sound became muted, but it was coming from one of the stalls.

"You okay in there?" he asked. "It's Mr. Robertson." He heard toilet paper being unrolled from the spool and some gulping noises.

"Yeah," a voice said.

"You sick?" Buddy persisted.

"Nope. I'm fine." With that, the stall door opened and Ben Jameson stepped out. Buddy could see he'd been crying, and as usual his hair was disheveled and his glasses were filthy. He walked slowly out of the stall and started to leave the lavatory, and Buddy found himself saying what every adult says to a kid leaving the bathroom: "Wash your hands."

Ben kept walking, and Buddy peeked into the stall, seeing that the toilet had blood in it. The toilet paper Ben had used was stained with red, the water showing a dark pink in the bowl. Buddy closed the stall door, went to his cart, and grabbed a piece of scrap paper from his recycling box. He wrote "Out of Order" on the paper and stuck it on the lavatory door with a piece of painter's tape. As he turned, he noticed a utility knife on the floor, the razor blade exposed. He bent to pick it up, noted blood on it and the floor, and thought better of it.

His hands were shaking. He went to advise the principal, Blair Hopkins, of what was in the boys' bathroom. Macy Pierce stood outside her classroom, waiting to see what had happened, but he didn't say anything to her, taking the opposite direction to reach the school office.

Of course Mr. Hopkins was also in a meeting, probably with

the superintendent at the other end of the building. Buddy asked Samantha, the secretary, if she had a minute.

"What's up?" she asked.

"Well, I don't know, but I think Ben Jameson has something wrong with him," Buddy said. "I just found blood in the toilet after I heard him crying in there, and there's a razor on the floor. You might want to come take a look."

Samantha gasped and got up to follow him. She never walked anywhere, but pretty much jogged, as she was always tending to this kid or that parent or another teacher and had no time to dilly-dally. Buddy lagged behind as she entered the bathroom. She only took a moment to check the stall.

"I think Mr. Hopkins needs to see this and talk to Ben," she said. "Thanks, Buddy."

"Sure," he said. A few moments later Blair Hopkins stepped into the restroom. Next, Buddy saw Ben being taken into the principal's office.

Buddy went on with his day. A kid puked, so he had to clean that up, and he ran out of trash bags like he did about every other day, meaning he had to listen to the custodial manager whine about how many consumables the buildings were using. All Buddy wanted to do was get home, go outside, and watch the way the blue snow and sky turned to lavender as the sun started to set. It wouldn't yet be dark if he got out of work on time. He wanted to be in the woods, where the sap was running. He wanted to smell spring coming like it did every year, without fail.

Life was funny. Crap happened, and sometimes you didn't think you'd recover from it, but then another crappy thing happened to take your mind off the last thing. This was pretty much Buddy's philosophy of human existence. Some things were better left in the past.

Buddy tried to forget bad things. He had gotten pretty good

at it through the years, and now, past the age of 60, he figured he could coast without being scathed by anything but dying. Death wasn't so scary. He had managed to keep a job for over a quarter of a century. It wasn't a great job, but he knew from the time he was a kid that he wasn't going to be blessed with greatness. He only wanted to be blessed with the absence of trauma. Childhood was traumatic enough.

Damn James Shearing for that. He hoped he was long dead, and that his death was a nightmarish, drawn-out, painful one. James Shearing robbed the Earth of oxygen for no good reason.

At the end of the school day, Buddy squeezed his cart into his small storage room and headed for home. No one said anything to him about Ben. He was just the school custodian, after all.

Buddy didn't usually need an alarm to rouse him from sleep, especially with sap running outside. This morning, one of the cats was sleeping on his chest. Buster was the alpha cat of the house, and he set his claim on Buddy from his first day there. Buddy grudgingly accepted the cat's affection.

"Hello, Buster," he said. The cat was unmoved by his greeting. Buddy stared into the animal's half-lidded eyes for a few seconds, then let his own eyes wander around the bedroom. The closet door was open, clothing both hanging up and lying on the floor. Buddy couldn't remember the last time he'd taken anything out of that closet. An old painting of a whitetail buck hung on the wall near his side of the bed. Mags was already up, or maybe she hadn't come to bed again. On her bedside table was an empty glass, her latest collection of paperback mystery novels, and a statue of a black bear. Buddy started to take his covers off, pissing off the cat, but Buster didn't move until Buddy began to sit up, finally huffing away into the kitchen. Buddy quickly reached for his pants, as the wood stove needed to be filled again and the house was more than chilly. He stepped into the slippers Mags gave him for Christmas last year. He didn't think he would wear slippers, but he found them useful.

He'd gotten to sleep last night after tossing and turning for a bit. He wondered what was going to happen with that kid from school. Well, it wasn't up to him, he told himself. Let the authorities deal with it.

Buddy poured himself some of the famously awful coffee that Mags made, and it met his expectations. He fished cream out of the fridge and stirred it in with a fork, since there weren't any clean spoons. Just then Mags came in with a few wedges of wood, and he took them from her, starting to load the stove.

"Good thing we still have lots of wood left," Mags said. "It should last us enough to get into next year."

"That was what I thought, too," he said. "It was good having Lennie here to help split it and stack it last fall."

"Well, he was out of work, so he could do that," Mags said. "I hope he isn't out of work this year."

Lennie was a construction worker, but he was always mouthing off and leaving job sites. He bragged that he never got fired because he was good at his job, though he didn't usually stay at the same place for too long. It seemed to Buddy that he'd run out of places to work. However, foremen always took him back.

"If he kept his mouth shut, he could work wherever he wanted," Buddy muttered. "That's too hard for some folks."

Mags shrugged. "There are lots of idiots out there," she said. "Lennie is smart."

"Smart-*ass*," Buddy said.

"Don't start," Mags warned.

"Wouldn't think of it," he said. He took another sip of the godawful coffee, watching as Mags took off her coat and threw it on a wall peg before heading toward the couch. Her morning always started with the game show network. Buddy couldn't stand that station. He might be able to tap more trees today and actually finish, in spite of the snowflakes coming down. The downy woodpecker was at the suet ball, pecking the hell out of it before the rest of the birds swarmed in.

Buddy got suet from one of the local farmers in exchange for maple syrup. Buddy and Mags used to have a few farm animals, but when Mags started refusing to help with them he gave them away. Mags really didn't like to go outside, and she didn't like moving around too much. Sad, because when he first met her at the cherry plant she was a good worker and liked being outdoors with him. Her back started bothering her, though, and she hated doctors as much as Buddy did, so she endured the pain. She pretty much stayed in the house, which she also stopped any attempt to clean once she quit working. With seven cats, hair was everywhere. Caesar, Buster, Rooney, Ned, Sparty, and Cheech and Chong had reign over the entire place. Mags didn't want them to go outdoors after her all-time favorite cat, Dude, made it back to the porch one night with his ear gone and his stomach punctured by a coyote bite. He died in her arms.

She didn't get out of bed for days after, and Buddy was helpless to assist her. He liked Dude, too. Yet he had to go to work. And he still went outside, where the woods gave solace.

Mags was talking to the game contestant on TV, goading him to give the right answer. When the time expired, she threw up her hands and rolled her eyes. "Pack your suitcase, you're gone," she said.

Buddy slipped outside. The birds were starting to get noisier, beginning their seasonal courtship rituals. Spring birdsong always reminded him of Grandpa. Birds were loudest in the spring, unabashedly calling for mates; Buddy noted the calls of each bird, wondering when the first red-winged blackbird would trill from the cattails at the end of the driveway. Soon, he estimated. He headed toward the trees, savoring a few spare minutes before the drive to school.

"Fire drill at 1:40," Samantha said as Buddy passed her in the hallway. The school was required to have a specified number of fire and storm drills, as well as lock-downs. Some were announced to staff and some were not. Buddy always appreciated the warnings from Samantha, as they gave him time to rearrange his schedule. It was frustrating to mop the halls and then have 200 pairs of wet boots track through as soon as you were done. Buddy would concentrate on the walkways and steps instead, which were impossible to keep clean in northern Michigan winters.

As he donned his coveralls, Principal Blair Hopkins poked his head into the custodial room.

"Got a minute?" he asked.

"Sure," Buddy said.

"That incident yesterday with Ben," Blair said, trailing off.

"Yeah?"

"I called the student's doctor's office and they wanted to see him. It seems Ben was cutting himself with that razor you found. We agreed to turn it over to Child Protective Services, who will investigate what's going on."

"That's good," Buddy said. "It should be investigated."

Blair nodded. "I couldn't get him to tell me anything. What did he say to you?"

"I asked him if he was alright. He said yes and left the bathroom. I saw the blood in the toilet, then the utility knife, and thought I should report it."

Blair nodded again. "Yes, that was the right thing to do. I would like you to write a statement so I can give it to the folks looking into it."

"Okay."

"If you need some paper, ask Samantha."

"I'll take care of it," Buddy said.

"Sometimes you wonder how some of these kids learn anything, with everything going on at home," Blair said. Buddy felt awkward and unqualified to make a proper reply.

"That's for sure," he finally said.

Blair tapped twice on the door casing and left. Buddy considered getting some paper now, but he thought better of it and zipped up his outdoor gear. He could at least tackle the north side of the building before the fire alarm sounded.

Outside was starting to smell different. In the winter, Buddy noted to himself, there were hardly any odors. If snow had a smell, it was dry and sharp. Spring smelled like what it was, earth returning to life; a wet scent, something Buddy loved but couldn't describe. He pushed the shovel along the steps leading to the side entrance of the school, breathing in the rich air.

When he got home he'd start pulling the sap buckets. Taking a peek this morning, he was happy to see the buckets from yesterday were filling nicely. He would have a long weekend of boiling the sap, but anticipated it with eagerness. Maybe he could even get Mags to help him watch the boil while he kept the buckets coming into the shack. Maybe, if she wasn't working at the restaurant the entire sugaring season, Jenna could help again.

The snow was letting up, and it was fairly warm. Buddy carried the shovel back into the building. As he was taking his coveralls off, the fire alarm sounded. He decided to leave them on and walk outside with the kids and staff.

He noticed Ben standing in the line of kids. He was obeying the rules of the drill like everyone else, keeping to himself and watching for the cue to return to class.

At the end of the day, Buddy used some old paper from his office for his report on finding Ben in the bathroom. He kept his report short, four brief sentences. Buddy couldn't remember the last time he'd actually had to write something down.

I heard something in the boys' bathroom. Ben Jameson came out of a stall. I found blood in the toilet and a utility knife with blood on it. Ben didn't tell me what happened.

Going to the office, he handed it to Samantha.

Over the next few days, Buddy found himself looking for Ben and noting how apart he was from the other kids. At lunch he sat alone. At gym he stood back and didn't participate. At recess he sat on one of the swings, but kept it still.

Ben reminded Buddy of himself.

Chapter 2

New Kid in Town

1969

Buddy was the new kid at school. His teacher, Mrs. Bell, announced his presence in the morning.

"Buddy is from Pennsylvania," she said, "which is to the east of Ohio. Can you tell us about your family, Buddy?"

"I have a sister in ninth grade, and that's about it," Buddy said.

"What about your parents?" Mrs. Bell asked.

"I have a mom and James — I mean Dad, and we live on Maple Road," Buddy said. He was supposed to call James Shearing "Dad" in public.

"Well, we welcome you here," Mrs. Bell said. "We always have someone from class take the new kids around for a few days. I would like to have Enoch Lewis do that."

Enoch was a big kid with red cheeks. He smiled and nodded at Buddy.

"Now, let's keep working on the story we are reading," Mrs. Bell said. "Buddy, here is your copy of the story."

He took some stapled papers from her. They smelled like they just came off the mimeograph machine, and he always liked that scent. It reminded him of brownies. "We are going to answer some questions about it when we're done reading," Mrs. Bell said as she returned to her desk at the front of the room. "Class, you may read silently for the remainder of the afternoon. If you finish early, you can have some free time while the rest of the class finishes. Then we'll get to the short set of questions."

The story was titled "Sucker." It was about a kid named Pete and his cousin Richard, called Sucker, who lived in the same house. Buddy read it along with everyone else in the class, feeling sorry for the kid named Sucker. Pete, the kid telling the story, told Sucker he could jump off the garage roof with an umbrella without being hurt, but Sucker tried it and got injured. Sucker wanted the attention of Pete so much it was embarrassing; he practically begged Pete to notice him. Pete had a girlfriend, and when she dumped him he got really mean to Sucker. Then Sucker got mean, too. The story ended with Pete realizing how he'd hurt Sucker, but it was too late to fix it. Buddy looked around the room for a few minutes, noting where the pencil sharpener was. It was in the same spot on the wall as his classroom in Pennsylvania. Maybe that was a rule for schools all over the place.

"Mrs. Bell, if we're done, can we play checkers in the back of the room?" someone asked, but Mrs. Bell shook her head.

"It looks like everyone is finished reading," she replied. "We are going to write answers to a few questions about this short story. Turn to the next page in your mimeographs and write answers to these questions. When you are finished, you can go out for recess."

The questions were easy until he got to the last one. It asked if Pete and the kid named Sucker ever made up. Buddy didn't know. He squirmed in his seat as he considered how to answer. He wanted to be a nicer person than the kid in the story, so he answered that they did make up. He walked his paper to the teacher's desk and went outside.

Enoch Lewis and some other kids found him.

"So, what's it like in Pennsylvania?" Enoch asked.

"Well, it's nice there," Buddy said. "There are lots of woods and it's real pretty, and I get to see my grandparents a lot."

"Why'd you move here?" one of the boys asked.

"My dad got a job here," Buddy said.

"Do you want to walk around and we'll show you our school?" Enoch asked.

"Sure."

The boys showed him the cafeteria and the courtyard, the audio/visual equipment room, and the auditorium. At first he felt nice as they asked him questions and pointed out where things were. As they walked, though, they started talking about people Buddy didn't know, about things Buddy didn't share with them, and he found himself feeling weird and strange. A blackness came over him. They were talking about their dads and moms and stuff, and what could he say that wasn't made up because his dad wasn't around and the jerk he had to say was his dad really wasn't, and he could never be friends with these people because he didn't know anything that they knew, and he never would. His dad was gone forever. He was in this strange place, being led around by a bunch of unfamiliar kids. As they turned the corner to head toward the gym, Buddy found himself walking straight ahead by himself.

"Hey, Buddy, where ya headed?" Enoch yelled. "We're going to the gym!"

Buddy kept walking.

"Buddy!" Enoch yelled again.

He kept walking.

"Huh. He's weird," someone said.

Buddy kept walking. After recess he went back to class and

ignored everyone because he didn't have the energy to make any
effort at friendships. Enoch and his friends ignored him, too.

A few days later, Mrs. Bell handed back their answers about
that short story. Buddy read her notes, written in red pencil. He
had messed up on the author's name, calling her *Carson McCu*
because her name was cut off by the mimeograph machine. He
felt dumb for that; her real name was Carson McCullers and
she was some famous writer who had died a few years earlier.
Mrs. Bell did not like his answer about the boys making up.
She had put a question mark beside his answer.

Buddy wondered how many of the kids in class had answered
correctly. He wanted to ask, but kept his mouth shut. If he was
the only one who got it wrong he'd feel even dumber than he
already did.

He took the story home for Anna to read, but shortly after
that James Shearing got worse than ever, and Buddy forgot all
about it.

James Shearing was a machinist. He had lots of tools, and since
their house in Ohio was so small, he kept them on a bench right
in the kitchen. On one corner of the bench was a vise James
Shearing would put things into and squeeze tightly so he could
work on them. Everything near the bench was neatly placed,
wrenches hung on pegs according to size. Buddy and Anna
knew not to touch anything on or near this space.

One night a priest came to their house to chat. He was the
minister where they were going to church, and both Buddy
and Anna liked him. He had round glasses, and his wife was a
tiny lady who wore blue eye shadow and lots of red stuff on her
cheeks. They had four kids who were what Mom called "busy."
Father Parker was an Episcopalian priest; he wore a collar but
wasn't Catholic, so he could get married and have kids. Buddy
and Anna were going to be confirmed in the church, which
meant they had to take classes and learn about God and Jesus.

They didn't mind the classes, and had memorized the names of the books in the Old and New Testaments. James Shearing was always nice in church. He wanted the kids to be confirmed there because it would help them learn how to act better. He said he had never seen two kids less respectful than Buddy and Anna.

In Pennsylvania, James attempted to win over the kids at first. He gave Anna an *Archie* comic book, and bought Buddy a kit of sea monkeys. Buddy had read about sea monkeys, and when he put them in water swore he could see their little faces as they swam in their fish tank. Both thanked James Shearing for the gifts, though they were leery of Mom's boyfriends by then, since none of them ever stuck around longer than a month or so.

The gifts soon stopped, the criticism beginning immediately after they moved to Ohio. Mom made dinner the night the priest visited — meatballs and spaghetti with garlic bread — and James said he didn't want to eat until the game was over. Mom had two plates dished up by then, so she told Buddy and Anna to go ahead and start. This was one of Buddy's favorite meals, and he always used his bread to sop up the sauce.

"What the hell?" James said as he came to the table. "You couldn't wait five minutes?" He glared at Mom, who was tidying up the counter.

"I had theirs dished up already," she said. "I figured you and I could eat when you were ready."

"Kids should know to wait for the man of the house," James said. "I knew that when I was their age."

"It was my fault," Mom said.

"You always take the blame when your kids don't have any manners," he grumbled. Yet he sat and smiled at her when she set down his plate. "It does look good."

"It's Buddy's favorite," Mom said.

"So that makes it alright, not waiting and eating like a little piggy?" James motioned for Anna to pass him the Parmesan shaker. She slid it across the table. He grabbed her hand.

"Then you've got this one," he said, staring at her with his eyes purposely bugged out. "She sleeps with her hands covering her little titties, as if they're the only thing in life worth having."

Anna pulled her hand back and then pushed her plate to the side.

"James!" Mom said.

He chuckled. "I know, she's developing," he said, putting his hands to his chest and fanning them out.

"I'm full," Anna said, starting to stand up.

"You'll sit here until I'm done." It was a statement filled with menace, and Anna sat back down. Buddy watched her while wanting to throw his plate at James, but stayed motionless in his chair, stiff and scared.

Mom set her plate on the table. Buddy thought she might stand up for Anna, but instead she took a seat and picked up her fork. She didn't eat, instead twirling her noodles around with it. Then she put the fork down and picked up her napkin, unfolding and placing it in her lap. From the living room came the sounds of post-game chatter. James's team had lost.

"Pretty good," James said. "Might have some more if Buddy lets me." He winked at Mom. "Eat up, honey," he said.

Mom picked up her fork again. They got through dinner, and the priest arrived. He had a cheerful face, like priests were supposed to, or so Buddy guessed. You couldn't really be grumpy and be a priest.

Tonight the priest was talking to them about what it meant to be confirmed in the church. James Shearing got all puffed up about how he took on the kids as his own, raising them, as he said, "in the way they should go."

"So many parents don't care," Father Parker said. "You are obviously going about things in the proper way."

"I got these kids as part of the package with their mother," James Shearing said. "They're pretty much feral."

Buddy didn't know what that meant, but he knew it wasn't good.

"They seem like fine children to me," Father Parker said.

"Well, we are working on it," James said. "We got married with the commitment to teach these kids respect for their elders."

Father Parker pushed his chair back a little and crossed his ankles. "When did you two get married?" he asked. Buddy waited for a response.

"It's been some time," James said.

"And then you recently moved here," Father Parker said. "A lot of change for young children. I imagine it has been hard for them to adjust."

James snorted. "You gotta head where the work is," he said. "Their mother knows a wife follows her husband wherever he needs to go."

"Well, the Bible does indeed refer to that principle. 'Whither thou goest, I will go,'" Father Parker quoted, nodding. "Marriage requires sacrifice. It is so much more than a piece of paper. Most people take those vows for life, don't think about them much, and just get on with the business of day-to-day, trying to survive. Matter of fact, I'll bet most people don't even know where their marriage licenses are. Do you?"

Buddy was partly frightened and partly thrilled by this question. He held his breath. Anna nudged him under the table.

"Well, ya got me there, Father," James Shearing said. "With our move and everything, I can't say I know where ours is either. Do you know, honey?" He looked at Mom, whose hands were flat on the table. She was watching her fingers. She cleared her throat and glanced at James, then at Father.

"I don't," she stated. "I'm afraid I don't."

Father Parker chuckled. "I'm with you on that," he said.

"If Eliza doesn't know where it is, it could be anywhere." He uncrossed his legs, leaned forward and set his eyes on Buddy, winking at him.

"Young man, you and your sister have been good students in the religion classes," he said. Buddy managed a nod.

Father Parker then moved on to grown-up chatter, though Buddy and Anna stayed at the table. Buddy wanted to say that James Shearing was not their dad and had never married their mom, but knew it would be disastrous. Mom always said people should never sleep together unless they were married. Buddy knew they slept together, so wasn't that a bad thing?

He learned what sleeping together really meant while watching a James Bond movie with his friend Truman.

"Those people are having sex," Truman whispered. Sean Connery was kissing a girl with long dark hair as both of them lay in a bed. The girl was smiling a lot.

"How do you know that?" Buddy asked.

"Oh, my cousin told me," Truman said.

The scene got a lot more interesting with this new knowledge. Buddy stared at the screen and then looked around the darkened theater, wondering if everyone else knew what was going on. All the James Bond movies he'd seen, and he'd never realized why James Bond took pretty girls to bed in every one of them.

It was different when James Bond did it. He was a secret agent. He was supposed to have lots of adventures with naughty girls. Buddy's mom wasn't like those girls in the .007 movies. Was she?

With Father Parker still at the table, Buddy tried to shift his attention to what was being discussed. Now they had moved on to the awful shows on television, like *Laugh-In*. Buddy didn't usually get to watch that, but he liked the guy who looked through the leaves as he spied on people and said, "Very interesting…"

"You kids can go to your rooms now," James Shearing said. "Get your homework finished and then get ready for bed."

As he and Anna walked down the hall, she whispered about what a liar he was. "And she is no better," Anna said. "No wonder they found each other."

"Very *interesting*," Buddy said, and Anna cuffed his head.

"You goofball," she laughed.

In his room, Buddy curled up on his bed with a notepad and pencil. He was going to write to Grandma and Grandpa, telling them what Ohio was like. He wanted to tell them it was horrible, but he didn't want them to think he was a baby. He told them he hoped to visit them soon, how he and Anna had a short ride to school, and that he noticed Ohio had the same types of trees as Pennsylvania, but they weren't stacked up on hills like back home. The roads were straighter, too. He mentioned a big poster at school of Neil Armstrong walking on the moon with the saying "One small step for man — one giant leap for mankind" on it. Buddy told them he missed them and loved them. He folded the letter into thirds, as he'd seen Mom do when she wrote letters, and wondered if they had any envelopes. He put the letter aside and started doodling on the notepad. He knew Anna kept a diary, but that was for girls.

He heard Father Parker's chair scrape across the floor in the kitchen, then Mom and James seeing him to the door. "Good night; thanks for coming!" James said.

The door closed. He could hear muttering, followed by his mother's muffled voice. Buddy recognized her begging tone and found himself holding his breath.

"I'm sure he wasn't," his mother said.

"Bullshit!" James shouted. "He was trying to bait us! That son of a bitch!"

"Oh, James. We are going to be married as soon as we can anyway, so that really doesn't matter," his mother said. "We can go to the courthouse, like you said."

"If you think I'm marrying you and your rotten kids, you're

nuts," he said. "I'd sooner put that pussy kid's hand in my vise than marry you."

"My God," Mom said. "Why would you say that? I came to Ohio with you because you promised to take care of us."

Mom, stop! Buddy wanted to say. *We don't need him!*

"That was before I knew your kids very well," he said. "That girl of yours is evil, and that boy is a queer if I ever saw one."

"I can't believe what you're saying," Mom said. "My kids are good kids. They haven't ever been any trouble to me."

"You have rose-colored glasses on, Bonnie. Always did, always will. If I could take you without your two kids I would. But I hate those children. One day you will see why."

Buddy caught movement out of the corner of his eye and saw that Anna was leaning against his doorway.

"Anna!" he whispered. "What are you doing?"

"If he doesn't shut up, I'm going out there," she said. She had her pajamas on, the ones with tiny daisies on them. Buddy could smell her Noxzema from where he sat on the bed.

"If you won't marry me, I need to go back home," Mom said. "I never wanted to live together in the first place. It was your idea to do this."

"You sure jumped at the chance to have someone take on the job of raising your children," James said. "Don't make me the bad guy."

The telephone rang, and Anna jumped. James came down the hallway before she could move.

"Get to bed, you little slut," he said.

Anna hesitated. For a horrific moment Buddy thought she was going to say something sassy, but she cowered as James passed her, then went into her room and slammed the door. Mom appeared at Buddy's doorway, leaned in and closed his door, gently. She didn't even look at him. Maybe she thought he was asleep. *How could someone sleep in this house?* He realized he still held the letter for his grandparents, but had gotten it all messed up. It was wrinkled into a ball in his fist.

"Don't keep calling here!" James yelled, and Buddy heard the phone slam down. He turned off his bedside lamp and lay down in the semidarkness. An outdoor light was on, and it attracted night visitors. Sometimes Buddy would lie on his side and watch bats flit about, though tonight he stayed flat on his back, looking at nothing.

"I'm going out," James announced. The door slammed, and it went quiet. Buddy let the mangled letter drop to the floor.

The next morning Buddy entered the living room to find Mom curled up on the couch. Eyeing the clock, he realized he and Anna had missed getting up for school.

Mom glanced at him. She looked awful, like she'd been crying all night, and still had on her clothes from yesterday.

"James didn't come home," she said flatly.

"He's mean."

"Not all the time," Mom said. "He is under a lot of pressure with this new job." Mom looked so tiny on the couch. She rubbed her face. "He isn't used to being around kids, either."

"I can tell," Buddy said. "Are we going to school today?"

Mom looked at the clock. "Oh," she said. "I didn't realize it was so late. Go wake up your sister and I'll get you there."

Buddy had to pee, but he wanted to ask Mom something while James wasn't around.

"Are we ever moving back to Pennsylvania, to be near Grandma and Grandpa?"

"I can't go back," she said.

"Why not?" he managed to squeak.

"For reasons that a kid can't understand," she said. "When you grow up, you'll see how things get complicated."

"It doesn't have to be complicated!"

"Buddy! Your dad died on me, leaving me two kids to raise,

and a woman needs a man to love her and help her. I am trying to make a new life here!"

"But it's awful!" he said. "James is awful!"

"Yeah, he is," Anna said from behind him. She shuffled over to the armchair and plopped into it. "Mom, he obviously hates us and he's just gonna get worse. Don't you see?"

"I am not having this discussion with my children," Mom said. "Everyone tells me what to do all the time — at work, in Pennsylvania, at home — and I won't have my kids doing it, too! Now, get ready for school!"

Anna had to get her last words in. "Mom, maybe *we* are the ones you *should* listen to." She huffed into her room and started slamming dresser drawers. "I'm getting ready!" she shouted.

On the way to school Mom's car stalled, and a man stopped and poured water into the radiator. He told her she'd need to get it fixed, but it would get her as far as school and her job at the grocery store. This was in 1969, but Mom's car was a 1956, with a passenger door that didn't work and lots of rust.

"My nerves can't take any more," she said.

James came back that evening; he at least knew how to fix Mom's car. He said he'd slept at the shop the night before. Mom cried and begged him not to do that again. Later, Buddy heard noises coming from their bedroom. He sat up, stood, and tiptoed toward the sounds. Looking in, he saw his mom rolling around naked on the bed. Her nipples looked like raisins. James knelt behind her, his bare hips moving back and forth.

He tried not to make any sound as he turned and went back to bed. Hatred roiling in his chest, Buddy covered his head with his pillow. He hated not only James Shearing, but his mother. A poison heat raced through him, and he threw off his covers, then tossed his pillow onto the floor. He stiffened his body and put his hands behind his head, then reached to grab the bedposts and squeeze them with all his might. When he woke up the next morning, he felt sore and cold.

"Do you want a boyfriend?" he asked Anna a few days later. She turned her face to him and looked surprised.

"No. Why are you asking me that?"

"Just wondering. It seems like when girls get boyfriends, they get stupid." He was holding his pencil and trying to finish his vocabulary words. Anna sat beside him at the table, working on her essay for social studies.

"Some do," she said. "Guess I want to concentrate on school first, and then worry about romance later."

"You are smarter than lots of other girls, Anna," he said. "I don't think I want a girlfriend right away, either."

"Then you are smarter than lots of other boys," she said.

"Do you know about sex?" he asked.

"Where do you get this stuff?" she replied through a laugh. "Jeepers, Buddy!"

"Well, I know about it, and I just wondered what you think."

Anna got a funny look on her face, and she didn't answer him for a time.

"I know more than I should," she said at last. "And what I know, I hate." Anna stood up and headed toward the kitchen. "Now, get busy on your homework. I don't want to listen to that jerk yelling at us."

"Okay," he said.

"I thought I'd make some goulash for supper tonight," she

called out while opening the refrigerator. Anna almost always cooked dinner, as Mom and James didn't get home until after six; she was a pretty good cook, but burnt the meat sometimes. Buddy always felt scared for her when she did that, because James yelled.

"Sounds good," he said. "Do you need me to help watch the meat?"

"Ha ha! If it burns, I'm blaming you!"

"Then I'm definitely watching it," he said. "You might want to put the burner where it says L-O."

"Oh, don't worry. Even if I don't burn the meat he'll find something to complain about."

"That is something we can always count on," Buddy said. Writing down his last vocabulary word, it struck him as funny that the word was *dependable*. He finished writing the definition, closed his book, and placed his pencil on the little indentation in the binding. "He's very dependable that way," he said.

Anna peeked around the kitchen door. "A dependable asshole," she said. "I like that."

Chapter 3

A Girl Named Carrie

Buddy poured the sap into buckets for the lengthy process of making syrup. He faced a long weekend. So why was James Shearing on his mind so much lately — James Shearing, whom he'd tucked away years ago? He had promised himself he wouldn't let that sorry excuse for a man rent any more space in his head.

"Mac!" Mags lugged herself over to the sugar shack. "Can you grab me one of those old chairs to sit on while I babysit this sap?" She pointed to the wooden seat by the porch. "I brought me a blanket, and the heat from the fire should keep me warm."

"Just give me two minutes to get this batch poured," Buddy said. He turned to glance at Mags, and failed to stifle a laugh. She was wearing one of the boys' old stocking hats, with a red barn jacket she couldn't zip up and a pair of leggings, striped knee-socks peeking over her boots.

"What?" she asked.

"I'd say you're kidnap-proof," he said.

"Ya think?" She stuck her tongue out at him. "Hey, don't knock free labor."

"I don't think I'll overwork you," he said. "And I know you'll be safe if any creepers come around looking for someone to take."

"Hardy-har-har," she said. "Just get me the damn chair."

"Okay." He gave the pot of sap a stir and handed her the long spoon. She motioned like she was going to hit him with it, but then pulled it back.

Buddy was dragging a chair over when Jenna showed up. She had the weekend off, and said she was happy to help with the syrup. As she closed the car door another opened, and a girl about Jenna's age got out of the passenger's side. She grabbed some gloves and a hat from behind her as Jenna hollered, "I brought more help!"

The girl with her smiled as they approached. Jenna said, "This is Carrie, and she has some experience with making syrup."

"Hi," Carrie said. "Hope it's okay if I help."

"Sure," Mags piped up. "The more the merrier. Good you got that car fixed!"

Buddy went to grab a few more chairs, as he was sure the girls would spend a good bit of time talking to Mags. She had that way about her; Mags loved to talk, and didn't do it enough anymore. He wouldn't mind the chatter so long as it didn't slow them down, and he trusted Jenna to keep things moving. The girl was a worker, something she'd proven over the past several seasons.

"I helped my dad with maple syrup when we had a farm downstate," Carrie said. "We put up a lot of it."

"You don't have the farm anymore?" Mags asked.

"Nope. My dad lost it," Carrie said. "I don't live with him anymore. I miss being on a farm."

Buddy started to lift another bucket from the strainer, and sure enough, Jenna was at his side to help. She held the bin below the strainer so Buddy could pour the filtered sap into her bucket easily. Jenna lifted the bucket herself after they were finished and placed it on a burner. He knew he could count on her to follow through with the entire process.

Carrie approached the burners, grinning as she took a deep breath through her nose.

"Ah…I remember that smell," she remarked, and closing her eyes she smiled. There was something about her that struck Buddy at that moment; he couldn't quite put his finger on it, but he felt a strange, unbidden awakening. Carrie was a pretty girl. She had honey-colored hair and hazel eyes, and her lips were naturally dark pink and full. *She has a knowing way about her,* Buddy thought. He suddenly felt like he was staring at her, and turned the other way. He was embarrassed for some reason, like he'd shown a part of himself that should be kept concealed. He hadn't felt that way for a long time.

He didn't say anything as he grabbed his sled and headed back out toward the trees. They wouldn't think anything of it. He was only going back to get more sap. No one would realize that he felt disoriented and strange. He walked the path he'd walked hundreds of times on his property, yet somehow he felt lost. Carrie reminded him of someone. As he pulled a bucket from its place on a tree, he realized that person was Leah.

Didn't he think about Leah every day, in some small way? He supposed he did. But it was a distant memory, and he always told himself he was over it. He was just a dumb kid when he met her, and everyone knows when you're a kid, your feelings are uncontrollable and magical nonsense. Yet, sometimes when he walked in the woods in spring he'd see a fern emerging from the forest in its fiddlehead shape and remember how she loved the way they looked as they unfurled. She wanted to go to school to study plants, she'd said. She loved being in the woods as much as he did.

Well, maybe she did that. He hoped she did that. He left long ago, coming to northern Michigan so he could learn how to breathe again. At first, just taking in air seemed like such an effort. It was all he felt capable of, although he had to find a job and go through the motions of life. What did he think was going to happen? Did he think they'd live happily ever after — her, so beautiful and exquisite, and him, just Buddy? The kid nobody thought would amount to much?

He leaned against one of the trees and tried to collect himself. His love for Leah might have been back in the Middle Ages for all it mattered now. He noticed how his hands were chapped, his nails dirty from scuffing his fingers along the bark and getting them sticky with sap. He never cared much about how he looked, but for a time he believed that Leah saw something in him. Sometimes you believe what you want to. He pulled another bucket from a tree and exchanged it with an empty one. Sap was really running; he would be back here trading out buckets again later. He might need more bottles. He'd better keep moving along.

"Gotta strike while the iron is hot," James Shearing always said as he stood in the kitchen near his workbench. Now Buddy knew what that meant. Seasons changed, and sap only ran for a short time — and time kept on marching. He tugged his sled forward.

Carrie did know about making syrup, and once she familiarized herself with Buddy's setup she and Jenna worked well together. Mags seemed to be enjoying their company. Buddy found himself amused by their laughter as he went back and forth with the various tasks of sugaring. He tried not to look Carrie's way very often.

"You springing for pizza?" Mags asked, as the sun cast long shadows along the tree line. Buddy's back was starting to stiffen, and he leaned backward to stretch.

"I suppose I could do that," he said. "You girls interested?"

Carrie and Jenna exchanged a glance, and shrugged at each other. "Or do you have plans?"

"Nah, not until later," Carrie answered. "I could eat pizza."

"I can always eat pizza," Jenna said. "I'll go pick it up if you want."

"I'll buy if you fly," Buddy said. "Deal?"

"Deal," she said.

"Call it in, Mags," he said. "Whatever you want on it is fine with me. Just no little fish."

"Got it," Mags said. She called in their order and announced it would be ready in a half hour.

"Can I go wash up?" Carrie asked, and Buddy nodded, though he was embarrassed for her to see the interior of their house. She'd have to go inside to eat anyway, he realized, and then he wondered where they would all sit. Their tabletop had long been overtaken by piles of stuff. Nothing could be done about it now. He gestured toward Jenna.

"Can you show her the way to the palace, and tell her how to work the sink?"

She nodded. "Yup. They have creative plumbing."

Mags laughed. "Creative plumbing, and creative housekeeping too," she said. "But make yourself at home."

"Won't be anything I haven't seen before," Carrie said. "I've lived in a lot of creative situations with my mom and half-brother. One summer we lived in a tent — only summer didn't end for us that year until late October."

"Where was that?" Mags asked. "When you were in Missouri?"

Carrie swung her hair away from her eyes, and Buddy again felt disoriented. She brushed her face with the sleeve of her coat, trying to keep her sticky hands from touching her skin. He purposely moved his eyes from her to Mags, who was folding her blanket. Her cheeks were pink from being outside. So were Carrie's.

"No, when we were in Wisconsin," Carrie said. "Much colder than Missouri."

"I'd say so," Buddy remarked.

Jenna took the blanket from Mags and held out her arm to help Mags stand up. "Whew, I sat too long in one spot," Mags said. "Just gimme a minute and let me get my legs awake."

Buddy moved toward her. "You girls go on inside, and I'll tend to Mags," he said. "By the time you get finished cleaning up the pizza will be ready, and my stomach is growling."

The girls headed toward the house as he took Mags by the elbow.

"Did you make good progress today?" Mags asked.

"Sure did. Those girls were a huge help."

"It seemed like it. Wish I could help out more," Mags said, then she lowered her voice. "That girl has been through a lot of crap. I only heard a little tip of the iceberg. No good can come from having a kid see what she's seen." Mags slowly turned toward the house. "No good at all."

"All I heard was laughing," Buddy said.

"That's how she copes with it all," Mags said. "That is her way of dealing with it."

"Is that your expert opinion?"

"Nope. Just experience," she said. She wasn't smiling. Buddy directed her past the chairs, glancing behind him to make sure everything would be okay until he got something in his stomach. Yes, things would keep.

Buddy stood outside the north entry of the school, spreading rock salt on the landing. A strung-out bearded man and an equally disheveled woman marched along the walkway, and Buddy could tell the guy was primed for a fight. The man flung a cigarette over the snowbank; as he passed, Buddy smelled the unmistakable reek of alcohol, tobacco, woodsmoke, and body odor. He recognized it, and it repulsed him.

"Where's the office at?" the woman asked.

"Just inside the door, to your right," Buddy said. He had no time to warn Samantha. They entered the building.

Buddy emptied the coffee can of salt and stepped inside. He set the can in the bin marked *WINTER*, then decided to sweep around the area. He convinced himself he wasn't being nosy, as a gut feeling told him to stay near.

"You'd best get him right now," the man said. "I want to know who the hell he thinks he is, and I ain't leavin' until I see him."

"Have a seat in the hall, and I'll go find him," Samantha said. She followed them out and glanced at Buddy. "Could you just stay close and watch the office while I'm gone?" she asked, and Buddy nodded. Samantha headed toward the south wing of the building. "I'll be right back," she said.

"She better be," the man said under his breath. "This is bullshit."

Evidence of a hard life was on the woman's face. She had a yellow pallor, and her hair was severely tied back in a ponytail. Her eyes betrayed years of lost sleep and lost chances. The man had thick eyebrows and a haughty look in spite of his obvious self-abuse. Buddy knew them. He'd seen their type before. He hated them instantly.

Blair Hopkins came around the corner and introduced himself. "How can I help you?" he asked.

"By keeping your nose out of my fricken' business," the man answered.

"May I get your name?" Blair asked.

"You know who I am," the man responded. "And you got no business talking to anyone about Ben without our permission."

"Well, based on the circumstances, I beg to differ," Blair said. "But I would like to speak with you privately." He ushered the couple into his office, but he left the door ajar. Buddy's feet seemed to be planted. He made a fair attempt to look like he was sweeping. At first he could only hear half of what was being said, but as the conversation got louder he heard clearly.

"I'll sue you and this whole damn district," the man yelled. "And if you don't think I will, you got another think coming!"

"Do what you feel you need to do," Blair said. "This meeting is over. And if you come in here like this again, I'll call the police."

Samantha, now returned to her desk, had her impenetrable face on as she watched the visitors lurch from her space. Buddy grabbed the dustpan and bent to use it, but kept his face to them.

"Assholes," the man muttered. "He ain't coming back to this school once this crap is settled."

Buddy watched them retrace their steps, noting the man never shut up and the woman said nothing. They got into a gold Chevy with a dent on the passenger side and screeched away.

Blair came into the hall, shaking his head and grinning. "Some people have more nerve than sense," he said. "He's apparently upset that he's being investigated."

"I'd say so," Buddy said. "Too bad."

"I'm going to let the police know about his visit and have him notified he's not welcome here," Blair said. "Ben doesn't need that on top of all the stress he's under."

"Do you want me to get them on the line?" Samantha piped up.

"Absolutely," Blair said. "Good thing Ben doesn't have to go home to that."

"Where is he?" Buddy asked.

"He's staying with a good foster family while this is being checked out," Blair said.

"Good," Buddy said. He placed dustpan and broom against the wall and headed to his cart. He was relieved for the kid. It never occurred to Buddy that Ben wasn't abused. Buddy knew what happened. He saw a kid who was doing what he used to do, what he'd done pretty much his whole life. Ben was trying to be invisible.

Later on, Buddy watched Ben in the lunch room. He sat by himself; he had a school lunch, barbeque chicken with mashed potatoes and salad. Ben only stirred things around on his plate, but he did finish his milk. He never looked up, never seemed interested in the shenanigans of the other kids. If he didn't show up tomorrow, no one would miss him. *At least he's staying with a good family,* Buddy thought — and then he wondered who decided which family was good and which wasn't. Was it so easy to tell? Were there actually homes where kids were loved and terrible things didn't happen? Well, he could at least say that his two, or Mags's two, didn't suffer while they were at his place. Was that enough to qualify as a "good" family?

"Mr. Robertson," one of the kids said, "I accidentally dropped my tray." Sure enough, a pile of food lay on the floor, right where the first group of kids would be erupting toward recess in about eight minutes.

"Go get yourself another lunch before it's too late," Buddy said. "I'll grab my stuff to clean up the mess."

"That's why we have janitors," one of the other kids said. "They clean up after us."

Oh, yeah, that's what I do, Buddy thought. He fetched a roll of paper towels and started collecting the slop from the floor. The kids trampled around him as they headed outside, and then it was quiet.

"Can you take care of that for me?" Mags asked from the living room as he came into the house after work.

"Take care of what?" She assumed he knew what she was talking about, which she often did. Buddy felt about ready to tell her he wasn't a mind reader.

"You don't smell that?" Just as she asked, Buddy realized the house didn't just smell like old bacon grease. Unmistakably, he detected the odor of cat shit.

"I do now," he groaned. "Which one did that?"

"I didn't watch it happen," Mags responded. "I only found it afterward with my nose."

Buddy grabbed the roll of paper towels from the counter and made his way into the living room. Mags pointed to the corner by the old turntable. Sure enough, a pool of diarrhea spread over the floor.

"You couldn't take care of that before I got home?"

"My back is killing me today."

"Well, one of the cats is obviously sick. This is disgusting." He gagged as he tried to sop up the worst of the mess. Here he was, in his happy home, scrubbing at something gross. The janitor. "I cleaned up messes all day at work, and now I come home and clean up another one."

"Sucks to be you," Mags said. "I haven't been able to get around at all today. Haven't eaten since breakfast."

"Maybe it's time to see a doctor," he said.

"Why, so they can tell me my back hurts? It even goes down my leg now."

"Maybe they can do something to help."

"Nah. I don't want to start that whole thing. They get you in there, want to run tests, see this doctor and then that one, and they tell you what you already know. When it gets warmer, I'll feel better." She was still wearing her robe.

"You need to move around so you don't get so stiffened up, Mags." He placed the soiled paper towels in a plastic grocery sack, then got a rag from underneath the sink and soaked it with soapy water. He finished cleaning up the poop and put the rag and all into the bag, tied it shut and tossed it in the trash. He'd have to find the sick cat. It was probably Cheech. None of them happened to be around at the moment. They were just like kids that way, hiding when they sensed trouble.

"Want me to make you something to eat?" Buddy asked.

"If you help me get up, I'll try to do it myself."

He walked over to the couch and held out his hand. He could smell her stale breath. A half-hearted ray of sunshine shone through the window into the room, and as she moved, dust motes and cat hair floated in the air. Mags sighed as she rose from her seat.

"Damn, this is getting old," she said.

"Aren't we both," Buddy remarked. He turned his head as her face neared his. "You need to brush your teeth, m'lady."

"Excuse me all to hell." She laughed, and he smiled. "You aren't any sweet-smellin' gentleman, either."

"Well, I did just clean up shit after cleaning up shit all day."

"Oh, get outside to your syrup. I'm fine once I get into the kitchen. I'll make some goulash for supper."

"Sounds good. I'll come in when it's dark."

Cheech crept from behind the couch and blinked lazily at them. Then he yawned. *Goulash for supper*, Buddy thought. *Anna used to make that.*

Chapter 4

The Sad Room

1969

One day pretty much rolled into the next in Ohio. Buddy and Anna were alone at the house much of the time, which they grew to appreciate. James came home later and later, working at his bench when he was there. He always played Charlie Pride or Ray Price or some twangy singer on the radio; Buddy and Anna hated country music, but knew each word by heart. Once Buddy made the mistake of changing the tuner on the radio, and they brought in a station from Chicago that had good music like The Rolling Stones and Blood, Sweat and Tears. They danced around the kitchen until James came home and had a fit because they touched his radio. Anna said he needed to go back to school and learn sharing.

Anna had started openly displaying her disdain for James. She wouldn't look at him, except to glare if he tried getting her to talk. She still had to cook dinner most nights, but she ate little and kept her arms crossed at the table. She was often in her room, or on the porch if the weather permitted. Neither one of them had friends over. Once in a while they would go down the street and hang out with other kids, but no one ever knocked on their door.

Buddy missed his grandparents like crazy. The letter he finally sent came back, and Mom said he'd put the wrong address on it. "I don't want you writing and telling them how much you hate it here," she said. "In fact, I don't want you to write them again."

"Why not?" Buddy asked. "I miss them an awful lot."

"Maybe you can go visit them soon," his mother said, and Buddy perked up.

"Really?"

"We'll see."

For days this gave Buddy hope. Then one night at dinner, James said he needed to replace their mom's vehicle.

"Where are we getting the money for that?" Mom asked.

"I asked for a bit of overtime," James said. "It just means we can't do anything else. It's not like we have big vacation plans or anything. Your kids are eating up every spare cent."

Buddy couldn't help it; he started to cry. "Does that mean we can't go visit Grandma and Grandpa?"

James glared at their mother. "What the hell is he talking about?"

"I mentioned a possible visit," she said meekly. "It was just an idea."

"Unless they pay for it, that's not going to happen," James said. "I don't need those kids going to see the people who helped them become spoiled brats, anyways." He stood up so quickly his chair tipped over. He didn't bother picking it up.

"Don't you ever think?" he yelled. "I work my ass off, and you make them promises!"

"It wasn't a promise!" Mom said.

"Good, because it's not happening."

"No surprise there," Anna whispered. She glared angrily at their mother.

"What did you say?" James snarled, although everyone knew he'd heard. "You little bitch. You walk around here with your piss-poor attitude and a burr up your ass! Like we'd do anything for you with the way you act!" James had a vein that stuck out on his forehead when he was mad, and now it pulsed blue and thick. Anna moved her glare from Mom to him. She knew better. Buddy couldn't help but admire her, though, because she still had the nerve to stand up to James. As for Buddy, he wanted to be anywhere else but there.

"Go to your rooms, both of you," Mom said. She looked at James with a plea in her eyes that Buddy realized was an attempt at calming him down. He was tired of her trying to calm James Shearing. He got up and headed toward his room, not coming out for the rest of the night. Lying in the dark, he thought about running away; maybe Anna would want to come with him. He pictured them arriving at Grandma and Grandpa's, being greeted at the door with hugs. He'd go outside and smell the dirt from the garden, then he and Grandpa would walk down the grassy road together behind their house. He'd catch frogs, Grandpa chewing on a long piece of hay as he watched. Grandma would smell like cinnamon when they got back. Anna and she would have flour on their aprons.

He daydreamed a lot, always picturing himself back home. Sometimes at school his mind wandered and he missed entire classes, not even knowing what the teacher said. Buddy found each day a challenge to endure. He waited for something to change, but had this bad feeling nothing ever would; he was going to be lonesome and sad until he grew up, when he could finally go home. By then Grandma and Grandpa would be very old or dead.

He found himself playing games in his head. For example,

if he walked past a certain tree before a car came by, it meant he would go back to Pennsylvania soon. If he held his breath long enough to reach a red light, he pretended his mom would shortly decide to take them back where they belonged. He did the same as he dried spoons after dinner, telling himself if he got them all taken care of before needing to breathe something good was bound to happen.

One night he awoke in bed to James Shearing cussing. He said really bad words and Buddy sat up, his heart racing.

"Goddamn it! I am going to kill that stupid sonofabitch cat!"

Buddy and Anna ran into the hallway as James exited his and Mom's bedroom. He was holding his knee; Buddy saw something greenish and wet on it.

"What happened?" Mom said from their bed.

"I went to get into bed and that cat had puked in it!" James said. "Where is it? Somebody get me a towel!"

Mom rushed into the bathroom, wet a hand towel, and handed it to James. She had curlers in her hair, the spongy kind she and Anna liked because they didn't hurt your head when you slept in them. James wiped off his leg and went in search of the cat.

Too late, Buddy saw Sunny hiding underneath the kitchen table. James grabbed the cat by the scruff of its neck, holding it away from him, and threw it out the back door, hard.

"If I see that thing back inside this house, I'll strangle it," he said.

"It's just a kitten! It can't be outside all the time," Mom pleaded.

Anna only got the kitten a few days ago, but already she and Buddy were attached. One of the people at church had a box of kittens they were giving away, and his sister had convinced Mom to let her take one. Now she was quiet, but tears were running down her face. "I just wanted a pet kitty," she said, her voice flat and barely above a whisper.

"Shut up and go back to bed," James said.

The next morning Buddy and Anna went out to look for Sunny. The kitten was lying dead on a mound of grass in the yard, neck bent in a strange way. Anna wrapped the body up, and she and Buddy buried it. They put a little stone over the burial spot and said a prayer — only, Anna said her real prayer was for James Shearing to be down there instead of their cat. Mom watched them from the window. She was crying, too.

"I should have made you keep Sunny in your room," she said as they came in through the back door. Anna started to sob.

"He would have found a way to take Sunny away from me sooner or later," Anna said. She walked over to James's work area, took one of the wrenches from its space on the peg board and hit his radio hard enough to break the plastic casing. "Damn Conway Twitty all to hell," she said.

"You will not behave like that, young lady!" Mom lunged for Anna, who dodged out of the way and sauntered down the hall, bawling and laughing at the same time.

Mom stood looking after her, but didn't bother following Anna. She still had curlers in her hair. It was a Saturday, and she had the day off; Buddy always wondered why she set her hair on days when she wasn't going anywhere special. Buddy sat down at the kitchen table, noticing his shoes had tracked dirt in from the yard. He was too exhausted to stand up and grab the broom, was too darn tired to do much of anything. Mom sat down at the table across from him and held her face in her hands. Then she reached up and removed the curlers, placing each one in her lap. The curls on her head were tight and coiled.

"I'm going shopping for a bit," she said to herself. Rising, she held her nightgown below the curlers like a little pouch and headed to the bathroom. Buddy was still at the table when she left.

Mom came home a little later with some bread, some hamburger, and a head of lettuce. She also had a brand new radio, which she said she found on sale at True Value. She unplugged the broken old one and replaced it with the new one.

"Everybody agree. We decided to get James a new radio," she pronounced.

Anna hid the old one in her room. It had a big crack on top of it, but it still played; when Mom and James were both gone they always tuned into the Chicago station. Every time The Rolling Stones sang "Satisfaction" they would bounce around Anna's room and bellow along with it at the top of their lungs.

Sometimes Buddy thought about his real father, but it was getting harder and harder to remember him. He could only recall Dad being angry a few times.

Once, when Dad got home from work he stretched out on the couch and soon fell asleep. Buddy wanted him to play, so he started crawling on him, tickling him and trying to get him to open his eyes.

"Stop, Buddy," Dad warned, but Buddy didn't. He kept crawling around, when suddenly Dad grabbed him roughly by the arm, sat up, and swatted him hard on his butt.

"Damn it!" he yelled. "I've been up all night and half the day, and when I tell you to leave me alone, I want you to listen!"

Buddy was stunned, then sorry he made his dad so mad. He ran into the kitchen and slumped against the freezer. He hated it when Dad shouted like that, because he was usually so nice. He worked at night and Mom worked in the daytime, which meant when they got home from school Dad was the one waiting for them. Sometimes he'd make a toasted cheese sandwich to "tide them over" until dinner, Buddy and Anna splitting it with each other. Dad worked at a factory, but said he didn't want to work there his whole life; he wanted to get a better job and live someplace warm.

Dad always wore a white T-shirt and light green slacks with creases from the iron down the front. His hair was dark and curly, his face marked by lots of scars Grandma said came from acne. But Dad also had a piercing blue gaze and long black eyelashes, Mom often saying his were the most beautiful eyes she'd ever seen. Sometimes Mom and Dad sat close together on the couch and held hands. On Sunday nights the whole family would watch Walt Disney's *Wonderful World of Color*, the kids lying on the floor with blankets they'd tote back upstairs once the show ended. Usually Buddy was so tired and content he drifted off immediately after his head hit the pillow.

Dad and Mom were poor, but they were working to have a better life, and Buddy never felt poor. They went to Grandma and Grandpa's a lot, and had big dinners of Grandma's good cooking, made with food from Grandpa's garden. Grandma always sent them home with leftovers, Dad putting some in his lunch for the next day. He had a black metal lunch box with a special nest for his Thermos. He put so much milk and sugar in his coffee Grandpa said he liked a little coffee with his sugar-milk. Buddy sometimes got to drink what was left in the Thermos when he got home from school. His dad told him he could always have the leftover pieces of sandwich or cookie that were still wrapped in wax paper.

Buddy started finding most of Dad's lunches remaining in the bucket. At first he didn't think much of it, but one day, when it had gone on for a while, he asked his dad if he didn't like taking lunch to work anymore.

"I haven't had much of an appetite lately," Dad said. "Think I caught a stomach bug or something. There's always stuff going around in the shop."

"All the more for me," Buddy said. He folded the wax paper neatly into a square and stuck it back into the bucket.

"Don't say anything to your mother," Dad said, winking. "She'll get on my case about not eating my lunch, and you know how that feels."

Buddy giggled. "Yeah, but she hasn't been saying much to me lately other than I am gonna eat you guys out of house and home."

Dad ruffled Buddy's hair. Buddy thought his dad did look a little skinny.

"Are you on a diet, Dad?" he asked.

"Nope. The only figure I watch is your mother's."

"Why would you do that?" Buddy asked, then looked at his dad's face and giggled. "Gross!" he said.

"You won't always think that about girls," Dad said.

Buddy shrugged and closed the fasteners on Dad's lunch bucket. He set it on the counter, placing the coffee Thermos in the sink. Dad always rinsed it out and left it filled with hot water until he was ready to go to work. Then he'd make a pot of coffee, fill the Thermos back up, and leave a cup for Mom.

Buddy never heard his parents fight, but he did hear some whispering a few days later when Dad got home from work just as Mom headed out for her job. He caught something about not feeling good and needing to see the doctor soon. He wasn't sure who needed to go, and didn't think much more about it. There was a donkey basketball game at school, and Buddy heard there were going to be real live donkeys. He thought he'd get a dime from Dad to go. Maybe Truman could go too, and even spend the night after. Buddy rarely had friends over because of Dad's work schedule, but maybe it would be okay.

Later at school, Buddy waited his turn in the lunch line and went to sit beside Truman, who had a habit of being fidgety. Today was no different.

"Did you know there's a donkey basketball game on Saturday?" Truman asked, and Buddy nodded, smiling.

"I was gonna see if you wanted to go," Buddy said. "Want to?"

"Sure," Truman said. "If I can. I might have to watch my little sister, though. She is such a brat." Truman's sister was a little kid. It surprised Buddy that Truman had to watch her, since he was only in the fifth grade.

"You don't have a babysitter?"

"Nope. Mom can't afford it, so she lets me watch her. If I need something I call Grandma and Grandpa," he said.

"Where is she going?"

"She likes to go out on the weekends. She's probably trying to get a new boyfriend or something." Truman poured his peas into his carton of milk, inserted the straw and started sucking hard. The lunch lady came up behind him and asked why he always had to play with his food. Her hands were on her large hips, and she wore a hairnet, which made her look mean. But she really wasn't.

"I guess I didn't have many toys when I was little, Mrs. Johnson," Truman said, winking at her.

"Oh my, you poor boy," she said, then smiled and gestured toward the exit door. "Get outta here and go outside. Throw your garbage into the bin, and set your lunch tray where it goes."

Buddy and Truman nodded, both heading out.

Buddy was in the schoolyard when the principal came to get him, telling Buddy to follow him to the office. As Buddy watched the back of Mr. Gentry's balding head, he wondered what he did.

"Have a seat, Buddy," Mr. Gentry said. "Your grandparents are coming to pick you up."

"What did I do?" Buddy asked, stricken with fear. "Am I in trouble?"

Mr. Gentry shook his head. "Oh, no, Buddy, you are not in trouble. Your grandparents just wanted to come get you from school early today." Mr. Gentry had a sad expression on his face, like the look movie actors get when something bad happens. Buddy was about to ask why he looked that way when Anna came to the door.

"Hello, Anna," Mr. Gentry said. "They should be here any minute."

"Why?" she asked. Her face was pale, and she clenched her sweater around herself, like she was giving herself a hug. Buddy noticed the picture of Mr. Gentry's wife and two kids on his desk. His wife looked small and what he thought grown-ups would call pleasant, and his kids were older than Buddy and Anna. One was a boy and one was a girl. The boy had long hair like a hippie. The girl had very straight teeth and big circle earrings. Mr. Gentry gestured for Anna to sit beside Buddy, but she remained standing.

Mr. Gentry's helper, Miss Jordan, poked her head inside and announced Grandma and Grandpa were there. Mr. Gentry stood and followed Buddy and Anna.

Grandma and Grandpa were both in the office, and it looked like they'd been crying. Buddy had never seen them cry before; a knot formed in his stomach as he approached them, and Grandma put her hands on his shoulders.

"What's going on?" Anna asked.

"Your dad is in the hospital," Grandpa said. "We need to get there. Your mom is with him."

"What happened?" Buddy croaked.

"We'll tell you on the way," Grandpa said.

"Please let us know if we can do anything," Mr. Gentry said.

Buddy allowed himself to be guided to the car. He and Anna

sat in the back seat, and Grandma got in on the passenger's side. She then turned to them, tears bright in her eyes.

"Your dad is very sick," she said. "He's got cancer. He passed out in the yard at your house, and the neighbors called an ambulance."

"Cancer?" Anna asked, like she didn't hear it right. "When did he get cancer?"

"They just discovered it today after he got to the hospital," Grandpa said. "He's had it for a while, and it's pretty bad. It's in his stomach or his insides somewhere." Grandpa's voice broke, and he pushed his hand through his full head of white hair. "Damn *cancer*," he said, like he couldn't believe it; Buddy couldn't believe it, either. Not his dad. Not Grandma and Grandpa's son. There must be a goof somewhere. Buddy never knew anyone who had cancer before, but when he heard people say the word it was always bad. There was no way his dad had that.

Grandpa pulled into a big parking lot. They all went inside the hospital, he, Anna, and Grandma waiting by the entrance while Grandpa talked to a lady behind a big counter like the one at school. He motioned them over after a minute, telling the receptionist his son was asking for his kids.

"We normally don't allow children in there," the lady said. "I will have to make sure it's alright."

"You do that, ma'am," Grandpa said.

She turned and went into a little room behind the counter, then came back a few seconds later. Handing Grandpa a piece of paper, she said it had Dad's room number on it. "You'll have to keep the children quiet," she advised.

"That won't be a problem," Grandma said.

As they went down a bunch of halls, Buddy's stomach started to hurt from being scared. He heard someone moaning, only realizing it was his dad when they rounded a corner and entered the room the sound came from. His dad lay in a big white hospital bed, holding his belly with one hand and the bed's railing with the other while Mom stood beside him, rubbing his right arm.

"Kids, your pop isn't feeling so hot," Dad said. "I got a nice ride in an ambulance, and they're gonna fix me right up." He attempted a smile, but it turned into a look of pain.

Buddy blinked. Were Dad's eyes yellow, or was it his imagination? He walked up to the bed, and Dad held out a hand. Anna gulped like she was either trying not to cry or resisting the urge to throw up.

"Dad, you have to get better," Anna said, like she was begging.

"I know, honey. I am going to do my darnedest." Again, the attempted smile.

Anna came forward. Leaning into Dad, she started to sob. Then everyone was crying, Buddy also stretching across the bed to hug Dad. Not too hard, but he wanted to comfort his dad the way Dad always did him.

A man in a white jacket came into the room and made a funny noise in his throat, causing everyone to look toward him. "Doctor, this is my family," Dad said. Grandpa shook the doctor's hand, Grandma just taking and holding it.

"Do everything you can for this one," she begged.

The doctor didn't seem to hear Grandma. "I need to speak with the patient and his wife," he said. "I'll let you folks back in when I'm done." The way he said it, everyone knew they had to leave that second. Not even Grandpa hesitated. They filed out, and another lady in a white dress and funny hat told them to go to the family lounge. It was a big room with a couch and chairs, just like a living room. *The Newlywed Game* was on TV, with nobody watching. There was a little table with an orange plastic jug and throwaway cups on it over in a corner. Buddy sat next to Grandma, and she put her arm around him.

"This is when you pray," she said, but Buddy closed his eyes and couldn't do it. What should he ask for? He wanted to ask God to make Dad better, but in church every week they said, "God's will be done." Well, it would be God's will not to let Dad get sick in the first place, right? Buddy decided he'd listen for Mom's footsteps as she came down the hall to get them after the doctor told her Dad was coming home.

Anna sniffled, and he opened his eyes. She wasn't praying either. Instead she was crying, not even looking around for something to wipe her nose on although a box of tissues sat on a nearby end table. Grandpa handed her the red and white hankie he always carried in his pocket.

"It's a little used, but it'll do," he said. He tried unsuccessfully to smile at Anna, then looked back the way they had come. "I think I'm going to walk down the hall a bit," he said. "You kids wait here with Grandma."

Buddy noticed a stack of blankets on a shelf. "What are those for?" he asked.

"They're for family members to use if they want to take a little nap," Grandma answered. "Sometimes, you don't want to leave if you have someone here who's sick."

"Could I stay here?" Anna asked.

"Oh honey, no, they don't let kids stay too long," Grandma said.

A bird landed on a ledge outside. They watched it together in silence after Grandma said it was a pigeon. The sky was blue, a few white clouds visible from the window. Buddy always remembered the weather that day, and the room where people got bad news about those they loved.

Grandpa and the doctor came into the little space. Grandpa opened his mouth to say something, but his chin quivered and he sat down. The doctor didn't sit.

"This is not good news, and I'm very sorry," he said. "I've been asked to tell you what's going on. Mr. Robertson — that is, your son and your father — he is very sick, and I'm afraid there isn't much we can do. He has cancer in his stomach that has spread to other organs, including his liver, and I suspect other places we haven't been able to confirm yet. I'm afraid it's at a very advanced stage, and the best we can do is to try and keep him comfortable —"

"How did it get this bad so quickly?" Grandma asked. "I don't understand."

"He's been feeling ill for some time, but didn't say anything to anyone," the doctor answered her. "Maybe if he'd done so we could have treated him, but now it's broken through to the — well — the other organs."

How could the doctor be so calm? "Is my dad dying?" Buddy asked.

"His condition is very bad," the doctor stated.

"No!" Anna cried. "Not my dad!" Grandpa's face collapsed into sorrow, and he grabbed Anna and held her close.

"Can I see him again?" Buddy pleaded.

"He's very tired and upset with the news, but you can go in for a brief time," the doctor said. "Again, I am very sorry."

With that, he was gone. Buddy hated him. After delivering a deadly blow he was allowed to leave them sobbing in the sad room. Buddy noticed there were boxes of tissues by all the chairs, and even a box on the coffee table. People got their lives ruined in here all the time. The pigeon was still on the outdoor sill, facing away from them, not knowing.

Dad was quiet. He stared at his kids.

"I love you, Dad," Anna said. A tear rolled down the side of Dad's face.

"You have no idea how much I've loved being your dad, you two," he whispered.

Three weeks later, he died. After that first visit Buddy and Anna only got to see him once more, and he was in so much pain he didn't seem to want them there. Buddy didn't even get a chance to say goodbye. After the funeral, Mom stayed in her room a lot, crying or just staring. Buddy and Anna went back to school a few days after that, and Mom eventually went back to work, but she announced they were moving in with Grandma and Grandpa for awhile because she couldn't afford the house by herself. Buddy was sad to leave, but at the same time relieved they were making the move. The house was too quiet without Dad. All the life in it left with him; at least Grandma and Grandpa wouldn't be alone while mourning their son. They put their stuff in boxes and stored everything on Grandma and Grandpa's enclosed porch.

"You'll always have a home with us, Bonnie," Grandpa said as he shoved Buddy's dresser into the tightly packed space. "Don't worry about anything. The kids will be better off coming here after school than going back to an empty house while you're at work."

"I know," Mom said. "I just hate to impose on you."

"No problem at all," Grandpa said. "It will do us all good to be together."

It was spring, and since his retirement Grandpa loved being out in the woods this time of year. He took Buddy with him often. Buddy and he dug leeks from the wet, muddy ground, and Grandma made ham dinner to go with them. Sometimes he and Grandpa would rub the dirt from a leek, pull off the skin and eat it from the earth. The women would yell at them because they stank so badly. "It gets in your pores!" Grandma complained.

Buddy loved the colors of the leaves in spring, the way the buds first turned red, then fresh lime, then suddenly exploded into deep summer greenery. Grandpa showed him Dutchman's Breeches, little white flowers that looked like upside-down little Dutch boy pants, and trillium — hardy flowers that Grandpa warned him not to bother.

"Don't pick those, because you're not supposed to," Grandpa said. "They're meant to live and fade off in peace." Grandpa also said spring flowers were special because they had to hurry up and grow before the leaves came out and stole their sunshine.

Sometimes after school, Buddy and Grandpa went out into the woods and stayed until dusk, when they could hear the peeper frogs from the swamp. They'd leave their muddy boots on the porch and come inside to find Grandma in the kitchen stirring or mashing something delicious for supper. Anna would either be sitting at the table working on school stuff or helping Grandma. Even though they'd just lost Dad, Buddy felt lucky every day they lived in this old house. Grandma and Grandpa were sad, but they still did all the things that gave Buddy and Anna comfort. Grandma's arms were still soft and warm and wrinkly, and Grandpa still picked on her like he always did.

Tonight they'd come in later than usual. Grandma flicked her dish towel at Grandpa as he swiped a dinner roll from the counter. "Go wash your hands," she ordered. "Who knows what you've picked up out there."

"Just a few slimy slugs and worms," he said.

They scrubbed their hands with Lava soap and made their way to the dinner table. Anna placed her books on the buffet behind her, and she got up to help Grandma put the meal into big bowls. Mom should be there any minute. They all missed his dad, but this absence was not a gaping wound to Buddy, largely because of Dad's parents.

Buddy took the big bowl of mashed potatoes, made a pile with an indentation in the middle, and passed the bowl along. Then he took a pat of butter, placed it in the middle of the potatoes, covered the butter and let it melt while he took a pork chop, corn, salad, and a roll. He liked honey on his roll, just like Grandpa did.

The windows in the kitchen were wet with steam from all

the cooking. Grandma took off her glasses and said a short blessing, and they dug in.

"Bonnie must be running late," Grandpa said. She'd been running late a lot recently, and had told everyone not to wait on her for supper.

Grandma gave Grandpa a look that Buddy knew was significant, but he didn't know what it meant. He shrugged and continued eating.

The next day while going downstairs to the kitchen, he heard Grandma say that Mom hadn't come home until early in the morning.

"I don't like it, and I don't think we should just allow it," Grandma said.

Buddy stood in the stairwell.

"Well, she's an adult, so what do we say?" Grandpa asked.

"She is an adult, and a mother to those two kids upstairs," Grandma said. "I know she's lonely and all, but she can't continue to live here if she's going to stay out all hours of the night."

"Alright, honey. I'll have a talk with her," Grandpa said. "She tends to take what I say better than your sage words of advice."

Grandma made a noise.

Buddy walked into the kitchen as Grandpa was stirring sugar into his coffee.

"Look who's up!" Grandma said. She smiled and smoothed her apron. "Hungry?"

"Yeah, I am," Buddy admitted. "Do you have any mashed potatoes left?"

Grandma chuckled. "Just like your dad, you are."

"I am?" Buddy felt like he'd just been given a present, but he also teared up. *Dad.* He had a vision of Dad sitting at that very kitchen table, and an ache spread in his chest.

"Your dad always liked leftovers for breakfast," Grandma said.

"I could never believe he'd want to eat a bunch of taters and gravy over a good dish of eggs and bacon."

"He liked cold spaghetti, too," Buddy said.

"I know, I know."

"I miss him," Buddy whispered, then feeling bad because he didn't want Grandma and Grandpa to be sad for the rest of their day.

"Oh, we do too, honey," Grandma said. She hugged Buddy against her, and he found himself crying.

"Sorry, Grandma," he muttered into her ample breasts.

"I'm sorry too, Buddy," she said. "It's alright to miss your dad, and it's also alright to cry. Lord knows I do it about every day."

"You do?"

"Oh, yes. I do. But I don't want you and your sister to divide your lives into happy times before your dad died and sorrowful times after. That would make me sadder than anything."

Grandpa was still standing by the coffeepot, and he cleared his throat. "I cry over my son, too, Buddy," he said. "I am glad he gave us you and Anna, though, and I agree with your grandma. She is a smart cookie."

Anna thumped down the stairs and glanced at everyone.

"Nice hairdo," Buddy blurted. "More like a hairdon't."

Everyone laughed, including Anna.

"Buddy wants leftover potatoes for breakfast; how about you?" Grandma asked.

"Oh, yuck! I want toast and eggs, over easy," Anna replied.

"It's time to teach you both how to cook," Grandpa said.

Mom slept until noon, and when she woke up she was quiet. Her face looked pink, and Buddy caught her watching herself in the living room mirror. He surprised her when she thought she was alone.

She had her neck turned and was pulling her hair back, like she was looking at herself with someone else's gaze. Buddy felt like he shouldn't see her doing that. She gave him a little smile and raised her eyebrows, then put her hand down. Her hair fell back into place. Her eyes, the color of moss, were filled with excitement.

While they all watched TV that night Buddy attempted to shuffle a deck of cards the way Grandpa taught him, so it looked cool and all the cards fluffed into place. Between TV and the deck, he glimpsed at his mother. She was mostly staring into space with a far-off look. Lately she seemed to live on some other planet. He wanted to startle her, see if he might somehow bring her back, but instead he sat with the deck of cards in his hands.

Chapter 5

Brother and Sister

The lingering daylight meant Buddy would soon put an end to another season of making syrup. He marked each of these seasons with a sense of accomplishment and nostalgia, since the sugaring days were so fleeting and special to him. Yet, the smell of awakening in the forests helped him make the transition into spring. He nestled the sap buckets into their resting spot for another year, tucking them away like old friends he looked forward to seeing once again.

He was happy with this year's production. Jenna and Carrie helped quite a bit. At the thought of Carrie, he forced himself to turn away from his sugaring equipment and continue past the shed. He ought to check for any new growth emerging from the woods. In the old flower bed, crocuses were flaunting themselves already. He tucked away the thought that he should go get Mags right away and bring her out to see them. She had been mixing up a batch of johnnycake when he'd headed outside, intending to cook it on the wood stove. Soon they wouldn't need to keep that going, so he'd have to clear space on their range to make room for her to cook. She damn sure wouldn't think to do it ahead of time.

Reflecting on their cluttered and dirty kitchen caused Buddy to curse out loud. He wasn't one for outbursts of profanity, but the enormity of the household projects that needed doing filled him with frustration. How did they let their house get so out of hand? He remembered Grandma's kitchen, so busy but organized, with its delicious smells. He knew he'd eat that corn-bread tonight and find cat hair in it — what the hell! However, the state of the house wasn't just Mags's fault. Buddy knew he shared much of the blame. Maybe he'd finally tackle the bath-room this weekend. But as quickly as that thought occurred to him, it was gone.

He found no signs of green in the snow-free moats around the tree stumps, so he headed inside.

"Those girls are coming over tonight to clean our kitchen," Mags announced as he shut the door behind him, shooing three cats away.

"Funny, I was just thinking about doing that," he said.

Mags snorted. "Yeah, I bet."

"No, really. I was thinking how you wouldn't be cooking on the wood stove much longer, so we'd best get the kitchen tidied up."

Mags looked at him skeptically. "Huh," she said. "Well, I told those girls I'd feed 'em cornbread and chili."

"Sounds good," Buddy said.

"I think I'll clean up the table a bit, even," Mags said. "Maybe you want to get a head start on the kitchen before those girls get here?"

"Nah, I'll supervise," Buddy said, grinning. "Do we even have dish soap around this place?"

"Yeah, somewhere or other," Mags said.

"We are pathetic, aren't we?" Buddy asked. "Are you

embarrassed that two young girls feel so bad for us they want to come clean our kitchen?"

"Nah," said Mags. "Them girls like it here, dirty or not. They both have too much going on in their own homes, and they say when they're here, at least we're not yelling all the time. Mac, you are about the only man they've ever seen who doesn't drink his supper and wash it down with more drink for dessert."

"Huh. Guess I'm what you'd call a role model for young children," he said. "Now, isn't that a sad state of affairs?"

"You don't know the half of it." Mags leaned into the cupboard below the sink. "I thought I had some cleaning rags in here for the girls to use, but I can't find 'em."

"Well, you don't need cleaning rags if you don't clean," Buddy said.

A car rattled down the drive. Mags and Buddy watched as Carrie and Jenna parked, the girls reaching into the back seat of their ride, a very old Chevy Jenna's mom had driven for years, to pull out piled rags and a bucket filled with cleaning products. "Will ya look at that," Mags marveled. "I do have hopes for those two."

Jenna stuck some keys in her pocket and made her way up the stairs. She smiled at them as they gazed out the window, Buddy then moving to open the door.

"How's that car running?"

"On a prayer, and I'm sure it won't be for long," Jenna said. "Louis keeps banging on crap, and somehow it keeps going." Louis was Jenna's mom's latest friend.

Carrie passed by him, and he caught her sweet scent. She smelled clean and green and alive, like the outdoors, only different.

Since he wasn't quite sure what to do with himself as the girls toiled in the kitchen, Buddy decided to go through an old toolbox, complete with assorted tools, that he'd picked up at a yard sale last year for five bucks. He pushed aside piles of assorted stuff atop the coffee table, laid out an old towel, and fetched the toolbox from beside the boxes near the front door. He pulled items out, laid them one by one on the coffee table, and started examining them more closely. Buddy was pleased to discover several screwdrivers with wooden handles, along with some drop-forged wrenches that were made in the USA. He retrieved a level that had the name of the previous owner, "Ansorge," etched in its side with some type of crude instrument. He remembered hearing that surname before — probably one of the students at school. After nearly nicking his finger on an old razor blade that had been left in the top tray, he found a utility knife in the box and tucked the rusty blade inside, making a mental note to empty it when he was finished.

Buddy didn't need tools. Grandpa left him many, and he still used those. Finding a well-crafted hand tool, though, gave him pleasure. You simply could not go to the hardware store anymore and find quality tools. The thought of someone using these items, letting them go, and Buddy somehow finding them for a five dollar bill — well, he felt fortunate to know their real value. He lined each tool up on the towel according to size and purpose. He would wipe out the box, oil the latches, and place the tools back inside, now stored properly.

"Do you have to do that inside?" Mags asked, standing over him with her hands on her hips. "Those girls are busy cleaning, and here you are creating another mess. Just like a kid."

"I'm going to take care of it," Buddy said. "Settle down."

Mags sputtered. "I had my magazines and my remote here just where I like 'em."

"I'll put them back," Buddy said. Like it mattered! He could have pointed out the clutter and crap throughout the house, but he didn't. Instead he forced himself to continue his task, even though Mags remained near him, staring at him. As usual, her stretch pants were tight and covered with cat hair. He would see little pockets of fat along her thighs if he took his eyes from the tools. Well, he wasn't going to.

"What should we do with all this stuff on your counters?" Jenna hollered from the kitchen. Mags sighed and turned away.

"Just a second," she said. "Let me see what you're talkin' about." Buddy was about to have a reprieve, he thought, until he heard Mags say the clutter on the counter was his. He remembered the box of old bottles he'd found at another yard sale.

"I want to go through those before you move them," he said, standing up from the couch. The cats were milling around the kitchen, curious about all the activity, so Buddy walked gingerly to the spot where the women stood. He saw the girls had managed to clear away most of the items on the counter. Where had they put them?

"How about if I put these bottles in the soapy water and let them soak, and you can go through them later?" Carrie asked.

"Okay, guess that'll work," Buddy said.

"That chili is about done," Mags announced. "When do you want to eat?"

"Anytime," Jenna said. "Just let us get these bottles in the sink."

Dinner was fun, Buddy listening to the chatter of Mags and the girls. He missed the liveliness young people brought to a house. When still at home, the boys were always entertaining at the dinner table. That was when Mags was still pretty active, though. They used to stuff the weekly shoppers into plastic bags at the table, getting them ready to deliver along routes they had to make some money. Buddy helped sometimes. The boys could usually convince Buddy to drive them to the delivery boxes on the rural routes. Those rides were some of the best memories he had with them. Sometimes he took them on back roads and purposely chose muddy, rutted trails. When they returned to the house Mags would make some remark about how Buddy was as much a kid as the boys, but smile while she said it.

Buddy reached for the ladle, angling for another scoop of chili. The girls were on their second piece of cornbread, and Mags was showing them how she liked it. She slathered butter on a square, topped it off with some maple syrup, and passed the bottle on to Carrie.

"As good as dessert," she said.

"Oh, wow, it is!" Carrie exclaimed. "I usually put honey on it, but I like this even better. Can I get your recipe for cornbread?"

Mags chuckled and reached behind herself for the round container of Quaker cornmeal. "I'd tell ya it's a family secret, but I'd be lying," she said. "It's here on every box. The trick is to underbake it just a touch."

Carrie was genuinely interested, taking the container from Mags to scan the recipe. "I think I could do that," she said. "My little brother might like it."

"What grade is your brother in?" Buddy asked.

"He's in elementary school, fifth grade," Carrie said. "His name is Ben, but his last name is different than mine. Mine is Elliott, and his is…"

Buddy knew the name before Carrie spoke it. Her brother was Ben Jameson. The kid in the bathroom. The invisible kid.

"…Jameson," she finished. "Ben is a sweet kid. He's my half brother, and I try to take care of him."

Buddy felt heat rush to his face as he tried to look past the others at the dinner table. He thought of the kid in the bathroom, the parents who came to the school, and the burden this young girl Carrie endured. She shouldn't have to care for her brother. It was wrong that such responsibility fell on her. Again he thought of his own sister, Anna, and the load she'd been forced to take up. Like Carrie, her little brother could not escape the evil of men.

Buddy could never find the courage or the desire to tell Mags much about his childhood. Each of them hinted at times that their youth was not ideal, but these revelations were shared in passing, almost casually, when observing other families or raising the boys. Buddy found it difficult to show the brothers physical affection when they were young. He would tousle their hair or playfully slug them in the arm, but he never hugged them or told them he loved them. Mags only asked about it once, after Dude the cat died and the boys cried with her out on the porch. Later that night, she wondered out loud why he hugged her but not her kids.

"I know you care about those boys, but you sure are stingy with your hugs," she'd said. "Sometimes a kid needs a hug from someone who is like their dad."

"Those boys know I care about them," Buddy remembered saying. "I don't have to get all mushy about it."

Mags had snorted. Her sinuses were still clogged from crying, and the sound was loud and wet. She'd wiped her nose with her sleeve.

"Don't get all preachy on me, Mags," Buddy had muttered. "I'm just not the huggy type."

"Don't I know that! I'm not either. Sometimes it's important, though."

That was all she ever said. Buddy knew she was curious at times, but Mags somehow knew to leave the lid on the box. Neither sought what the other couldn't or wouldn't give; it was how they endured so many years. They found company with each other, which was usually enough.

They weren't together for physical reasons, for sure. It had been, what, 20 years or so since they'd had sex? At first they did have a sexual relationship, but it was like both of them drifted off to sleep one night and forgot about it. They settled into companionship, something they both appreciated. Did Mags miss the intimacy? Somehow, Buddy thought not. He didn't, either. That is to say, he didn't until Carrie came along and he felt his pulse quicken, remembering all over again what it was like with Leah.

It saddened him to think that Leah was his first love, yet he'd hardly spoken her name aloud after seeing her for the last time. She might as well not have existed, like a character in a fairy tale — and there were no fairy tale endings. Or at least, Buddy wasn't inclined to put forth the effort for one. He knew better. Any time a person had the daring to ask for something like that, the Fates or God or whatever put him in his place. Buddy knew this like he knew the woods. The less you asked for in life, the kinder your future. If you had very little, bad fortune would look to someone with more to take.

"Mac, she's talking to you," Mags said. She was still at the table, as were Carrie and Jenna.

"What? Sorry," Buddy said.

"I just wondered if you know who my stepbrother is," Carrie said. "Probably not, because he's really quiet. Not like his sister."

"Oh, I just know who he is," Buddy said. "I don't really know him."

A lie. Buddy knew that kid better than he knew any other kid he'd come across since he started pushing a broom. He couldn't even glance at Carrie as he answered. He stood up, grabbed his bowl and spoon, and headed to the sink.

"I'll wash these bottles up and handle the dishes," he said.

"Miracles never cease," Mags said.

Chapter 6

No Good Men Left

1969

Mom's first boyfriend after Dad died was a guy called Mohawk. It turned out he was the reason she was so distracted all the time. She started dropping his name at the dinner table, when she was even at the dinner table. Usually Buddy and Anna were with Grandma and Grandpa, Mom either working or gone. At first she always said she was working late, but then she mentioned meeting someone who was a good friend, and then he was more than that. Buddy and Anna were not ready for anyone to take the place of Dad. Grandma said they should allow it to happen; Dad wouldn't want Mom to be lonely the rest of her life.

"But she has us," Buddy said. He was learning how to plant seeds in little peat pots so they would be ready to transplant when it got warmer. He put his thumb into each little pot, following it with a seed as Grandma watched. They set the trays of pots under a special light. Grandma assured Buddy that in just a few days he would see sprouts emerging from the soil.

Buddy liked the smell of the dirt, as it reminded him of being outside with Grandpa.

"I know she has all of us," Grandma said. "But your mom is a young woman who needs an adult man in her life to keep company with. It's hard for me, too, because I wish your dad were still here to be that man, but he isn't."

"I don't get it," Buddy said, shrugging.

"You will someday," Grandma said.

"Dad used to tell me that, too," Buddy said. "But I sure don't get it now."

Grandpa came inside from fetching the mail at the end of the driveway. He slipped his galoshes off and headed toward his recliner, where he took a letter opener and neatly slit the envelopes. "Bills and junk," he pronounced.

"The usual," Grandma said. "Buddy, would you like an orange?"

"Sure," he said. Grandma always got the best oranges, and she started them for him so all he had to do was stick his thumb under the opening and pull the rind away.

Grandma rose to go to the kitchen just as a racket sounded from the porch. Buddy looked up from the peat pots to see Mom stumble through the kitchen door, holding her purse against herself and crying.

"Bonnie, what happened?" Grandma asked.

"He tried to rape me!" Mom yelled. Snot was all over her face, her lips looking swollen.

Grandpa went to her quicker than Buddy had ever seen him move. "Who?" He reached Mom and took the purse out of her hands, grabbed her elbow and sat her down at the table. "Who?" he asked again.

"Mose Bingham," Mom said. "My car wouldn't start, so he offered to bring me home. Instead he pulled down some back road and tried to rape me!"

"That sonofabitch," Grandpa said. Buddy didn't remember

him ever cussing. "Get Bonnie a little bit of whiskey," he said to Grandma.

Buddy watched as Grandma reached way behind the Club crackers in the cupboard and pulled out a bottle. He'd never seen his grandparents drink before, either. Grandma poured some brown liquid into a tiny glass and handed it to Bonnie. Bonnie shook her head, but Grandpa nodded and she took it in one gulp. She rubbed her eyes and started to shiver. "Do you want me to call the police?" Grandpa asked. "Or should I just beat the hell out of him?"

Grandma gasped. "I don't think you want to do that, Clarence," she said.

"No one would believe me," Mom said. "Who would? I'm a widow with two kids, and Mose is a foreman at the shop. Nobody saw it happen."

"He shouldn't get away with it," Grandpa said. "Tell me exactly what he did."

Mom took a deep, crackly breath. Buddy hadn't moved from the spot where he'd been planting peat pots.

"Well, he took a turn on the way home and I asked him where we were going. He told me he always liked me," Mom said. "He stopped along some woods and moved in to kiss me. When I tried fighting him off, he held my hands down and told me I was going to do what he wanted and I was going to like it." Mom gagged as she spoke, and Buddy thought she might throw up. But she just started crying harder. "I had to do something I can't talk about, and then he said he'd make me feel as good as I made him feel. He tried to get my nylons off, which hurt because I was still trying to fight against him. I lied and told him I had my period. He seemed to calm down after that, saying he'd wait until the next time. How can I go back to work and see him there?"

"Christ, Bonnie," Grandpa said.

"I always had a bad feeling about that sorry excuse for a man," Grandma said.

"I really don't want you to call the police," Mom said. "They won't believe me, and they'll just make it worse! Please promise me you won't do that!"

Anna came through the door at that moment and sensed the gravity of the situation. She didn't ask what was going on, but removed her boots silently and went to sit by Buddy. It seemed like all the adults woke up and realized there were two children in the room, and they put covers on their feelings.

"Anna, take Buddy into the den," Grandma ordered. She had one orange in her hand, and she grabbed another along with two napkins. "I was just giving him an orange, so here's one for you, too."

Anna took the oranges, Buddy following her from the kitchen. She only had to look with a question in her eyes for him to relate what he'd heard.

"Wow," Anna said. "That bastard should learn a lesson."

"What did Mom mean by saying she had to do something that she can't talk about?" Buddy asked. The whole conversation was like a riddle, but that part was very confusing.

"She had to touch him and kiss him in his privates," Anna said. "Disgusting."

Buddy cringed. "I guess so!" A picture of the act formed in his head, and it was totally gross. He had to order his brain to stop.

Mom sat at the table with Grandpa and Grandma for a while afterward, and then Grandpa left the house for a bit. When he got home, he walked up to Mom as she sat on the couch, squeezed her shoulder and went on. The next day he took Mom to work.

That night, everything seemed normal again. Buddy was dying to know what happened. He asked Grandma when they were alone.

"Your grandpa has lived his life right and earned respect in this town," Grandma said as she pared the skin off some carrots. "A few words from him can ruin someone who has not lived in such a way. Don't worry — that man won't be bothering your mother again, and that's all you need to know about it."

"Okay," Buddy said. "Tell Grandpa thanks from me."

Grandma smiled a funny little smile. Her hands stopped in the sink. "I will, little man," she said.

"I thought that guy's name was like Moses from the Bible," Buddy said. "But he's not a good Moses, so he's just Mose."

Grandma laughed. "He's not a leader of his people, for sure."

If the incident was unofficially forgotten in the house, Mom didn't seem to be shaking it off. She stayed quiet, and Buddy worried about her. He knew Grandma and Grandpa did too.

Anna, meanwhile, was so busy working on the school paper that she seemed removed from everything at the house. She also got a job helping in the school office so she could learn about making mimeographs and typing. Grandma said Anna was going to rule the world one day. Mom was a more fragile person, Grandma said. That was why it was so important she found Dad. Too bad he couldn't stick around to take care of her forever.

Mom was a little cheerier than normal one night, and she informed everyone that Mohawk wanted to have her and the kids over for dinner. Anna rolled her eyes and said she wasn't interested.

"You're going," Mom said. Grandma and Grandpa didn't say anything.

"Why do I have to? I'm not dating the guy," Anna argued.

"He was nice enough to invite us, and we are going," Mom stated. "He's picking up hamburgers and fries from McDonald's, since he drives by one on his way home from work."

"Cool! I've only had McDonald's once," Buddy said. He felt

Anna kick him under the table and glanced guiltily at her. "I probably won't have fun, but the food will be good," he muttered.

"We are going on Friday night," Mom asserted.

"Oh, joy," Anna said.

Friday night came, and Mom, Anna, and Buddy went to Mohawk's house. It was a nice house once, but it looked worn out and tired. Buddy liked the porch because it had an old swing on it, and a railing he wanted to jump from. But there was a rotten board on the steps, Anna almost breaking through it on her way up.

"Nice place," she said.

"Quiet, Anna. I'm warning you," said Mom.

"Why is his name Mohawk?" Buddy asked.

"Not now, Buddy." Mom tucked her hair behind her ears and knocked on the door. "You kids just focus on acting presentable."

A man with long hair and a mustache answered. He wore glasses with wire frames, and Buddy thought he kind of looked like John Lennon. He'd been expecting someone more like a warrior, what with the name Mohawk.

They entered a room with dark paneling and a couch, chair, and a television. Towels were draped over the seats of the chairs. Buddy noticed an ashtray with lots of butts in it. *Not too dirty,* he thought, *just busy.* There wasn't a lot of furniture, but there was lots of stuff.

"This is Anna and Buddy," Mom said. "Kids, this is Mike."

"I thought your name was Mohawk," Buddy said.

"That's what they called me when I was in the Army," Mike said. "It kind of stuck."

"Are you an Indian?"

Mike looked at Buddy like he was an idiot. "Kid, I was in 'Nam. You flunk history or something?"

"I was just trying to figure out where the name Mohawk came from."

"In the Army they shaved my head. When it started to grow back, I let it get long in the middle and kept it buzzed on the sides. Hence the name, because my hair looked like a mohawk."

"Huh." Buddy didn't know what he expected, but he was hoping for a more dramatic tale.

Mike had their burgers and fries in a bag on the table. They circled around it, and he handed everyone their meals. Halfway through, Buddy realized he was thirsty and there were no drinks in sight.

"Think I could have something to drink?" Buddy asked. "I'm a little thirsty."

"The kitchen sink is right there," Mike said, pointing.

Buddy's mom stood up. "I'll get drinks for everyone," she said.

"Suit yourself," Mike said. "But I'll take a beer."

Buddy noted that his mom knew where things were in the house, so she must have spent some time there. He was enjoying his fries, as they were awesome, and he liked the pickles and onion pieces on his burger. McDonald's was a treat; they didn't eat restaurant food often. Too bad Mike didn't get any pop.

Anna ate slowly, watching Mike and Mom from the corner of her eyes. She hadn't yet spoken. Mike and Mom were talking about work and what a jerk someone was. Mom said it was because he had never done physical labor a day in his life, and Mike agreed. He said it was important for everyone to learn to work with their hands. That was real work.

"My dad was a hard worker," Buddy piped in. "He worked

with his hands, but always wanted a better job, saying we would get more money that way. He died, though."

"Yeah, I know. He was a good man, but he's cold and dead," Mike said. "Don't go comparing me to him."

"I'm sure he didn't mean to," Mom said. "Isn't it nice, kids, that Mike treated us all to this?"

"Sure is," Buddy said. "Thanks." He was still trying to shake off what Mike said about his dad being cold and dead. Like he didn't know Dad was gone forever. He decided he was full. He set his burger inside the wrapper and bundled it up.

"You kids can go do whatever you want," Mike said. "Your mother and I are going to have a chat."

Anna rolled up her trash and stood. "Let's walk, Buddy."

"Can't we watch *Perry Mason* reruns instead?"

"Let's *walk*, Buddy," Anna repeated.

Buddy and she went outside, and Anna made a funny noise. "What an asshole."

"Maybe he's just nervous," Buddy said. "I know I was." He tried to keep up with Anna, but she always walked faster when she was mad. There weren't very many houses in this neighborhood, though Buddy heard a dog bark and caught the sound of some kids playing nearby.

"I look at everyone with a different way of thinking than you," Anna said. "You always think people are nice, and I like to have people prove it to me. I don't know where I got it from, but that guy proved nothing to me. And I don't think it had anything to do with being nervous. I just don't think he likes kids."

"Why'd he invite us over, then?"

"To get to our mom," Anna said. "The most trusting person in the world." She kicked a stone as she said the last word. It landed a few feet ahead of them in Buddy's path, so he kicked it when he reached it. They kept kicking it back and forth until they got to a spot in town with a traffic light, where they turned around and started walking back. Somewhere along the way the stone landed in the grass and neither one of them went after it.

Anna stomped up the stairs when they got back to Mohawk's house. Buddy thought she was loud on purpose, though he didn't know why. She turned the knob and pushed against the door, but it was locked.

"Told ya," she said.

"Told me what?"

Anna stomped from the porch to the sidewalk.

"Told me what?" Buddy repeated.

She didn't reply.

Mohawk didn't last long in their lives. He never asked the kids over again, telling Mom she had too big of a burden with two children. After that, Mom resumed moping around the house like she usually did. Grandma and Grandpa tried to cheer her up, but she was, again, in a remote place.

Their mother's next boyfriend was Lance, a salesman who visited Mom's work. Lance was so white that he seemed transparent, and to Buddy he smelled like fluffy, clean toilet paper. Buddy couldn't imagine his mom wanting to kiss someone like that, but Mom said he was a very nice person who had a good job and a wonderful home. She also said he had never been married before, so he didn't have a lot of complications in his life.

"He took me to a fancy restaurant and we had chicken cordon bleu," Mom said. "It was like nothing I've ever had. It melted in my mouth. And he was such a gentleman."

"What's chicken Gordon blue?" Buddy asked.

"Chicken CORdon bleu," Mom stressed. "It's a special kind of chicken that has ham in it. You probably wouldn't like it, but it's very good."

"I just like regular chicken and mashed potatoes," Buddy agreed.

Lance was okay, but he didn't talk to Anna or Buddy. He wasn't used to having children around, and almost seemed afraid of them, looking to Mom if they raised their voices to each other. Lance drove a nice car and had a nice house, but the kids weren't ever in his car, and they only went to his house twice. Once he had them all over for what he called pasta, which was really spaghetti with red sauce and meatballs. After sitting down at the table Buddy asked why there were two forks.

"The smaller fork is for your salad," Lance said. "The larger fork is for your meal."

"Why get two forks dirty when you don't have to?" Buddy asked. He looked to Mom, but she was shaking her head at him with very tiny movements.

"It's the proper way to eat," Lance said.

"Huh."

Upon eating the salad with the little fork, Buddy began to eat his noodles, sucking up the long strands like he usually did. Lance didn't say anything, but Buddy got the feeling he again wasn't being proper.

The next time Lance invited them over was to swim in his pool. Anna didn't want to go, but Mom made her, so she was in a horrible mood and everyone knew it. Buddy did a cannonball in the shallow end, where Anna happened to be dangling her feet in the water, and he splashed her. She hollered and told him he was a pest, so he went over and started slapping the water to get her wetter. She kicked water back at him, got up and stomped into the house.

"I have towels here for you kids before you go inside," Lance said, too late. He followed her in and used one of the towels on his wooden floors.

"You kids mortified me," Mom said on the way home. "I didn't realize how terrible your manners are."

"If Lance has a pool, why is his skin so white?" Buddy asked. "Doesn't he ever sit outside by it or swim in it?"

"I think he's an albino person," Anna said. "He's like a ghost. And he doesn't have much personality."

"You kids are ungrateful and rude," Mom said. "He could provide for us very well."

Anna cringed. "Ooh, the price you'd have to pay for that," she said. "Not worth it. I'd rather be poor."

"You have no idea," Mom said.

Lance didn't ask them over a third time, and Buddy heard Grandma say he got engaged to Sharon Watkins, a lady from town who owned a clothing store. Buddy thought of Lance's smell, relieved he'd never have that in his nostrils again.

Then there was someone named Jules. He took Mom to see Robert Goulet, and she thought Jules was very sophisticated and handsome. But he didn't want kids, either. He told Mom to put their photos back into her purse when she tried to show them to him.

Mom had a few more dates with different people, but nothing materialized. She said she hated living with Grandma and Grandpa, as a grown woman should not live with her husband's parents. Buddy loved all of it, feeling he could live there his whole life. Anna said Dad probably would have wanted them with his mom and dad.

"Dad knows we're safe here," Anna said. "I think he'd like that."

Mom was folding a load of towels on the table, and she paused. She looked like she was going to say something, but then closed her mouth and picked up another towel. She gave it a good shake, folded it twice, then folded it the other way before placing it on the pile of previously folded towels, all facing in the same direction. Mom said laundry was a never-ending job, especially since Anna needed a towel for her body and a towel for her hair and refused to use the same one twice. Buddy once pointed out that she was clean when she dried herself so she should be able to reuse them, but she glared at him like he had warts. Mom said it was a battle that wasn't worth fighting.

Months had passed since they'd moved in with Grandma and Grandpa. Mom got more and more itchy about it. She insisted on paying a little bit of rent, but couldn't convince Grandma and Grandpa to take any money. Instead of getting closer to her in-laws, Mom seemed like she was trying to get further away. Sometimes a knot formed in Buddy's belly from all the worry. He didn't know why he got that hard spot in his stomach, and would try to persuade it to go away. It happened mostly at night, when he thought about how his mom looked far away when he desperately wanted her to see what was right in front of her.

"I know it's hard living with us," Grandma said one morning. Buddy was up early because he had to pee, and he heard her and Mom talking. "We love having all of you, but you obviously aren't comfortable here."

A pause followed. Then Mom said, "It's just that I can't keep depending on you. You've been so kind, and I can't make it on my own, but I can't take advantage of you, either."

"Is that the real issue, Bonnie? Or do you feel like we are watching you? We know you're going to move on with your life. We're trying to prepare ourselves for that. You are responsible for those kids, but we don't want anything to get in the way of your happiness."

"Sometimes I don't think I'll ever be happy," Mom said. "I had everything I ever wanted, but guess I didn't deserve it. I feel like I asked for too much, and God is punishing me."

"It doesn't work like that, honey," Grandma protested. "You have to know that."

The clock above the dining room table went *click, click, click.* As if what came next was normal.

"I feel like he saved my life, and I couldn't save his. He was everything to me. The fact that he loved me even after he found out I was pregnant with Anna, and he married me, and then we had Buddy...I couldn't believe I was so lucky."

"I know, Bonnie," Grandma said. "Now you are all with us, though, and we have to find God's blessings where they are."

Buddy stayed behind the bathroom door. The sun was coming up, shining a golden sliver through the window over the sink. He could maybe sneak back to bed for a few minutes and think about what he'd just heard. His feet were cold from the tiles on the black and white floor; he wasn't sure he understood the significance of Mom and Grandma's conversation, but knew it meant something. The door squeaked when he finally opened it, and the women stopped talking.

James Shearing came along right when Buddy thought maybe his mom would accept that they needed to stay with his grandparents. She still acted restless, but seemed to have given up on the local pool of men. She even joked that she'd met all of them, and they were all losers. She'd been lucky to find Dad, the only decent man in the area.

"Having two kids only makes it harder," she said to someone on the phone that particular afternoon, Buddy listening in nearby. "No man wants to take on another man's children. Well, there are a couple, but they are few and far between." Mom dragged the cord around the kitchen with her as she talked. Grandma and Grandpa were at the grocery store.

"Are you serious?" she asked. "Where is he from?" Mom motioned for Buddy to hand her the Coke bottle fitted with the special top for sprinkling clothes. She used it to put water on a shirt sleeve, cradling the phone with her neck as she picked up the iron. "Huh," she said. "Well, if he's new to the area, and Andy says he's lonely, maybe I'll give him a chance." So Mom was talking to Sylvia, one of the other ladies at her work. She and Andy had been friends of Mom and Dad's. Mom didn't seem to have a lot of women friends; maybe Grandma was the closest friend she had.

"Friday night? Oh, alright," Mom said. "What's one more attempt to find a nice guy?" She and Sylvia chatted a little longer before Mom unwound herself from the phone cord, hung up, and resumed ironing. She started to hum a Neil Diamond song.

A few weeks later, Mom announced she and James Shearing were dating.

"He's smart; he's a mechanic, and he moved here from Georgia," Mom said.

"What brought him to this part of the country?" Grandpa asked. "When are we going to meet him?"

"The plant where he worked shut down," Mom said. "And you'll meet him soon, I promise."

That first meeting was unremarkable. He came by the house to pick Mom up for dinner, stepping inside for just a few minutes. Buddy didn't know what he was expecting, but was surprised at how much older James looked than Mom. He stood very straight and tall, and had a skinny nose. He shook Grandpa's hand and smiled at Grandma.

"You must be Buddy," he said, extending his hand. Buddy grasped it, making sure to use his right hand.

"I am," Buddy said.

"What's your real name?" James asked.

"Buddy," Buddy said.

"Can't be," James said. "No one names their kid Buddy." He chuckled. "It has to be Robert or Clifford or something, maybe after your dad."

Buddy shook his head. "It's my real name. My dad named me Buddy when I was born because he said I would be his best buddy."

"That's right," Grandma said.

"Well, that's a new one on me," James said. "Kinda silly."

There was an awkward pause. Mom grabbed her sweater and purse, saying she was ready to go.

"Nice to meet you," James said as they left. Anna, who'd been ignored, said nothing.

Grandma snorted after the door shut. "First impression not so good," she whispered.

"Doesn't it bug you?" Anna asked. "Having someone who isn't our dad come to pick up our mom?"

Grandma raised her eyebrows. "What bugs me is that your dad had to leave us. Beyond that, I just have to turn things over to the man upstairs."

"Is there someone upstairs? If so, he's taking a nap and has forgotten about us," Anna said.

"Oh, come now, Anna. You can't understand everything that happens in life; it's all beyond our comprehension." Grandma turned and tucked her into a hug. "Let's have some soup and toasted cheese sandwiches. Sound good?"

Mom seemed to be floating on a cloud those first days of dating James Shearing. Buddy wanted to be happy for her, but another part of him hoped she fell through those clouds. The bad feeling in his stomach wouldn't go away.

James didn't come to the house often, but Mom spent a lot of time with him. He was renting an apartment, and when the kids visited never took his eyes from them. While there they were uneasy and afraid to make a mess. Mom seemed not to notice, though they never stayed long.

Buddy and Anna also saw that James was pretty fussy about

his food. He didn't like chicken. He didn't like leftovers, and said they meant the cook was lazy. He didn't seem crazy about anything but their mom.

Then he lost his job, and they moved to Ohio.

Chapter 7

Smells Like Spring

Late **April, and snow** in the forecast. Buddy knew he couldn't yet move the sidewalk salt to the storage room, but he was getting irritated by it. He was eager for the weather to change.

The kids were, too. They tracked in mud, snow, and boundless energy, spilling things and leaving trails in their wake. The time from spring break to June was brutal for a custodian. Not only were the kids wound up, but teachers were getting grumpy, too. Everyone was leaning toward summer, like the wildflowers in the woods. Now that syrup was finished, the next season Buddy craved was greenness. As soon as the trilliums opened, that meant morels; he could actually feel his fingers itching to forage among last fall's leaves.

Morels were elusive for some folks, but Buddy knew where to look. He carefully pinched them from their stems, leaving the base in the ground. Trout lilies, wild violets, and fiddleheads were a bonus, along with the smell of the forest waking up. Oh, and the leeks, scenting the earth with that sweet young onion smell. He'd coax them from their skins and eat them raw, knowing Mags would say something about his breath but not caring. Even black flies circling didn't bother him. He rarely got bitten, maybe because he didn't bathe every day and the bugs weren't drawn to his scent.

"Hey, Mr. Robertson," someone said, and he turned from the baseboard with his broom. It was one of the fourth graders, Liam. The boy came walking down the hall toward him.

"Hey, Liam," Buddy said. "What's up?"

"Oh, I need to go to the eye doctor today, so I'm getting out early," Liam said. "Then my mom and I are going to a movie so we can be in the dark for awhile until the eye drops wear off."

"That's a good idea," Buddy said. He had never gone to a movie with his mother. *Huh.*

"Yeah, and we always get popcorn," Liam said.

"That's nice of your mom."

Buddy continued his way down the hall. At home he'd load up the wood stove, hoping it was getting to the end of doing that for awhile. Vainly optimistic, but eventually it would come to pass. All too soon he'd be wishing for the kind summer weather to take time in leaving.

When Buddy walked in the door he was surprised by the warm smell of cinnamon. Following his nose to the kitchen, he found Mags dressed and cooking.

"What's the occasion?" he asked. Mags even had her hair brushed. Her blue eyes crinkled around the edges as she smiled.

"Our boys are coming for dinner," she said.

"Both of them?"

"Yup. And the kids." Mags tossed a brick of frozen hamburger into a skillet and put a lid on it. Two jars of store-bought spaghetti sauce were on the counter, along with a large box of noodles.

"Oh boy," Buddy said. "The cats are probably already in hiding. They always know when those kids are coming over."

"Last time I thought they were starting to settle down a bit," Mags protested. "Little Caleb even let me read to him."

"I'd better move those tools from the other night, or the kids will run through the house with them and impale themselves," Buddy said. He set to his task, noting Mags had put her remotes in their customary spots. He rolled the tools up in the towel and placed them inside the toolbox without closing it. He tucked it behind some of the boxes along the wall, where little hands couldn't reach.

When the boys and their families arrived, Mags grinned widely and hugged everyone tight. Buddy got hugs from the two youngest kids, and he gave a head rub to the oldest. Although they lived in the area, Lennie and Luke rarely visited together. Buddy was grateful the girls had managed to straighten up their kitchen. Kelso, the oldest of Luke's kids, was 11, and he looked like Luke spit him out. Juke was seven, and little Caleb was three. They were energetic and curious. Buddy showed a great deal of affection toward them, feeling less restrained than he had with Luke and Lennie. They all liked going into the woods with him, where they scared every wild critter for miles.

"What's that you have?" Buddy asked Kelso, pointing to a device in his hand.

"It's a cell phone," Kelso said, vainly attempting to conceal his pride. "My mom got it for me."

"It stays off while we're here," Luke ordered. "Damn kid has his nose in it far too often for my taste."

"He's not the only one," Buddy commiserated. "They've all got 'em."

"Did you hear what those cost, not only to get but maintain?" Luke snorted. "No way would I have paid for that."

Kelso shrugged and slid the gadget into his pocket. "What's for dinner?" he asked. "It smells good, Grandma."

"Snail tails and roadkill, if I remember dinners from when I was a kid," Lennie said. That got a small smile from Kelso, but a belly laugh from Juke.

"It's only gotten worse," Buddy said, and now even Kelso laughed out loud. Buddy had a feeling of everything being right in the world. He hardly ever felt that way. It was like a prayer you say before climbing into a warm bed.

Dinner was loud and happy, carrying him into the evening. He felt drowsiness overtaking him after they had apple crisp for dessert. Mags used the frozen apples Buddy harvested last fall from an old orchard over by Elk Rapids.

"Hey, can Lennie and I work on your bathroom for you guys?" Luke asked, just as Buddy was about to put his feet up in the recliner. For some reason he wanted to object, but Mags brightened, her finger marking the place in the book she'd been reading to Caleb.

"You want to tackle that?" she asked. Buddy knew it would be a lost cause to argue.

"Well, I'm off until the weather improves, and I've got some supplies in my garage that I think will work," Luke said. "Lennie said he ain't doing much, either, so we got the time."

"I'd have to tear it apart first, see what all's back there," Buddy said. "That's gonna be a huge mess."

"Like it isn't now," Mags said. "I'd love to be able to shower again."

"We got this," Luke said, nodding to Buddy. His cheeks always shone pink, and he had blue eyes inherited from Mags. He wore a hat to conceal his receding hairline; his hair had always been thin, also like his mom's. He bore no resemblance to Buddy, and why would he? Luke carried himself differently, with a confidence so foreign to Buddy it almost made him jealous. Yet he loved that kid, and his brother, like they were his from birth. Why couldn't he just let them fix his bathroom and be happy they were willing?

Because it felt like a judgment, just one more thing Buddy didn't do around the house he and Mags lived in, another task fallen by the wayside. He knew he had to swallow his pride and let it happen, so he managed to say, "Sure," and even, "Thanks," feeling like the loser he'd always been.

He woke up in the night, wondering if the boys knew he wished he'd been their real dad, if they ever felt like he at least partly filled that role. They'd never even come close to discussing it. He regretted not expressing himself more when they were little, when their chubby fingers touched Mags's face and he'd yearned for the freedom to accept their sloppy caresses. That was a lifetime ago, too late to make up for. He thought of Ben Jameson, how his life was set on a track leading down a cold, lonely, darkened route. Buddy decided to show that boy some kindness. He'd try to convince one lost, little soul there was someone who cared.

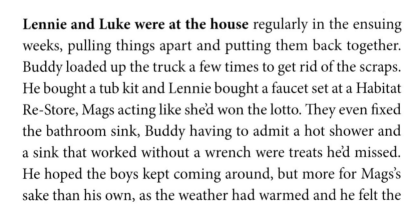

Lennie and Luke were at the house regularly in the ensuing weeks, pulling things apart and putting them back together. Buddy loaded up the truck a few times to get rid of the scraps. He bought a tub kit and Lennie bought a faucet set at a Habitat Re-Store, Mags acting like she'd won the lotto. They even fixed the bathroom sink, Buddy having to admit a hot shower and a sink that worked without a wrench were treats he'd missed. He hoped the boys kept coming around, but more for Mags's sake than his own, as the weather had warmed and he felt the woods beckoning.

His first day out in the forest a barred owl stared down at him from a budding maple, fixing Buddy with its black eyes. Buddy marveled at its markings and its unflinching stare until it lifted from the branch and whooshed away.

Finally the woods came to life, fulfilling the promise they'd whispered through the long winter. Both the black and white morels were plentiful this year. They thrived during warm, wet weather, and Buddy made sure to take advantage of their short season. Today his mesh bag bulged full; if he didn't get back to the house soon he'd likely end up stepping on more mushrooms in the dark. A garter snake slithered through the leaves, tempting Buddy to pick it up, but last time he did that his hands got covered with stinky excrement from the frightened reptile. *Never mind that,* he thought, hefting his load. Reaching out to touch a beech tree, he appreciated the smoothness of its bark, remembering when he and Leah carved their initials into one so long ago.

Someday he should tally the trees on his property, so he knew how many hemlocks, beech, maples, and oaks were on it. He'd grid areas off so he could make sure to get an accurate count. Why hadn't he done that before? Buddy shrugged as if asked the question by someone else. How good it was to have so many different trees he could touch and be among every day. Each species had its own feel to the bark, its own leaf, its own cone or acorn or nut.

"I swear, spring has a peculiar smell to it," Mags said as he entered the kitchen. "It stinks."

"Whaddya mean, it stinks?" Buddy asked as he eased out of his boots. "I love the smell of spring."

"It stinks like dampness and trees mating," Mags said.

"Trees mating?"

"Yeah, like old, rotten wood and old, rotten leaves on steroids."

Mags took the teapot from the stove and filled it with water. "It's a nasty odor."

"You are a crazy woman," Buddy said. "It smells better than almost anything else in the whole world."

"Smells like a scummy pond."

"What's wrong with a pond?" Buddy held up his bag of fungoids. "That smelly place gave up all these gems today," he said, which got a nod even from Mags.

"Well, at least there's something good that comes from the smell," she said. "How about me frying some up for dinner?"

"Sounds amazing," Buddy said. "I think I'll pull some steaks out, too."

"Beat ya to it," Mags said. "I knew you wouldn't come outta them woods without some 'shrooms."

"So I'm good for something, eh?"

Mags grinned. "Every so often," she said. "I hang around here for some reason."

"Besides my looks?" Buddy asked.

Mags pulled a teabag from a box on the counter and looked at him sideways. "Well, there's that," she said, winking. Buddy should have hugged her, but he didn't.

Today the fifth graders were trying out for middle school band, a tradition that took place every May. All Tuesday afternoon, Buddy listened to the horrid sounds of kids blowing on trombones or clarinets or flutes for the first time. *Good lord, make it stop,* he thought to himself more than once. The poor band teacher must wear earplugs.

The hall floors had been polished over spring break, but you'd never know it. The kids dragged in sand constantly, and Buddy was repeatedly pushing the broom. Northern Michigan sand was particularly abrasive on floors; no clay here like in Pennsylvania, though that was probably tough to clean up too, he figured. Still, at least it was good dirt. He made another pass down the hall, ears perking up as he heard raised voices, a horn instrument also squeaking like a dying pig.

"…Faggot," Buddy picked up from a boy near the lockers. He looked to see a tall kid standing next to Ben Jameson. Ben attempted to grab a book from his locker, and the kid slapped his hand.

"I said, you're a faggot."

Ben was still. Buddy turned the broom around and headed their way.

"You kids should be in class," he said.

"Who says?" The kid bothering Ben was Isaac Calder. Buddy didn't know him well, but he recalled that his brother was a bully, too.

"We can ask Mr. Hopkins if you want," Buddy said. "But I think you know where you ought to be right now."

Isaac sneered harder, as if he were going to spew something, but then it weakened and he backed off. "You're just the janitor," he muttered.

"And you're just a bully," Buddy answered. "Get to class."

Ben wouldn't fix his gaze on anything, including Buddy. He pulled the book he'd been retrieving into his arms and started to walk away.

"You okay? Do you want to talk with Mr. Hopkins about how Isaac was treating you?"

"No. Wouldn't do any good," Ben said.

Buddy opened his mouth to say something, then closed it.

Ben was right. It wouldn't. If anything, it would make Isaac worse. He watched as Ben slunk down the hall.

What a terrible word, faggot, he thought. Tossed at someone else to inflict insult and pain. The person who called Buddy that was a straight man who hurled words alongside physical abuse and sexual cruelty. What type of word could define someone like that? Depraved? Savage? He couldn't think of anything to match the contempt of "faggot," an empty and hateful word that should be abolished.

Later, Buddy decided he would at least mention the incident to Blair Hopkins. Maybe if the principal knew he could keep an eye on things. He pushed his broom down the east side of the building toward the office, stooping to pick up a few pieces of trash along the way and crumpling them into his pocket.

"He really needs to see a dentist," he overheard as he neared Samantha's office. "Why would someone with dental insurance not go? I just don't get it." It wasn't until Buddy rounded the corner that he realized he was the topic of conversation. The look on Sage Carmichael's face when she saw him betrayed this. And it was the way the talk stopped. Sage was a teacher known for her mouth, and Buddy tried to steer as clear of her as possible. Now he tried to ignore her. Samantha was a little too eager to look at Buddy with a kind expression, the same one she wore when she dealt with the kids.

"Need something, Buddy?" Samantha asked. Sage strutted over to the copy machine, where papers were shooting into a pile on a tray. *Huh.* So she did know how to run the copier by herself. Some of the teachers treated Sam like their own personal secretary.

"Is Mr. Hopkins in?" Buddy asked.

"No, he had to go to a conference. Is there something I can relay when he checks in?"

Buddy surely wasn't going to say anything in range of Sage's hearing.

"No, it can wait," he said. "Not important."

He turned and pushed his broom down the other side of the hall. Reaching his work cart, Buddy put the broom in its place and just stood there for a few seconds. Then he pushed open the door to the boys' room. Approaching the mirror, he looked at his teeth. No denying the fact: they were a mess. He'd lost a canine tooth years ago, along with some in the back. The remaining teeth were brown and crooked.

He avoided the dentist: no denying that, either. By the time he'd qualified for dental insurance through the school, his teeth were sorely neglected. He pulled one out himself following a course of antibiotics for an abscess, prescribed after Mags finally talked him into seeing someone. By that time it had been about 20 years since his last visit, and the asshole dentist remarked how people in this town didn't take care of their teeth, adding that poverty seemed to be an excuse for ignorance. He wanted Buddy to remain on the medicine for another 10 days and then come in for a root canal. Even with insurance, the cost was hundreds of dollars. Buddy walked out without stopping at the desk, headed home, and took a pair of pliers to his mouth. He finished the antibiotic, hoping he wouldn't get an infection, and it worked. He hadn't been to a dentist since, would rather poke himself in the eye than go (let alone pull his own tooth with a pair of rusty old pliers).

The scorn he felt for Sage Carmichael burned. As he looked at his image in the glass, his reddened face with the brown teeth showed no mercy.

When he saw Samantha escorting some kids outside after school, she smiled at him. He knew Sam was a good person, that she was someone who sympathized with those "less fortunate."

Still, she had no idea what it felt like to be from Buddy's world, much less Ben Jameson's.

Even in the woods later that day, Buddy felt the sting of what he'd overheard, the reproach and condescension. He knew the feelings he was having would pass; they always did. He'd find some sort of redemption in the outdoors.

Chapter 8

Thou Shalt Not
Steal Candy

1969

Buddy held a small television set in his lap the whole way to Ohio. His mom drove her old car and James Shearing followed with a U-Haul. The trip took about seven hours, but it felt like a world away from where they belonged. Buddy pictured Grandma and Grandpa at their dinner table, quiet and alone.

Anna stared out her window from the front passenger seat. Lately her eyes were hard and mad. Even Grandma told her she needed to keep an open mind about moving.

"You might surprise yourself and like it," Grandma had said.

"I know this isn't going to go well," Anna had countered. "It's awful not having a choice about where you go and who you're with."

Grandma had sighed. "I know, honey."

Mom turned the radio up so she could hear a song she liked. It was something sappy by The Lettermen. Buddy put his hands over his ears and groaned. "Jeez, Mom," he whined. She paid him no attention.

Everyone stopped for dinner at a truck stop, and James held Mom's hand over the table. "This will be fine; you'll see," he said. Mom's eyes got all watery as she said she was a little scared.

"Nothin' to be scared of," James said. "I have a job, and you'll find one soon."

"I won't know anyone," Mom said.

"You know me," James whispered.

Buddy saw Anna roll her eyes.

They ate hot beef sandwiches and mashed potatoes, and James said the kids could have root beer, though they couldn't drink it until their meals came. Their waitress was nice; she wore a white apron with a big brown stain on it in the shape of a turtle. She said she couldn't make it through one day without spilling coffee.

"I could clean that up for you," James said.

The waitress didn't say anything back. Instead she gave Buddy a straw and said, "Here you go, sweetheart." Buddy liked her for saying that. Her hair was piled real high on top of her head, like a bunch of cotton candy on a paper cone. When she brought their meals she carried all four plates at once, impressing him. She set the bill at the end of their table. The hot beef wasn't as good as Grandma's, but they were hungry. Even Anna ate most of hers.

On the road again, Anna dozed. Buddy didn't realize he was sleeping until he dreamed that a big dog was on his lap. He opened his eyes, and the TV reminded him of where he was.

Not long after that, they pulled into a driveway behind James. A house with gray shingles stood at the end.

"Is this it?" Anna asked.

"I guess," Mom said. "Let's get out and start unpacking."

"So this isn't a nightmare," Anna said. "I was hoping I'd wake up and it would be."

"Shush."

Buddy managed to wrest himself from underneath the television set and crawl out of the car. "Can I pee first?" he asked.

"Sure."

He started to run toward the house, and James whistled. "Whoa, aren't you gonna help?" he asked.

"Yeah, but I need to pee!"

"You need a key first!" James left the U-Haul door half open and came up to the house. "Don't think you're gonna wheedle your way out of unloading," he barked. "Hurry up and get your ass back out here."

Buddy burst through the door, hoping he made it to the toilet. "It's the first door on the left," James said, pointing.

The bathroom had green tiles and a yellow sink, with big green and yellow flowers in patterns papered on the walls. Buddy shivered as he peed, relieved to be out of the car. He left the bathroom after giving his hands a cursory rinse in cold water. The living room was bare, with dark paneling and a green carpet. They didn't have a lot of furniture, but Buddy could finally unpack what had been at Grandma and Grandpa's. He wiped his hands on his pants so he could get the door handle to turn. Mom and James were already at the U-Haul, pulling stuff out.

"I want my workbench stuff out first so I can get it into the kitchen," James said.

"The kitchen?" asked Mom.

"Yes, that's where I want my workbench. I'm not putting it in a garage with no electricity," James asserted.

"But why the kitchen?"

"I looked, and it's the only place where there's room," James said. "Better keep your mouth shut about it."

Mom's lips got tight, and she looked smaller. She took a box toward the house.

"What did I just say?" James yelled. "My work stuff first."

"This says 'tools,'" Mom said.

"Awright. Just make sure."

The day was long. By the end of it Buddy felt like he was walking on his tiptoes, trying to avoid James's attention and constant griping. Anna repeatedly wiped her sweaty hair from her face, which was fixed in a permanent scowl. Buddy's stomach was growling, but he wasn't going to ask about eating anything. He just wanted to have quiet.

Finally Mom said she was going to throw something together for dinner. There wasn't much, but she did have some Kraft macaroni and cheese and a few hot dogs.

"Don't make a habit out of that kind of shit," James muttered. Yet he ate three hot dogs and most of the mac and cheese.

Buddy fell into bed afterward, exhausted. James said they were no help, but Buddy's legs were sore from moving dressers and bed frames and boxes. James sure didn't remember what it was like to be a kid.

As he started to fall asleep, he dreamed of Dad. Buddy was holding his dad's hands, walking up his legs and doing a backward somersault, laughing. "Again!" he said in the dream, and Dad took Buddy's hands in his, over and over.

"I think we should explore outside," Anna said the next morning, standing over Buddy's bed.

"Huh?" For a second Buddy wasn't sure where he was.

"Let's see where we live," Anna said. "Before that bastard wakes up." She grabbed Buddy's covers and flipped them aside. As he started to yell, she put a finger to her lips. "Shhh!"

Buddy reluctantly sat up. Anna handed him a pair of pants. "Just put these over your PJs," she said.

They let themselves outside through the door in the kitchen, on the other side of the house from Mom's room. *Mom and James's room.* That was a weird thought.

The house looked ordinary in the morning light. The landscape was nothing like home, though. Buddy could see all the way across the fields, no hills and few trees breaking up the view. "Why is it so flat?" he asked.

"Guess that's just the way it is here," Anna said, shrugging. "Kind of barren without our hills."

"Where will I wander around?"

"I dunno. It's like someone laid a blanket over the earth and took out all the wrinkles, isn't it?"

"I like the wrinkles," Buddy said.

"Me too. Everything is strange; really, it's been strange since Dad died." Anna took a piece of candy out of her pocket. "I stole these from the refrigerator," she said. "Let's eat them for breakfast."

Buddy grabbed the chocolate and had a bite of it, savoring the caramel that stuck to each of his teeth. He took his time, slowly sucking every last bit out of every cranny, not indulging in another mouthful until the remnants were all gone.

"Where were these hid in the fridge?"

"Way in the back," Anna said. "There was a whole box, and I took one for each of us."

"My favorite candy bar is a PayDay, but these are delicious," Buddy said. "I'd sure like to have one while I read a comic book."

"Did I show you that *Mad* magazine I have?" Anna asked.

"It's really funny. The kid in it kind of reminds me of you. He has big ears and freckles."

"I have freckles?" Buddy asked, horrified. "I hate freckles!"

Anna laughed. "Oh, they're cute on you, little bro," she said. They walked side by side, and she bent to pick up a spent dandelion. Rather than blow on it, she tore a few tufts loose and released them from her palm. "Well, they have these here," she said.

"They have milkweed, too," Buddy said. "Did you know that monarch butterflies love milkweed?"

"Yeah, Grandpa showed me a chrysalis once," Anna said.

"Me too!"

"It didn't look anything like a monarch, though. I thought it looked almost like a piece of jewelry."

"Yeah."

They heard a door slam in the distance. Mom called out to them, and she sounded funny. They turned and headed back to the little house.

"Coming!" Anna yelled back. Then, "We probably have a list of chores by now."

Mom stood by the edge of the yard, watching them as they approached. "Which one of you stole the candy?" she asked when they were close enough. She still had sleepy dust on her eyelids.

"I took two," Anna said. "What's the big deal?"

James Shearing came around the corner of the house, one hand clutching a long and winding twig. Buddy thought it came from a tree called a weeping willow. Grandpa said they were pretty, though they made a mess.

"The big deal is that those were mine, and no one asked if they could have one," James said. "Now, who took them?"

"I did!" Anna said.

"Don't give me that shit; look at you," James spit. "You're too skinny to steal chocolate. I know who did it."

"It was me!" Anna eyed the twig that James gripped. "I didn't know it was a cardinal sin to take a few."

"You're lying for that little faggot," James said. "I know better. Tell me who did it, and maybe I won't use this."

Buddy realized what this meant for him, and he started to sob. "It was me," he said. "I did it."

"No, he didn't!" Anna protested. "If you're gonna whip someone, whip me!"

Her pleas did no good. The willow branch quickly unfurled, catching Buddy around his legs. The pain was lessened somewhat by his two pairs of pants, but it stung. He clutched his calves and hollered.

"Stop!" Mom yelped. "My word, James! Stop!"

Mercifully, James only used the whip once. He tossed it aside and went toward the house. "Keep your hands to yourselves," he ordered. "You got off easy this time."

Mom tried to comfort Buddy, but he pushed past her and stumbled inside, heading for his room. Anna followed him, but as she neared his door James told her to leave the "fairy kid" alone and get busy.

Buddy decided he wasn't going anywhere until he absolutely had to. He lay in bed and listened to the conversation coming from the kitchen.

"One day here and your kids are proving to be trouble," James said to Mom.

"Is this really a reason to hurt Buddy?" Mom asked. "I will buy you another box of candy."

"That's not the point! You don't get it! Didn't you people teach them anything?"

"They weren't brought up to be afraid of taking a piece of candy," Mom said. "Please, think about it."

"Shut the hell up." James slammed the door, then opened it again. "I'm going to the shop, and when I get back, this house better be standin' tall." Buddy heard the engine of James's truck, then squealing tires as he hit the road. At least there would be relief for a little while. He stayed in his bed, mad at Mom for bringing them here, for allowing this to happen, for not knowing that Ohio would be the worst idea ever.

When she stepped into his room, he couldn't help but glare at her.

"I'm sorry, Buddy," she said. "You didn't deserve that."

"No, he didn't," Anna said from behind her. "What the hell?"

"Watch your language." Mom sat down beside Buddy and touched his leg. "Did it leave a mark?"

"What do you care?" He couldn't resist.

"Oh, Buddy." Mom lifted his pants and rubbed his left calf. "Nothing there."

"Like that asshole said, that's not the point." Anna remained in the doorway. She threw her hands up and made buggy eyes at Mom. "I am not going to walk around worried about making that jerk mad."

"We are all adjusting," Mom said. "It will get better."

She was so wrong. What's more, she told herself that lie for far too long. In the meantime, they all — including Anna — began to try and anticipate what would make James Shearing erupt. None of them ever mastered the practice.

One Saturday, Buddy picked up the phone after it rang repeatedly. The person on the other end asked for James.

"He's at work," Buddy said. As Grandma taught him, he then asked, "Would you like to leave a message?" He carefully wrote down a number. The person on the line said it was extremely important that James call back right away.

James came in for dinner, his boots greasy, but he didn't remove them before sitting at the table. Mom had prepared a special dinner of homemade scalloped potatoes and Spam; she'd made corn muffins, too. Buddy was so hungry he could hardly wait for the food to cool on his fork, but he remembered the telephone call and told James he had a message. He gave James the number he'd written down.

"What the hell?" James muttered. "Why did you answer the telephone?"

"It kept ringing," Buddy said. "I didn't know I wasn't supposed to."

"What did you say?"

"I didn't know I wasn't supposed…"

"No, you idiot, what did you say to the person on the phone?"

"I said you were at work, and asked if they wanted to leave a message." Somehow, the thought of meeting James's eyes was terrifying. Buddy didn't know where to look, so he kept his head down. That was why he didn't see the fist coming toward him, giving him no time to react. Buddy felt the impact, and it took a few seconds for it to hurt. Then it hurt like crazy. He held his head and kept his eyes closed, waiting for another strike, but when none came dared to open them. His potatoes were half on his plate and half on the table in an oozy mess.

"You don't know shit from Shinola!" James yelled, just as Anna came over from her side of the table and scratched at his face.

In moments the two were down on the floor rolling around, Mom trying unsuccessfully to break them apart. Despite all this activity the only noise was that of grunting and panting. Finally Mom screamed, "STOP!" and James tore himself away from Anna. Standing up, he threw the full casserole dish across the room.

"Little bastards!" He went to hit Mom, but something stopped him and his fingers instead raised to his face, where blood now trickled from his cheek. James swiped a work towel from his bench and brushed at the wound. Then he grabbed his keys and left, sand and mud hitting the side of the garage as he peeled out.

Anna lay in a heap on the floor. She fought back tears, having to catch her breath before mustering the energy to let them out. Mom was trying to scoop the rest of their supper onto the bigger part of the dish on the floor.

"How can you even care about that?" Anna gasped. "Jesus, Mom! Do you think we can eat after what just happened?"

Mom paused and put her face in her hands. "I don't think anything anymore, Anna."

"Are you okay?" Buddy asked. He didn't know which one he was asking.

Anna used a chair to pull herself up. She had blood on her face, too, and she was holding her side.

"I can't breathe," she whispered.

Mom stood and got Anna to sit on a chair. She wiped Anna's face clean, Buddy relieved to see there was nothing underneath the blood. It must have all come from James. When Mom lifted Anna's blouse to check her left side, Anna grimaced and tried to push her away.

"I need to see," Mom said. "You are going to have a big bruise."

"But he's got marks on his face," Anna said, and smiled. "So I got 'im. Let's hope he doesn't bother to come back."

"What happens if he does?" Buddy posed.

"By that time he'll be calmed down. We'll have this cleaned up, and you kids will be in bed," Mom said. "You two just sit."

"Gladly," Anna said. "I don't think I can stand up."

Two days later, Mom took Anna to the doctor because she was still complaining about her side. It turned out she had two fractured ribs.

Mom told the doctor Anna fell down the front steps of their house. When Anna got home she said that was a joke, since there were only two steps. But no one in the outside world knew any different. Just the four people who lived there knew, and there was no one else to tell.

Of course James said they brought it all on themselves. He yelled at Mom that it was a bill collector calling, and thanks to Buddy they now knew he had a job somewhere. It would only be a matter of time until they tracked him down, and it was all the fault of that little faggot.

"It's not my fault you don't pay your bills," Buddy said from his room. Mom didn't even argue on his behalf. He saw her folding into herself more and more, and got angrier and angrier at her for forsaking him and his sister.

Chapter 9

A Dollar Store Puzzle

Buddy couldn't recall how long they lived in Ohio. He remembered events and days there like it was yesterday, but dates escaped him. Sometimes he'd hear a song and recall it came out during that time. He supposed they were there for a little less than a year. He held no grudges against Ohio, but sometimes wondered if the house where they lived still stood. It should have crumbled in on itself. Buddy didn't much care for talk shows, but he happened to hear Dr. Phil say once that every bad thought took energy from the universe. All the bad thoughts in that house could have sucked life out of a good portion of the Midwest.

It was time to get some clothes to the laundromat, he knew. He moved from the bathroom to the bedroom, gathering items as he went. He'd separate the darks and the whites once he got everything in one spot. Mags said she'd stay and watch the loads if he'd walk over to the dollar store and buy some cat litter and a puzzle for her to work on.

"What kind of picture do you want on the puzzle?"

"I don't care. Something pretty."

"You know those cats won't leave it alone, so you're gonna have a few pieces missing by the time you're done, anyway."

"Oh, quit it. I just want something to take my mind off things."

Buddy snorted. "What's that mean?"

Mags shrugged, tossing a few dishrags onto the pile. "I've just got things on my mind, you know, like people do sometimes. Been thinkin' too much lately."

"I s'pose." Buddy stooped to take a trash bag from underneath the sink, and used it for the dirty clothes. Shit, it looked like he'd need two. Good thing they had a change machine at the laundry. He got both bags into the truck, grabbed the detergent, and waited while Mags brushed her hair and got her jacket. Static caused her hair to click as she pulled it from the collar.

"It's hell being so hot that you give off sparks," she mused, and Buddy chuckled.

"Helluva thing it is," he said.

"Maybe we could grab something for lunch while we're in town?"

He nodded. "Want to go to Big Boy and get a Big Boy?"

"Sure! It's been awhile since I had a Big Boy."

"Tell me about it."

It was a beautiful sunny morning. Buddy liked the smell of the laundromat. He and Mags worked side by side, dividing their clothing and towels into several loads. Other folks were doing the same thing. An attendant was waiting on someone who brought in dry cleaning. Once they put the coins into the washers and got everything going, Mags grabbed a magazine and sat at a small table while Buddy set out for the store. The automatic door opened for him, and he stepped inside, heading toward the pet supplies aisle.

"Hey, Buddy!" he heard, and turning saw Carrie. She had a tube of some sort of makeup in her hand. At her side was Ben.

"Hi," Buddy said. "Doing some shopping?" *Dumb question.*

"Just a bit. I don't know if you heard, but Ben and I are in a foster home now. We're picking up a movie and then heading back to watch it. The people we're with are really nice. They let me use the car sometimes." Carrie's fingernails had the remains of dark blue polish on them, and her cuticles were rough. "You know Mr. Robertson, right, Ben?"

Ben barely nodded. He was holding a bag of potato chips and a two-liter bottle of Mountain Dew.

"Is that breakfast?" Buddy asked, pointing.

Ben made an attempt at a smile. Buddy appreciated it beyond measure.

"I'm picking up some things for Mags," he said. "She wants a puzzle, and I have no idea what she'd like."

Carrie raised her eyebrows. "Can we help? I think I could pick out something for her."

"Sure! She'd like that," Buddy said.

They didn't have much to choose from, but after a moment of consideration Ben picked up a 1000 piece box. Carrie took it and handed it to Buddy. "This is the one," she said. "She'll like that a lot."

The puzzle picture was a cat sitting on a bookshelf. It wore the expression of their cats, aloof and arrogant. Mags would love it. He couldn't have picked anything better.

"Perfect," he said.

"Purrr-fect," Ben said, making Carrie laugh. Buddy took great delight in that.

"Tell her my little brother picked it out," she said. Buddy said he certainly would. After grabbing the litter he went to check out, deciding to pay for their items as well.

"Oh, no, I have this makeup crap, and you don't want to pay for that," Carrie protested.

"No biggie," Buddy insisted. "Put your stuff up here."

They did. As he walked his purchases to the truck, he felt light and good. He even got a little wave from Ben as they parted ways.

Mags was still reading upon his return to the laundry, and he got her a pop from one of the machines. Three minutes left of the wash cycle. He walked to the window, jingling quarters in his pocket. A breeze had begun to pick up little pieces of litter in the parking lot, carrying them to a corner of the strip mall where they circled like a lazy mini-twister. He watched as people came and went. Samantha drove by after visiting the bank, and then one of the kids from school walked by with his mom and waved. Buddy acknowledged him with a grin.

Half an hour later, they had the trash bags reloaded with clean but unfolded things. Buddy knew the laundry would sit by the door until God knew when, but he sure as heck didn't intend to waste time folding when it was a nice day to be outside. He wanted to get a few tomato plants in some pots, then walk down to the creek at the end of his property.

They got into the truck and took off. "Ooh, nice puzzle!" Mags exclaimed as she took it from the bag. "How fun!"

"I can't take credit," Buddy said. "I bumped into Carrie and her brother at the store, and Ben picked it out for you."

"They should have come to say hi. Did you know they're in a foster home?"

"Yeah, she told me." Buddy didn't volunteer that he already knew about Ben. In fact, he'd never told Mags about Ben at all. He'd considered doing so, but decided against it because he didn't want to go there with her. It was ugly and wrong, and he couldn't begin to talk about it. *I think Ben was molested,* he'd say, and then Mags would want to know how he knew, what exactly he'd seen.

Buddy found himself holding his stomach at just the thought of having to explain. He could see Mags being horrified, wondering what Carrie had been through too; he saw her looking at him and somehow knowing what he felt. Forced to face her pity-filled expression, he'd have to look away. She'd know. He couldn't walk down that road with her. Not ever.

She was still examining the puzzle box, a slight smile on her face.

"Don't you just love those expressions cats get?" Mags mused. She looked up at the road, and then at him. "Do you know why those kids are in a foster home?" she asked.

"Not a clue," he lied. "Do you?"

"Jenna said the boy was beaten up. She said that's what Carrie told her. Isn't that awful?"

You don't know the half of it, Buddy thought. "Yes, it is," he replied.

That night one of the cats came into the bedroom, and Buddy sat up with a start. The sound of the door moving against the old carpet woke him immediately. He may have even made a noise from fear. He tried to calm himself, feeling his heartbeat thumping against his chest, thankful that Mags wasn't in bed with him.

Chapter 10

Shit from Shinola

1969

Had Buddy known James Shearing's abusive behavior was going to get worse, he maybe could have done something first. For weeks and months, he lived in fear of the slaps and slugs, the threats, the verbal hits. Then things changed, and he knew life could get much worse than it already was.

He should have figured that James would turn Mom against him and Anna. Mom had no energy to fight, and James was quick to point out every mistake the kids made. Anna was an ungrateful little bitch, and Buddy was lazy and stupid. Almost every day he told Buddy he didn't know shit from Shinola.

One weekend night, Mom cooked breakfast for supper. She fried sausages and eggs and made pancakes from scratch, James grumbling all the while how it wasn't really a fitting supper. But Buddy and Anna were looking forward to it.

Buddy took the Log Cabin syrup bottle and gave himself a generous dose. It wasn't Grandpa's good stuff, but it was sweet.

He could feel James watching him as he ate, but attempted to ignore him.

"You even hold your fork like a faggot," James said. Buddy kept trying to eat.

"I said, you hold your fork like a fag."

"Show me how a faggot holds his fork," Buddy answered.

James pounded a fist on the table, then jumped up from his chair. In a flash he put his hands around Buddy's neck and began to squeeze, dragging him from his seat. Buddy was now beneath him on the floor; he couldn't breathe, but the funny thing was he didn't feel like he was really there. Then he saw Anna's face over James's shoulder, her painted fingernails digging into the man's cheeks.

"Get off my brother!"

James shrugged her off. She flew backwards and landed on Mom, who was screaming at James to stop.

"Goddamn fairy!" James yelled.

"Who's the fairy?" Anna screamed back at him. "You need to pick on someone your own size!"

Coming forward, she landed a slap on his face. James released his grip on Buddy's throat and swung a punch that struck her squarely in the forehead. Anna tumbled and fell again. Mom finally threatened to call the police, and James backed away, pulling a handkerchief from his pocket. He wiped sweat from his forehead while staring down at Buddy, who was on his knees and elbows on the floor, watching and sobbing.

"Your kids make me do this!" James snapped. He stormed outside, and Mom followed him.

"See where she goes? Not to us, but to that damn asshole!" Anna reached for Buddy's hands and pulled him upright. He clung to her and couldn't stop crying.

"You've got purple marks on your neck." Anna grabbed a

cloth and wet it with cold water, wrapping it around Buddy's neck and face.

Nothing came of that nightmarish supper. For a few days the house was extremely quiet; Buddy's bruises faded, and if anyone noticed at school they didn't say anything. Anna had a lump on her head, but that went unnoticed as well. Buddy knew nobody noticed him, but Mom acting as if she couldn't even see their injuries was crushing. How could his mom, his good mom, let her kids live through this? He tried to ask Anna, but she only cursed.

Buddy picked up a cold that wouldn't go away, and James mimicked his sniffles and coughs, telling him to get the hell out of bed and help Mom around the house. Buddy's legs felt heavy, and he couldn't bring air into his lungs. He was so exhausted he just stood in the middle of the living room with the vacuum nozzle in his hand, confused about why he was supposed to clean when he should be at school. He felt the vacuum canister hit his cheek as he fell to the floor.

"My God, he's got a fever," Mom said after she knelt by him and felt his forehead.

"Anything to get out of a minute's work," James said, but he let Mom take Buddy to the emergency room.

He had strep throat and pneumonia, ending up missing two weeks of school. Mom didn't know anyone who could watch him, so on her work days Buddy tagged along and stayed in the car during her shift. He didn't care because all he wanted to do was sleep. Mom checked on him during her break and lunch hour. Once he started feeling better, he took some old comics and a few Matchbox cars with him. He got bored one day and started rolling over the front seat into the back, over and over, getting scared when a guy who worked at the restaurant next door came and peered into the window. He was glad the doors were locked. When he told his Mom she said it was a good thing it was Friday, as he'd go back to school next week.

"I'm really going to be behind," Buddy said.

"Yes, but Anna said she'd help you catch up," Mom said. "Just don't whine about it in front of James."

"I won't," Buddy promised. He didn't add that he watched every little thing around James, and it never helped.

The very next day Buddy was sitting at the table trying to make sense of his history homework, Anna beside him working on a composition paper, when James came in from work.

"Get your asses up and do something productive," he ordered.

"We are," Anna said. "It's called schoolwork."

James took Anna's papers from the table. "You get these back after you sweep the front porch and sidewalk."

Anna stood. Buddy tried to make it outside with her, but James grabbed him tightly around his shoulder and instructed him to clean the bathroom utilities. That was the worst job ever, and Buddy still had a bit of a queasy stomach from the medicine he was on for the pneumonia. He gagged as he put the Comet into the toilet and swished it around with a brush. There were hairs and yellow stains around the rim, and he tried to capture them with the brush so he wouldn't have to touch anything with his hands. He wondered where those blue gloves were that Mom used.

"Do it right," James said. Buddy turned to see James in the doorway, watching him. He had a funny look on his face, kind of like a grin but kind of like he was mad. He handed Buddy a rag. Buddy began to use it and gagged again. James gripped the back of his neck, and Buddy thought he was going to get smacked. Instead, James pushed his fingers into Buddy's mouth. "I'll give you something to gag on, you little fairy," he growled. Buddy wrenched away.

"Now use that rag, little girl, and clean up this bathroom right." With that, James left the room.

Buddy finished the job while holding his breath. He wiped tears from the end of his nose as he bent over the tub.

What was it about that day that changed things? Afterwards began a new world of cruelty and misery. Mom started to take James's side, and she blamed the kids for making her a nervous wreck. She said all she wanted was to be happy after Dad died, but Buddy and Anna wouldn't let her. It wasn't her fault he died, she said. Anna didn't even bother to argue. Her back would go straight, and she'd be quiet.

James Shearing started coming into his room at night, the door barely making any noise when he entered. It would all begin with a muffled scrape across the old rug. James Shearing never spoke when he came into Buddy's room, because there was no need. Fingers prodded, and a firm grip commanded. Buddy was afraid James would hurt them all if he yelled for help.

That first night, James touched him in places he knew should not be touched. He held his breath for as long as he could, and when he finally did inhale smelled James's breath, a disgusting heat of beer and tobacco and something sour. He was kind of relieved when James put the blanket up against his face. This way he didn't have to smell anything but the laundry scent of the covers. Each time he waited for the torture to be over, at first counting the nights this happened, but eventually he lost track and decided it didn't matter.

Buddy started having trouble staying awake at school. Every time he closed his eyes, he thought about what James did. Smells and tastes and fear rose in his throat. Classes went by, and he had no idea what the teachers said. He failed a spelling exam, then decided to cheat on a science test because he knew he was going to flunk that, too. He managed to fill in the blanks on the homework before the test, sticking the paper inside his desk so he could scrunch down and look at the answers.

During the test, the science teacher walked by his desk and paused. Buddy didn't look up. He saw her hand go to the paper and heard her make a small noise, like a sigh, before she grasped his shoulder.

"Come with me, Buddy," she said, and he hung his head. "Come on," she said, when he didn't immediately move. He couldn't look at any of the kids, but heard whispers and chuckles as Miss Tyler escorted him to the hallway.

"I can't have cheaters in my classroom," she stated.

"I know," Buddy said. "I'm sorry."

Oh, how he hoped she would not tell anyone what he did. He could feel the sting of James's slaps.

"Do you have to tell my parents?" he whispered. He hoped he could convince her by sheer will that he would never, ever do this again. Looking into her eyes, he saw concern and sympathy, and for a minute thought she would not. Then something changed, and she set her jaw. She was pretty for a teacher. Her hair was in a bun, and he liked how she had bobby pins all along the top, holding it in place. It must have taken a long time for her to get it like that.

"I do have to tell your parents," she said.

"I'll get whipped," Buddy said. A noise escaped his throat. "I mean, really bad."

"You should have thought of that before you cheated," Miss Tyler said. "For everything you do, Buddy, there is a consequence."

"Yeah, if you're a kid," Buddy replied. "Not if you're a mean grown-up."

Miss Tyler's face softened a little, though that stern look returned after a moment. Just then the janitor came around the corner with his keys jangling and his smell of mint.

"Mr. Peabody, would you please watch my classroom for just one moment?" Miss Tyler asked. She was already taking Buddy by the shoulder and guiding him down the hallway.

"Certainly," Mr. Peabody said, nodding. He went and stood with one foot in the classroom and one foot in the hallway, like he was afraid to step all the way over the threshold.

"This won't take long," Miss Tyler assured him.

Buddy had not been to the principal's office since the day his dad went into the hospital. Now he was attending a whole different school with someone else in charge, someone Buddy had never met. All the kids knew the principal on sight, but most of them were not known by the principal unless they got into trouble or were popular kids. Buddy knew he wasn't one of the popular kids, though he never thought he'd be in trouble like this, either.

He sank into a seat in the office, too afraid to cry. His palms were sweaty. He had to wait his turn. He saw another kid leave the office, his head held high and his ears pink.

"Mr. Robertson." The principal said it like a roll call. Buddy stood and went to the little box where the man had his desk.

"Tell me what happened today," the principal said. On the corner of his desk was a board with his name and title engraved on it: *Mr. Caprio, Junior High Principal.*

"Go on," the man urged.

"Well, we had a test today. I wasn't ready for it because I can't stay awake to study, and I got desperate so I used the homework to find the answers," Buddy started.

"You mean you cheated."

"Well, I didn't mean to, but I can't flunk my classes because I'll be in big trouble," Buddy said. "I couldn't think of anything else to do."

"Perhaps you could have made yourself study more?" Mr.

Caprio seemed like he was burning a hole into Buddy's head with his eyeballs.

"Perhaps I will next time," Buddy said.

"Are you being smart?"

"No, sir! I just mean I learned my lesson. Please let me do something to make up for this. I don't get into trouble."

Mr. Caprio gave a short nod. "I see that," he said, and grasped his chin like he was thinking. Buddy waited.

"I suggest you write Miss Tyler a note of apology and ask her how you can help her a bit in the classroom," he finally said. "Provided this doesn't happen again, we will keep this between us."

The tears started then. This was what Jesus called mercy in the Bible. Buddy wasn't sure he heard it right.

"That's all?" he whispered.

"That's all for now," Mr. Caprio said. "I will have my secretary walk you back to class, and you may tell Miss Tyler to speak with me during lunch."

Buddy couldn't look Mr. Caprio in the eyes after that, but he always nodded to him when they passed in the hallway and thanked him in his mind. Mr. Caprio had no idea what Buddy was spared. However, though he escaped punishment, James had other ways of hurting him.

James liked to pinch him when no one was looking, especially in the back of the arms. If he held up his hands in front of the bathroom mirror, he could see the bruises. So he wore long sleeves.

Sometimes when Buddy was in his room James would stand in the doorway, staring at him. Buddy tried not to look at him, but if he did, James would whisper something bad. *I hate you. You are a little shit. You're a sissy. Your sister is a whore.*

One night James Shearing did something different. It was way past bedtime, and very dark, but James came into his room.

He put his hand over Buddy's mouth and touched Buddy in his privates. Then he touched him in a sick way that hurt, his fingers thick and fast. There was fumbling and a forceful and painful pushing of something else, and Buddy puked a little into his pillowcase. Then the horrible thing was over.

Buddy discovered the next morning that he'd bled. The blood was on the sheets, and Buddy told his mother he was sick, hoping he could be home alone to wash the stains.

His mom must have remembered the man looking at him in the car when he was sick before, so she relented and told him he could stay home if he kept the doors locked.

Anna turned and shot a glance at him as she left. When she got home from school and found him sitting on the couch, not watching TV, absently flipping through a comic book, she sat on the other end and said nothing.

"We're going to surprise James tonight," his mother said when she got home from work. She didn't even ask how he was feeling. "We're going to go where he works and take him out for pizza."

He and Anna sat in the back seat as his mother headed to a nearby small town in northern Ohio. It was cold. He took his shoes and then his socks off, discovering his feet stayed warmer if he sat cross-legged on them and held them between his hands. Anna sulked beside him.

"You, Anna, need to straighten up and act like you care about something other than yourself," Mom said from the driver's seat. She was looking at her daughter in the rear-view mirror. Anna hugged herself and didn't budge.

Buddy concentrated on the back of his mother's seat. He still hurt from the night before. It was hard to clean the sheets; he'd used a soapy washcloth to rub the stains, then a towel to blot the wetness. Maybe he should have taken the sheets off, but it was hard making a bed with a fitted sheet. Maybe he could have ironed the wet spots. It wasn't bad, ironing, if you set the board up by the TV so you could watch reruns of *Gilligan's Island* or *The Beverly Hillbillies*. "*Come and listen to the story of a man named Jed, poor mountaineer barely kept his fam'ly fed, then one day he was shootin'...*"

"You have no idea what it's like to take care of kids that aren't your own," Mom was saying. "You need to treat James with more respect. I would like it if you called him Dad."

Buddy and Anna looked at each other, and Anna put a fake gun to her head. Since Anna hadn't been successful with her moodiness and surliness, Buddy would have to find some way to get rid of James. He wished he could explode and spew out the ugliness of the night before, but the words just wouldn't form. Shame and disgust washed over him. Anna's fingers were clenched against her stomach now. She was biting the inside of her cheek.

Maybe Buddy could hide a knife under his pillow and stab James Shearing hard the next time he came into his room. Maybe he could get some rat poison and put it in James's coffee. Maybe Buddy could just die, or maybe he could get a time traveler to zap him back to Grandma's house in Pennsylvania. They put a man on the moon a while back; couldn't they transport an 11-year-old to a different place in the past? He really did not want to die. He just wanted to be left alone. He wanted to get a good job someday and make at least 150 dollars a week. He wanted to live near Yankee Stadium so he could listen to people cheering. He wanted to own a car.

He sensed his mother's confusion before she said anything. When they pulled into the parking lot at James Shearing's shop there was only one car there, and it wasn't James's. Mom sat beside that strange car for a few minutes, and then she got out, walked to it and tried all the doors. The driver's side was open, and she got in and started looking around. She was concentrating very hard. Her hands moved quickly. She pulled down the visors and finally opened the glove compartment, coming back to their car with a piece of paper.

"That's Sara Hague's car," she said, although it didn't seem like she was talking to either him or Anna. "I'm driving to her house."

Uh-oh, Buddy thought. *This is not going to be good.*

It was starting to sprinkle. Everyone was silent. His feet were finally warm, but he made no move to put his shoes back on. His mother's lips made a thin, straight line across her face. He always thought his mother was pretty, but not pretty in a happy way. She was tense and distracted most of the time, and only seemed alive when she had a new boyfriend. James Shearing had been around for months, and had made them move to Ohio, where it was so flat there were no hills for resting your eyes. The kids at school were mean. He heard them whispering behind his back that his hair was greasy, and one time he was standing for the Pledge and someone behind him whispered, "What do you know, Buddy Robertson washed his hair!" Then he wanted to disappear.

Buddy came back to the present, looking closely at his mom. The glow she had when James Shearing first came into her life was long gone.

They made lots of turns, finally stopping at a tiny brick house. James Shearing's vehicle was in the driveway. Mom marched past it and went to the front door. She knocked, and a woman took a long time answering. She had blonde hair and a polka dot dress on. In moments James Shearing appeared behind the blonde lady, and there was lots of yelling.

"Holy shit," Anna said.

"Holy Shinola," Buddy replied. They started to giggle guiltily. The more they tried to stop, the more they did it.

"I can't stand that bastard," Anna said.

"Me neither." Buddy dared a sideways glance at his sister, who was staring at him. Oddly, even though they had just been giggling she was wiping tears from her eyes, the mascara she always liberally applied running down her face.

Buddy bent over in his seat, gasping for air. He couldn't catch his breath, and felt cold and hot at the same time, shivering and sweating. He wanted to get out of the car and run, but his mom and James Shearing still stood on the porch. Now Mom was sobbing as James Shearing talked to her alone. Was he going to try and get her to make up with him? Buddy shifted his eyes back to Anna, who reached over and took his arm.

"I could kill that guy," Anna whispered.

Buddy pictured himself rushing at the creepy, smelly man, screaming at him that he needed to die. He wanted to take turns with Anna cutting James and kicking him where it hurt. Over and over again.

The car door opened and his mother climbed inside. She gripped the steering wheel, her face and knuckles white. Buddy watched her, waiting for her to say James Shearing was coming out of that house to go for pizza with them. There was no way he'd be able to eat a bite of anything, not even pizza.

"I hope you children are happy," she muttered. Before Buddy could register what she'd said, she repeated it loudly, punctuating each word: "I. HOPE. YOU. CHILDREN. ARE. HAPPY."

He and Anna knew not to look at one another. They kept their eyes fixed straight ahead, also not looking in the rear-view mirror to witness their mother's hateful stare.

"My selfish kids have come between me and a man I love," she cried, starting the car and pulling out too fast. "He has someone new in his life now, someone he thinks will make him happy, and I'm alone again. He said you two made him feel so unwanted in his own home that he couldn't take it anymore. I guess I should just give up on being happy, ever, because you two only care about yourselves." Her sobs became heaves, but she kept driving, Buddy and Anna holding their eyes still as cats who just woke up from naps.

Suddenly, the car swerved over the centerline into the opposing lane. "You need to pull over and get a grip on yourself before you crash into something!" Anna yelled.

"If I knew it would take us all out, I'd do just that!" Mom screamed. "What happened to you kids? I just can't believe how you act! You only think about yourselves!" She got back in the right lane and stayed there, still crying but keeping her eyes on the road.

Well, his mom was right about one thing. He and Anna may not have been happy, but they were glad James Shearing wasn't going to be around any longer. No more listening to him saying Buddy didn't know "shit from Shinola" — what did that mean, anyway? No more awful visits in the dark. Buddy couldn't wait to get home. He just wanted rest. How long since he'd been able to sleep soundly?

He felt Anna's hand take his as he continued to stare straight ahead.

A few days later his grandparents came to Ohio, loaded them into a car, and moved them back to Pennsylvania. The trip was quiet.

All they took was clothing and a few items they could squeeze into the trunk, Buddy holding that black-and-white TV in his lap the whole way again. Watching scenery passing by the side window, he started to notice swells in the countryside after they passed lots of big buildings in Cleveland. Pennsylvania woods were so thick you could be in dense, green escapes before you knew it. He allowed his eyes to close when they got past Lake Erie.

They lived with their grandparents again. Grandpa had started to carry a roll of Tums in his shirt pocket. He still had a garden, with carrots you could pull up and eat right from the black dirt. He had a lot of potatoes growing, too. Buddy resumed the practice of following Grandpa around outside. Once they found a praying mantis and Buddy held it in his palm, watching it turn its head around like something from outer space.

Grandma was the same, too, just a little more wrinkly.

Buddy and Anna had their own desk drawer that held decks of cards, crayons, paper, scissors, dominoes, and checkers. The only rule was they had to put everything back when they finished playing with it. Anna didn't use this stuff much anymore, but Buddy was thrilled that Grandma and Grandpa kept everything while the kids were gone.

If he was happy, Anna was on cloud nine. She quickly picked up with her old friends, and Buddy knew she was doing well in school. Anna never seemed to struggle like he did. She helped him with his math, but it seemed like he forgot everything from one night to the next. Every time he felt like he did understand something, the next day the teacher added something new and he would panic, the numbers looking strangely put together all over again.

"You need to know this stuff, Buddy," Anna said.

"Why? Why would I ever need to know this?" Buddy asked.

Anna paused, then replied that math was something he would need when he learned to cook or wanted to build something.

"You have to know fractions for cooking, because if something calls for three quarters of a cup and you don't know what that means, you'll mess it up," she advised.

"I'll get a wife who cooks," Buddy said.

"What kind of wife is going to want someone who flunks math?" Anna asked, rolling her eyes at him.

"I'm charming. I'll get a smart wife," he said, and Anna chuckled. She had nice blue eyes, and she always seemed to take care of her hair and her face. It took her forever in the bathroom, but he liked it when she came out with the top of her head wrapped in a giant towel. She would sit in a kitchen chair every morning, drape the towel behind her, and comb her long golden hair, which smelled like Prell. Since their return to Pennsylvania, Buddy grew to like daily baths. Buddy liked that Prell smell so much he sometimes used it on his body instead of soap. Grandma and Grandpa didn't have a shower, just a tub with a huge orange stain that went from underneath the faucet to the drain. Grandma said it was from hard water, and that she gave up on trying to clean it. Their water was not only hard, as they called it; the hot was very hot. Buddy liked to get in when it was just hot enough to be able to sit down. He put the Prell on his head and went under, rinsing it out, and then he washed the rest of himself with the shampoo. When he got out, he would be red on his bottom half from the hot water. He didn't hurt any more from James Shearing, but he had trouble going to the bathroom sometimes, and then he'd have explosions. He didn't know it was from damage. He didn't know it would be with him for life.

Sometimes he'd wake in the night, shaking and afraid, and grab the string that ran from a knot around the bedpost to the light above him. The light would spring on, and he'd say thank you to God or the air that he was in a different place. If he never told anyone about what James did, maybe he'd forget about it. He still couldn't figure out why the man hated him so much, though Anna said there was no why, that James was just a purely bad person.

Sometimes in the night she whispered to Buddy that she wished people like James Shearing would die. Anna said she was going to get good grades at school, go to college, and never be like their mother.

Buddy often lay awake, worrying about how things would be when Anna left. Grandma and Grandpa would just have to live a long time. He asked God to make sure. After all, God made sure they got away from James Shearing, even if He was a little late.

Chapter 11

The Burden of Sparrows

The woods thickened with greenery. A grouse drummed in the distance. Buddy stood still, trying to determine where the bird was. It seemed to be down by the stream. Outdoor noise was continual, with the birds beginning his morning and the peeper frogs lulling him to sleep. He had the window open in spite of Mags's complaints.

Only a few weeks of school remained, and at work the custodial staff was organizing the summer schedule. Wax the gym floors. Scrub the walls. Sand the desks and refinish them, erasing all those declarations of love and hate from pen nibs and permanent markers. Touch up paint. At least Buddy would go to and get out of work earlier, leaving most of his afternoons free. He was hoping to talk Mags into growing lots of tomatoes and canning them. It would be good for her. He would help.

For now, the kids were hyped up like the critters outside, with warmth in their blood. Teachers were ready to be finished with another year. After spring break, the days got longer and the attention span of everyone got shorter.

Since their meeting at the dollar store, Ben waved to Buddy

every day. At first he did it tentatively, but then he started to smile. Buddy returned both wave and smile happily. He hadn't been called to pick up Jenna in quite a while. She still came by regularly, though, sometimes bringing Carrie with her. Now they were both working at Big Boy.

Buddy pulled into the lot at school and grabbed his sack lunch. He anticipated an easy day, as the fifth graders were going to Mackinac Island on a field trip. In Buddy's mind the island was just a tourist trap: you paid a lot of money to ride a boat to a place where you couldn't drive a car and had to walk through endless stores selling trinkets made in China. He had never been, but he'd heard about it. The kids said the boat ride was fun, and the island beautiful, but it smelled like horse poop because the only way to get around was by horse-drawn carriage, bicycle, or your own two feet.

That was all Buddy needed to know. He might like to see the old fort, but he sure wasn't going to pay money to ride a boat there. The Upper Peninsula was a different story. He'd ride across that Mackinac Bridge to go there. The UP was full of remote woods, and he'd managed to get up there a few times over the years. It soothed him to know there were still places like that, though of course the best place to be was on his own property.

He headed to the superintendent's office, hoping to mop the floor in there and get a couple other things taken care of. He waited for the secretary to let him in.

"Hey, Buddy," Hannah said as she held the door open for him and his cart.

"Good mornin'," he replied. "Is it okay if I mop in there?"

She grimaced and gave her head a slight shake. "I'm not sure. They're having a meeting today, so it's probably not the best time. But if you do your other stuff first, they might be finished by the time you're ready."

Buddy nodded. "I'll see how it goes," he said.

He maneuvered his cart down the hallway and left it on the opposite side of the building, then started emptying the trash. He smelled the coffee from the large urn, and noticed an assortment of doughnuts on the counter. Buddy's stomach was already growling; he only had time to grab a stale bagel and a piece of string cheese for breakfast. It didn't occur to him to take a doughnut, as they were for the administration. Sometimes, though, the gals in the office offered him one. He usually said no, but he could use one right now.

Hannah sat at her desk, staring at her computer. She did that a lot. Buddy thought she was watching a blank screen at first, but one day he realized she had a privacy cover over it so people couldn't see what she was doing. He tried not to look at what was on her desk. Once, a custodian got accused of reading something he shouldn't have. He made the mistake of repeating what he'd seen, but he'd read it wrong or told the wrong person, and almost lost his job.

As Buddy leaned over to grab the metal trash bin, words jumped out at him from the contents, and he found himself staring. He saw the name Fairfield, Kurt A. and the words "criminal sexual conduct." On Hannah's desk was what appeared to be a legal document, and Buddy was tempted to linger so he could read it. At the same time, he wanted to forget he saw anything. He set the bin down with a thud and kept moving.

He emptied all the bins save the one in the superintendent's office, walked outside to the dumpster and tossed a large bag inside. Then he went back to the main office, going through the front door this time, and waited for Hannah to re-admit him. He clutched a dust cloth, passing by her desk to reach the counters and shelves. He never dared move anything, but gingerly edged the cloth around. He opened the blinds so he could reach the windowsills, then closed them again on a diagonal so people could see out but visitors couldn't see in. Taking the broom, he went around the corners of the offices, saying little to Kara and Joyce as he passed through. Kara's office was always tidy and Joyce's office was always messy, with piles of paper, framed photographs, and knick-knacks scattered over her desk and on the floor. She still had Easter decorations on her desktop, and that was over a month ago.

"Think you could hang another shelf or two for me one of these days?" Joyce asked.

"Sure. Where do you want it?"

She pointed. "Right there, if you can drill holes into the cinder block."

"Not a problem. I'll bring the drill in tomorrow if that's alright."

"That's awesome. Thanks, Buddy."

He nodded and exited her space. Right then the super's door opened and the principals entered the hallway. Blair was the only one who said hello to Buddy. Two of the others nodded; two didn't bother acknowledging him. He stood awkwardly as they passed by him to refill their coffee cups, talking about golf, about which iron they used. Buddy didn't know what an iron was when it came to golf. He waited until they went back in before moving on, heading toward the front entry to wipe down the windows. The damn pollen had started, and it coated everything with a layer of yellow dust. He'd be able to get both the interior and exterior panes, though he wasn't much good at doing windows; he wished he had some newspaper. It worked best for cleaning glass, as it didn't streak or leave lint behind.

He finished that task and abandoned any hope of mopping. He'd just have to come back later, which irritated him, as he had hot mop water now. He pushed his cart back to the exit door that separated the administrative offices from the main school building.

No use fretting about it, he told himself. He continued down the hallway toward the fifth grade wing, which was quiet because the kids were gone. He might be able to use the mop down there, since they wouldn't be traipsing in after lunch. It was so silent he could hear the wind coming through the gap in the exit door. He needed to write up a work order for the maintenance crew to put in some new weather stripping.

By the end of the day he'd completed everything but mopping the central office, so Buddy held onto that nagging thought as he headed home. He would make it a point to clean in there tomorrow before he got reprimanded for the floor being dirty. He hoped the ladies in the office remembered he'd tried.

Mags looked up from the couch as Buddy passed her by. He'd just gotten home from work.

"They had a picture of Carrie's stepdad on the news," she said. "He's been arrested, charged with abusing a kid."

"Yeah, I know," Buddy said. Darn it, he shouldn't have let that slip.

"Do you think he abused someone in his family?"

"I don't know. What did the news say?" Buddy felt her intensity, and didn't want to sit down with her. "I'm going to till a spot for some tomatoes," he added. "I want us to can a bunch."

"This thing is serious," Mags said. "Do you think he hurt Ben or Carrie? The news said he's accused of sexually abusing a child under the age of 13."

"I said I don't know," Buddy repeated. "I don't know what that bastard did."

"Well, if someone did something to a kid of mine, they

wouldn't be accusing him in court," Mags pronounced. "I'd have to cut his nuts off and feed 'em to the dog." She crossed her arms. "Makes me sick."

"You and me both," Buddy said. "But we can't fix it."

"I feel so bad," Mags said.

"I see you don't even have the TV on," Buddy said. "Come outside and sit on the porch while I get the tiller going."

"I've been sittin' here for a couple hours," Mags admitted. "I don't understand how a grown person can do that to a kid."

"You and me both," Buddy repeated.

Carrie and Jenna stopped by later. They got sent home from work early because the dinner hour was slow. Buddy was afraid that Mags wouldn't be able to refrain from asking questions, but he didn't have to worry. Carrie brought it up.

"My evil stepdad is in jail," she said. She took off one of her shoes and rubbed the arch of her foot. "My mom said he didn't do anything wrong, but I hope he goes away for a long time."

"I saw it on the news," Mags said, putting her hand over her mouth when she saw Carrie's reaction.

Carrie's face reddened and she shuddered. "It was on the news?" she asked. "Crap."

"It was, honey."

"Exactly what did it say?"

"That he is accused of sexually abusing a child under the age of 13."

"That bastard!" Carrie yelled. "It has to be my brother!" She started crying, and Buddy moved toward her. To comfort her or something, he didn't quite know. Then he froze. He watched as Mags got up and went over to Carrie. She smoothed the girl's hair and let her cry while Jenna stood behind her friend, one hand touching Carrie's shoulder. Buddy felt his scrubby whiskers as he held onto his chin with one hand, gripping the counter with the other.

"Everyone will find out!" Carrie cried. "They'll realize it was Ben — they'll all know!"

"Ben has nothing to be ashamed of," Mags said. "He's safe now, and that creep is in jail."

"You don't understand," Carrie whispered. "You can't."

I do, Buddy thought. But he didn't say it; he only stood there, useless and powerless as he ever was.

He fumbled his way outside, letting the girls and the woman be together.

Later, after Carrie and Jenna left, he was on the porch when Mags opened the door and asked what he wanted for supper.

"I hadn't thought about it much," he replied.

"Me neither, but I haven't eaten since breakfast and I s'pose we should. How about breakfast for supper? I could fry up some eggs and sausage, make some gravy."

"Sounds fine," he said. Then he added, "How is Carrie?"

Mags shook her head. "As expected. A little too much for you to handle?"

"What?" Buddy's face paled.

"I just know it's uncomfortable for you to talk about stuff like that."

"What's that supposed to mean?" he asked.

"Well, you'd never do anything to a kid, and it makes you sick, don't it?"

He nodded. "Yeah, it does. More than you know."

"I think I know pretty damn well."

Buddy watched the door stick as it closed behind her. When she hollered that dinner was ready a short while later he was standing out in the garden, doing nothing.

He moved food around on his plate, but the gravy tasted like paste and his stomach didn't want to accept anything. Mags barely touched her food. She finally gathered her fork, plate, and glass of milk, setting them on the counter. She'd been trying to keep the dishes done since the girls cleaned, and she stood at the sink, staring blankly as it filled with soapy water. Buddy rose and put his stuff next to hers, then touched her shoulder before realizing he was going to.

"You're a good friend to those girls, Mags," he muttered. She grasped his fingers awkwardly and looked at him, her blue eyes filling with tears.

"I hope so," she said. "You are too, Mac. Know how I told you Carrie has seen too much? She shared a little bit. Just enough to rip me up inside."

He squeezed her fingers lightly, then went back outdoors, mind set on putting tomato plants into the earth.

Buddy admired the straight lines he'd strung along the garden. Earlier, he had worked some manure into the sandy soil of northern Michigan. His back only hurt a little as he settled plants into the dirt along the neat rows, each one the same distance apart. The spring sun was warm; he got a burn on his bald spot even though it was early evening.

Grandpa had a full head of hair until the day he died. Grandpa's hands were not idle until that day, either. Buddy noted his hands were starting to resemble Grandpa's. The knuckles had begun to look swollen all the time, and some mornings his thumbs would ache, just like Grandpa's had. Grandpa would appreciate this little garden, though. He'd probably have liked this area, although he'd miss those Pennsylvania hills.

A sparrow hopped into Buddy's line of sight and tugged a small twig from the edge of the garden, taking it to a tree nearby. *A common little bird,* he thought, flicking an ant from his hand. The breeze from earlier had stilled. For a second he heard nothing; then he noted the drone from the frogs. One bullfrog sent up a distinctive croak and another answered.

At church long ago, he'd heard a sermon about how God watched over all creatures in the universe, even the little sparrows. At the time, Buddy thought this was a huge responsibility. There were lots of tiny animals in the world. If God had to watch over every one of them, maybe He sometimes forgot about humans. Out of all living beings humans did seem the most likely to hurt, or be hurt by, each other.

The Lord always provides, Grandma used to say. Grandma was so wise, she couldn't have believed in something that didn't exist. Buddy hadn't prayed in, well, a very long time. He wasn't as wise as Grandma — really, he wasn't wise about too much. But he knew how to plant a heck of a garden.

He heard the door catch as Mags came back outside. This time she cast her bulk into the old chair on the porch. She carried a glass, probably mint tea. She glanced his way. He pretended he didn't see.

Chapter 12

The Diary
With Omissions

1970

To say things were strained between Mom and Grandma after their return from Ohio would be an understatement. Grandpa was his jovial self, but Buddy found himself holding his breath if Mom and Grandma were in the same room. Anna said you could cut the tension with a knife; Buddy tried to make sense of that saying but couldn't.

After school one day, Mom was standing in the living room when they got home. That was funny, because she had gone back to work at her old place. Why wasn't she at her job? Buddy always felt hungry after class, so he tried to get past her into the kitchen, but she wouldn't let him by. She held out a small thing, a little book, and pushed it toward Anna.

"If you hate me so much, why don't you just tell me?" she asked.

Anna moved toward the little book. "You read my diary?"

"I didn't, but someone in this house did, and I refuse to listen to the constant criticism and judgment around here. You think you have all the answers, don't you?"

"No, but I do think I make better decisions than you," Anna said. "It doesn't mean I hate you. A diary is supposed to be private."

"Tell that to the person who read it."

"I assume you've helped yourself to it now, too."

"Your mind is full of spite and venom," Mom said. "I know I've made mistakes. I don't need my children telling me that."

Anna shrugged. "You wouldn't listen, anyway."

Mom set the little book down on the coffee table. "You might want to do a better job hiding that, and you might want to keep your ugly thoughts about me to yourself." She turned away. Buddy wanted Anna to say she was sorry, but he knew better than that. Anna grasped her book.

A few days later Anna asked him to go for a walk with her, and they stopped at a creek. She pulled the diary from her jacket and started ripping the pages out one by one. Letting go of each, she watched them flutter, land, and float downstream, even walking over to the other side of the road to make sure they continued on their way.

"What did you say in there?" Buddy asked. "And who looked in it before Mom?"

"It had to be Grandma," Anna answered. "She maybe saw my journal when she was putting clothes on my bed." It was a gray day. Anna looked tired, the circles under her eyes matching the clouds.

"What did you write about?" Buddy asked again.

"I called her weak and helpless a lot," she said. "I didn't write down what happened during the night, though. I can't put that into words. If I ever wrote it down, I couldn't pretend it never took place. Do you know what I mean, Buddy?"

"Yes."

"So we just keep it inside and don't let it eat into our souls," she offered. "I wish I could have protected you from him. I thought if I let him do things to me, he'd leave you alone. At least that's what I tell myself. I knew he did something the day we found him with that woman. I recognized it in you."

"What did he do to you, Anna?"

"He just felt me up, put his hands under my shirt, pinched my breasts, and said if I ever told Mom he'd hurt us all. Once he backed me up against the wall and tried to get into my underwear, but then you came down the hall. I thought if I was clear about how much I hated him, it might make him stop or make Mom notice, but nope."

"He raped me, I think," Buddy whispered. "He really hurt me."

Anna covered her face with her hands.

"Do you know what rape is, Buddy? Please tell me so I can tell you you're wrong."

He fought back tears as he remembered. "I can't say it. He pressed into me very hard and made me bleed, you know, down there."

"That's worse than what he did to me! Oh, holy shit. I wish I'd killed him! Where was Mom? Where was God?" Anna wasn't really asking him; she was staring into the creek. Then she closed her eyes. "Buddy, do you want me to tell someone? I can if it would help. I just don't want people thinking I'm damaged for life. I won't give the bastard that satisfaction. But if you want someone to know, I'll do it."

"What would happen then?"

"I honestly don't know."

"Then no. No."

They stood by the bridge, looking down at the creek. A few minutes of silence passed before Anna finally threw the diary cover into the water as well.

When Mom decided to move out a few months later, the kids asked if they could stay with Grandma and Grandpa. Mom didn't fight it much. She had a new boyfriend, and must have figured the kids would ruin her happiness again. Grandma and Grandpa said they were getting old, but that they would love to have Anna and Buddy stay.

Buddy thought of that time as a blessing. He might still live there if the Pennsylvania hills had proven more comforting. When he moved to Michigan he was desperate to get as far away from there as possible. Back then, if he somehow reached the end of the world, if it were flat and he could jump off, he would have.

Chapter 13

A Magical Summer

1974

Buddy had just finished his junior year of high school when he met Leah. He wasn't a bad student, but he was the kind of kid who didn't get encouraged to attend college. Anna, well, she was already in university classes by then. She was studying English and philosophy, things Grandpa sure didn't understand and didn't care to. He said he liked coping with things by getting his hands in the dirt, not that there was anything wrong with what his granddaughter was doing. Grandma enjoyed hearing about her studies when Anna came home on breaks.

"You mean there is actually something you study in college to figure out the meaning of life?" she asked. "I mean, it seems funny to me."

Grandpa chuckled. "If you read the good book, you get a good idea."

"Well, Grandpa, there is a science to it. You and Grandma are salt of the earth types of people. You live your lives by the rules of God, and you are good. Not everyone thinks like that," Anna said.

"Just don't go burning your bra, and I'll be fine with whatever they're teaching you," Grandpa said.

"What the heck?" Buddy blurted.

"Oh, there's all kinds of things the hippies are doing," Grandpa said, and smiled. "I don't know what the kids today are thinking, but I guess kids in my generation sowed their wild oats, too."

"Grandpa, I hope I never embarrass you," Anna said. "You are one person who has never let me down. You too, Grandma."

Grandma's eyes misted, and she grinned. "You have no idea what that means to us," she said. "We are so proud of you and your brother."

"I wish Mom would tell us that," Anna said.

"Your mother is involved with herself right now, trying to figure life out," Grandpa said.

"Hence my wish to try and figure her out," Anna replied. "I love studying."

Buddy loved helping Grandpa. He didn't much like studying and books. He liked the way Grandpa's face lit up when he heard an owl in the evening as they walked back across the field. He liked knowing the difference between birch and aspen trees. He liked being able to distinguish between a downy and a hairy woodpecker. Nothing so dramatic as what Anna was doing. She even went to a special class in the summer, a study program in New York City.

He was content to see the same things each day.

If he hadn't been in the woods that summer, he never would have met Leah. Buddy had wandered off the path, picking some buttercups to give Grandma, when he noticed a young woman on her knees examining some sort of weed beside a tiny spring. Her hair first caught his eye. It was wild, untamed, golden. When she looked up and saw him, she didn't seem surprised to find a stranger in the forest with her, a bunch of wilting yellow flowers held in his hand. Instead of saying hello, she mused, "I've never seen one of these types of ferns before. It's a maidenhair. Look how it whispers into the air, with such fine stems and dainty leaves."

"Huh." Buddy glanced at the plant, appreciating the fact that it was pretty, indeed.

"Kind of elegant, isn't it?" he asked.

She looked at him, or rather stared at him, her mouth forming a smile. "Perfectly described," she said.

Buddy had fallen for her before he drew his next breath. Her eyes were not quite blue, not quite green, but aqua, with flecks of gold in them. Her eyelashes were long and dark, stunning really, since she was quite fair. A mist of freckles dusted her nose.

"I'm Leah," she announced.

"Are you from around here?" he asked.

"Aren't you going to tell me your name?"

"Oh, sorry — it's Buddy."

"Well, hi, Buddy. And I'm not from around here. I'm visiting my aunt and uncle while my parents decide if they want to continue making each other miserable or get a divorce. Personally, I vote for the divorce, since they don't know how to play nice. But nobody is asking me. Where are you from? Do you live nearby?"

"Yeah, I live with my grandparents, just down that hill." He pointed.

"You are lucky to live in these woods," she said through a sigh. "I love it here, and could stay outdoors all day. I wander around and forget I'm supposed to be sad while my parents screw everything up. I try to find one new plant each day, and then I write it down. Most days I bring my sketchbook out with me so I can draw what I see. I want to go to college and be a botanist."

"I didn't know there was such a thing," Buddy said. "What does one of those do?"

"Well, I suppose you could do anything," she said. "You could be an artist, or you could plan peoples' gardens, or you could try to cross-pollinate plants and make new ones that are resistant to disease and pests. I'm going to explore everything before I decide my direction. Being out here makes me even more determined to further my education."

Buddy realized his mouth was slightly open. He was sweating a little; the day had turned warm, bugs circling his head. Leah appeared to glow, her skin was so smooth. Her hands went up to her bundle of hair, trying to tame it. "This heat does crazy stuff to my hair," she remarked.

"I think it's so pretty," Buddy said. He quickly looked away, embarrassed.

"You do?"

"Yup."

"My mom says I am cursed with unruly hair. She tries to straighten it all the time."

"She should let it be," Buddy said.

"Thanks." Leah gingerly pulled a piece of the fern from a stem, opened a little book, and stuck it inside. "This presses my discoveries and dries them, so they stay like when I found them as much as possible. I have hundreds."

"What do you do with them?"

"I put them in special cases, labeling each one. You should see my room back home. Whenever I have a chance to get into the woods, wherever I go, I collect."

"That sounds so nice," Buddy said.

"And what are you doing in these parts?" Leah asked.

"I was getting some buttercups for my grandma. She likes them a lot," he answered. "I also come out here often as I can. I forget about bad stuff when I'm in the woods, just like you do."

"We are going to have a good summer together, then," Leah pronounced.

They did, Buddy following Leah as she went on her quests. He learned the names of many plants he would have tripped over before, such as yarrow, anemone, and Queen Anne's lace. Leah said Queen Anne's lace was not native, but a member of the carrot family introduced from another country. She said the bottom tubers could be eaten and tasted like parsnips, so Buddy pulled one from the soil just to see. It smelled like a carrot. He bit the rooted end, dirt and all, and it did taste rather like a parsnip.

"How do you know all this stuff?" he asked.

"There are books on all this information," Leah said. "One of my favorites is called *The Herbalist*, and I have a very worn copy of it. It was written in the 1930s by Joseph Meyer. I got it at a book sale the library held when I was just little; my parents thought I was such an odd girl. What I really liked were the renderings of the plants, and I didn't realize it was a botanical book until I got older. Now it's my favorite book in my collection of things."

"My grandpa knows a lot, but you know more than he does," Buddy said. "You should meet him, and my grandma." He paused. "Oh, and my sister." Who knew when Anna would be home next, though. She hadn't come back since Christmas, and Buddy missed her.

"I'd like to meet all of them," Leah said.

When she did meet Grandma and Grandpa, they were immediately taken with her. Grandpa asked Buddy how he found such a pretty little thing in the woods, and Grandma chuckled. Buddy felt his face get hot.

"We're just friends," he protested. "She and I like the same things. We both like being outside."

"I'll bet," Grandpa said. "Out with the birds...and the bees."

He laughed at his little joke. "You enjoy this time, Buddy. It's the prime of your life."

Leah came to dinner sometimes. She always brought something. A bowl of strawberries from the trail was so sweet they ate every one without any sugar. Another day, she found some black raspberries and drizzled honey over them from the apiaries her aunt and uncle kept.

"I thought about keeping bees, but just never did," Grandpa reflected. "Nothing like good local honey."

"My uncle said he'd trade you some honey for some syrup," Leah said. She stuck a finger in her bowl to get some honey on the tip, then brought it up to her mouth. Buddy looked at her as she looked at Grandpa, the light from the kitchen window seeming to settle on her bottom lip, where she'd just smeared the honey. Buddy wanted to put his tongue there, to taste that sweetness. He imagined Leah's breath warm on his face. It would be a gentle kiss, placed just where that light was.

"Buddy, go to the cellar and grab a jug of syrup," Grandpa said. "We're going to take up that offer."

He walked Leah home through the woods that evening, lugging the syrup. He didn't dare look her way too much, being overconscious of the space she took up, the shimmer she gave off without even trying. He then trudged back, carrying the honey. Leah's aunt and uncle seemed like very nice people, but they were more well-off than Grandma and Grandpa. Their house was modern, and they had two vehicles, a pickup and a fancy car. Leah's aunt styled her hair like Ginger on *Gilligan's Island*; Leah said she kept a standing appointment at a salon to get it done.

"What's that?" Buddy asked.

"It means she's on the schedule the same time, same day of the week, all year," Leah said.

Buddy had never heard of such a thing. He didn't know who

took care of Grandma's hair, but was pretty sure it wasn't a salon. Grandpa used clippers on his, and once in a while took them to Buddy as well.

On subsequent visits he noticed other things he hadn't seen before. They had pop in their refrigerator all the time — not the cheap stuff, either. Real Coca-Cola. Oh, and they had beer. Grandma and Grandpa didn't drink much; the bottle they brought out the day Mom got hurt by that Mose guy was the only time Buddy ever saw them with alcohol. Dad used to enjoy a cold beer now and then, but Buddy had never seen anyone get drunk. Leah's uncle seemed to have a beer in his hand all the time.

He and Leah didn't hang out around there much, though. They would usually meet halfway between his house and hers, spending their days outside. They were both getting brown, and he noticed that her freckles were a little more prominent. They only made her prettier.

Sometimes she would come to the house and chat with him and Grandma and Grandpa. Those were Buddy's favorite days. It was like having his favorite people all in one room. If only Anna were there, and Mom, when she was like she used to be.

"Someday I want a house just like this," Leah said.

"This old farmhouse?" Grandma asked.

"Oh, yes, with the butler's pantry and the woodwork and the big tub," Leah said. "And I want lots of flowers outside, with cold frames and a greenhouse and little paths everywhere."

"Buddy tells us you want to study botany," Grandpa commented. "I guess I've studied it, in my way. I sure do enjoy gardening and such. Where did you get your interest in that?"

Leah sipped her lemonade and answered, "I've always loved plants and what other people think of as weeds. But I can pretty much remember the day my interest came alive. I was bored, just sitting in my room, and it was stifling hot. Mom and Dad were gone, and so was my big brother, Jake. I used to sit in my room a lot and listen to music, but that day I decided to go out for a walk. I walked and walked, and found myself by this little trail, so I took it. It was enchanting. I could hear the birds, all different kinds of them, and I decided to sit on this rock."

Enchanting, Buddy thought. *Like her.*

Leah continued, "So, I'm sitting there, and I see this tiny chipmunk by this little plant. I watched as he pulled its vines toward him. He ate the flowers from the ends of the vines, one by one. Like we'd eat a sandwich!"

Grandma laughed. "Then what?"

"I was so taken by that moment. I had to know what type of flower the chipmunk was eating, and figured out it was a wild sweet pea. I went outside the next day, then the day after that, starting to notice all the drama that happens outside among the trees and wildlife. I had to be part of it, and began paying closer attention to different types of flowers and plants and animals. I guess I'm obsessed with it."

"What a wonderful thing," Grandpa said. "I drag Buddy around with me, but I think he only goes because he doesn't want to get stuck with housework."

"I think Buddy really likes it, too," Leah replied.

"Or he likes you," Grandpa said.

Did she blush, or did Buddy imagine that? Leah sipped her drink, set it down, and gathered her hair away from her face. She then looked at Buddy, and her eyes told him she liked him too. A feeling like gratitude or relief or disbelief — maybe all three mixed together — startled him, and he sat on his hands so he wouldn't float away. He saw a look exchanged between his grandparents, full of amusement and something else Buddy couldn't name. It filled him with warmth.

When he walked Leah back that evening he wanted to kiss

her, but felt shy and awkward. She was the one who turned to him, reached out, and touched his lips with hers.

"See you tomorrow," she said, and he nodded, gathering enough courage to cup her face in his hands and kiss her again.

That summer was bright and warm, filled with promise. Every day they went out to gather blossoms and flowers and berries. Buddy still had chores to do, and Leah usually accompanied him. Her presence became regular around the farm, as if she'd always been there. Their days were full and simple at the same time, and it seemed they could go on like this forever, neither Buddy nor Leah realizing the summer would eventually come to an end. They chanced upon a family of foxes one day, and stayed hidden among the trees as the kits frolicked in a field. Three performed somersaults and jumped through the brush right as Buddy and Leah heard a noise behind them. An adult fox, probably the mother, strolled past them, not threatened by their presence. She joined her kits and they happily greeted her, following her through the field and into the trees across the way.

"We are so lucky to see that," Leah said. "Just you and me."

"Yeah, we are," Buddy replied. "Not everyone gets to see something like that."

"I can't imagine living where you can't be around this," Leah said, stretching her arms out. "I sure wish I could finish high school here."

Buddy's heart leaped. "Is that possible?"

"Oh, I don't know," she said. "I just think about it all the time."

"I sure would like that," he said. Leah could meet everyone at school. They'd see how pretty she was, then be surprised at her being with Buddy. But this meant he'd have to share her, which he wasn't at all certain he wanted to do. He liked the way they were with each other, in their own world in the woods with no one else. She might find someone she liked better.

"I can't see Mom letting me," she was saying. "I just like to imagine it, staying here with you for our senior year of school."

"You're probably right," Buddy replied.

Leah sighed. "Let's just enjoy the summer, okay?"

"Yup."

Leah taught Buddy not to ignore the growing and changing environment of the woods. She pointed out plantain, red clover, chicory, chamomile, and rue, things he would have neglected to notice without her. Even Grandpa learned from her. She knew which herbs and plants had medicinal qualities, although she loved everything for its simple existence.

Everything was lovelier because of her.

In a thicket one day they came on some wild raspberries, eating them as quickly as they picked them. Leah found a fat one and held it out for Buddy, and he grasped her cupped hand and lifted the berry with his mouth. His tongue grazed her palm, and he felt electricity jolt his body from his jaw down to his feet, then back up to his face. He lifted his head, the berry nestled in his lips, and swallowed its juicy redness. Then she stepped closer, and he took her hand again and kissed it in the exact same spot the berry had been.

Leah's eyes shone like twin turquoise lakes. She leaned into him, and his hands went to her hair. They kissed eagerly, and she pulled him down so they were kneeling, still kissing. He smelled the grasses and the ground and the scent of her breath, fresh from the sweet berries, and then they were lying down together. She was all around him like a warm breeze, and he gasped as she pulled off her shirt and bra. He saw where her tanned arms changed to the white, precious skin of her breasts and torso. Everything happened both too fast and with such reverence and meaning Buddy knew he'd treasure it forever.

"I love you," he said as they fanned each other afterward. Her hair hung in tendrils around her face, damp and beautiful. She was sweating, pink, glowing.

"I love you, Buddy," she said.

It wasn't until nightfall, as he lay in bed reliving every second, that James Shearing entered his mind. What that bastard did compared in no way to what Buddy had done with Leah, yet shame washed over him. Buddy turned onto his side, pulling the pillow over his head, and then tossed the pillow onto the floor.

He couldn't breathe. Memories of James flooded into his brain. The smells, the pain, the humiliation. The hatred. Buddy wished he could find that animal and kill him. He allowed himself to feel the fury once again, and for a while worried that he somehow hurt Leah the way James hurt him. But then he remembered the way she smiled at him. The way she held him close, the way she said she loved him.

She loved him. What they shared with each other was the opposite of what James Shearing did to him. Buddy told himself, finally, that he wasn't going to let anything ruin what he had with Leah. He couldn't wait to see her tomorrow. If she never wanted to be together like that again, he would respect her wishes. Buddy only wanted her to know that he loved her, too, more than anything.

If he had any doubts, they vanished the next morning when Leah led him into the woods. He would always remember spending those days — the sounds of the birds, the rustling of leaves on the trees and bushes where they lay — together. The sounds of her as her breath quickened and she let out small, musical notes, soft as the summer air.

Chapter 14

The Curse of Being Right

Tell me how cats can possibly shed so much, he thought to himself as he looked under the bed for his left slipper. The slipper, finally located, was covered with hair. Buddy brushed his hands over it to get the worst off, stuck it on, and wandered into the kitchen. He threw the cat hair into the trash, or tried, but most of it drifted past the garbage bin and landed on the floor. *Never mind.* The floor was dirty, anyway. Mags had managed to keep the dishes caught up, but the rest of the house was still a mass of disorganization and life.

Buddy had to pee, but Mags was in the bathroom, so he grabbed a cup of her mud and started to go outside in his robe. No one would notice if he just peed among the trees. Just as he opened the door, though, he heard steps outside. It was Carrie, and she had Ben with her. Before Buddy could think, he was peering at them through the screen door.

"Hey, Buddy," she said as he stood there. She was smiling in a tentative way, and Ben was holding a box of doughnuts.

"Hey," he said. "Mags will be right out. Come on in."

"We can't stay long, but I told Ben about all your cats, and he wanted to see them," Carrie said. "Sorry we didn't call first. I was supposed to work today, but someone wanted to switch with me so they could have tomorrow off. I thought maybe you guys would like some doughnuts."

"I never turn down doughnuts," Buddy said. "Let me get changed, though."

"Did I hear the word doughnuts?" Mags hollered as she came around the corner. "Oh, my, you have your brother! Nice to meetcha, Ben!"

Buddy noticed Ben start to hang behind his sister, but Mags had a way of making anyone comfortable. Before long he was sitting at the table munching a nutty doughnut, although he remained quiet. Buddy went to the bathroom, returned to the kitchen, and swiped a plain one. He dunked it into his coffee. A few of the more outgoing cats came into the kitchen. Caesar made a move to get on the table, but Mags grabbed him and set him on the floor. Ben held out his hand, and the cat moved toward him.

"Ya like cats?" Mags asked.

"Yeah."

"We do, but we couldn't have any before, and the foster mom is allergic," Carrie said.

"Yeah," Ben repeated.

"I'm going outside," Buddy said. He slipped past the table and headed out the front door.

Soon he would put the beans up, so he set some beer out for slugs to drown in. Things were coming along. Buddy bent to pull a few weeds. His back protested, but he knew if he kept at it he'd limber up. Grandpa always claimed that.

It was Saturday. He had two days to be outside, and it was supposed to be sunny but cool. He'd have time to do some of that tree counting today, maybe. Buddy nodded to himself, then noticed a stirring beside him. He was surprised to find Ben standing there.

"Girls talk a lot," he said.

"Oh, they do that," Buddy agreed.

"What are you doing, Mr. Robertson?"

"Oh, just puttering. Thought I'd see how my garden is doing. Did you get bored with the cats?"

"No, I just got bored with the talking. I could help you." Ben gazed earnestly up at Buddy through his smudged glasses. Unlike Carrie's, his eyes were brown.

"Well, that's fine. Would you like to help me mark off part of my land so I can count my trees? Some posts will need to go up."

Ben snorted. "What would you want to count your trees for?" His lips had bits of doughnut stuck on them. His glasses were not only dirty; they sat crooked on his face, though his hair looked clean. His fingernails were clipped neatly as well.

"Well, I want to know how many types of trees I have and how many of each," Buddy explained. "I know they are mostly maples, but I have oak, beeches, poplars, pine, hemlock, and spruce, too."

"Trees are just trees," Ben said.

"Oh, no," Buddy protested. "Every type of tree is different."

Ben followed him to the lean-to, then onto the east side of the property, where Buddy placed poles in a 50-yard square. Well, close to a square, anyway. As they moved he pointed out different types of trees to Ben, showing him the tap scars on the maples. He wasn't sure the boy was paying attention, though Ben did feel the bark of each tree type and remark on their differences. Buddy lost track of how much time passed.

After a while Carrie burst onto the porch. "Ben! Stop bugging Buddy!" she yelled.

"It's okay," Buddy answered. "We're just counting trees."

"Why would anyone want to count trees?" she asked.

"That's what I wanted to know," Ben said.

"We have to get going in a few minutes. Joanne needs the car to get groceries."

Buddy continued after they left. He had a tablet and a pencil, and he took notes. It would take him weeks to finish, but it felt good to start a new project. It was easier to consider the trees than it was to ponder the mess in the house. Where would one start in there? He might finish up with the old toolbox he'd opened a while back, but was saving that job for a rainy day. It was too pleasant outside to be indoors. He could get the vacuum and tackle the cat hair, but it would just be back tomorrow. The dappled light was perfect. It softened the rough bark of the pines.

How long had he been out? The light had changed, lengthening and turning gold. Soon June would arrive. What is so rare? A memory of Anna came to him from when she was into Shakespeare. He wasn't so much, since he never understood what was being said until Anna explained it. She loved *Macbeth*, and memorized a verse from it he came to know through her. Aloud he recited: "Tomorrow and tomorrow and tomorrow, creeps in its petty pace from day to day…" Anna told him the verse was a tragic statement that there was basically no point to life. We were all players on a stage, and everything we did was meaningless.

Some of us are unimportant, for sure, Buddy thought. He kept his most precious memories close to his heart, sometimes taking them out and unfolding them, but they seemed to get smaller and more threadbare with age. Grandma and Grandpa, Anna. Dad and Mom. Leah. After all his losses, it felt like he was watching his little life from a remote spot. Detached and alone, he never seemed to share himself, to become a part of anyone else. Most of his memories were tied to outdoors, he mused. At least he still had the woods. Those cherished times with past loved ones were gone. They only mattered to him, and because of that didn't mean very much at all. What value do memories have if they die with people, leaving no one to remember? Is the world changed by anyone's unshared memories?

Buddy looked down at his boots, scuffed by both work and days spent in the woods. He always purchased the same type Grandpa used to swear by. How many pairs had he gone through since the first time he and Grandpa shopped for some? Who cared?

"Signifying nothing," he said, remembering the last two words of that Shakespeare verse.

Melancholy as he was, he snapped out of it by the time he got back to the house. The lushness of the trees, the calls of the flickers, and the grumbling of bullfrogs lifted his mood. Chuckling, he watched a crow swagger into his garden and pull straw from the earth.

"Wasn't that nice of them to come by?" Mags asked later.

"Sure was," Buddy said. "I'm surprised they came without Jenna."

"Well, I talk to Carrie on the phone sometimes."

"How often?"

"Oh, every couple days," Mags said. "A teenage girl should have someone to confide in, and she just needs me to listen. Her foster mom talked with me at first, I think to find out more about me. And you, of course. She said she already got a lot of info from Jenna."

"Doesn't Carrie have Jenna to talk to?"

"Jenna can't comfort her like a mom could," Mags said, shaking her head. "I never had a daughter, but I think she gets something like a mom's support from me."

"I'm sure she does," Buddy said.

"She's really worried about the publicity of this thing. Not only for Ben, but for herself. She doesn't want to be connected with it in any way. She's afraid of other kids at school knowing and wondering about her."

"Did she also get — hurt — by him?"

Mags shook her head. "Not him, but others."

"So what you thought about her life is true."

"You know, it's a curse being right all the time," Mags said. She sighed and turned on the television. "Sometimes I really hate it."

A few days later, Buddy took Mags to a local ice cream parlor for a treat. Buddy got a malt, and Mags got a chocolate marshmallow sundae. They ate in the pickup, Buddy walking their trash to the bin afterwards.

"Who's that woman, Mac?" Mags asked as he threw one leg into the truck and started raising himself up on the seat. He turned to see Sage Carmichael, the teacher he had overheard talking about his teeth. She was seated at a picnic table with a few other people, but was the only one facing him and Mags.

"Oh, she's a teacher at the school," Buddy answered.

"She just gave you a look that would make a new John Deere stall," Mags said. He looked at Sage and got mad all over again.

"She's not the nicest person I know," he commented. At that moment Sage looked directly at him, then past him, purposefully, like she didn't want him to feel he belonged in the same atmosphere. He turned to check behind him as he backed out of the parking lot.

"Obviously," Mags said. "She'd stop a clock with that glare. What did you ever do to her?"

"Got no idea," Buddy said. "She's just a..."

"Bee-otch," Mags finished. "It's written all over her face."

Thanks, Mags, Buddy thought. "I couldn't say it better," he agreed aloud. He glanced at Mags and noticed she had dripped some marshmallow or ice cream down the front of her shirt. She would still be wearing it when he left for work the next day.

Monday mornings in the summer weren't too bad. In June especially, no one was itching to get back inside the building yet. Summer was too new. Teachers weren't interested in accessing their rooms, and the only people Buddy saw were other maintenance staff. Central office was still open, but his schedule with them never changed. Today he was going to patch some holes in the drywall so the painting crew could get busy. He also had to remove the putty teachers used to hang stuff up in classrooms. It stayed on the walls in blue clay-like dots; easy to scrape off, but it was everywhere, every year. He had 16 rooms to prep before tackling the hallways.

Every year he started with a different classroom, working his way around counter-clockwise. He always circled back to the room he started on, but today his mind kept wandering so that he lost track. He opened windows in the third room, since it was getting warm and the floor fan wasn't doing much for his comfort. Using spackle, he filled in the holes and dents in the walls first, then took a putty knife to those pesky blue spots.

Ernie, the maintenance manager, entered the room. "Need anything?" he asked. Ernie was a good guy, but he liked talking, and Buddy wanted to stay on the move.

"Nope, I'm set," he answered.

"Alright, just checking." Ernie brushed his hand over one of the spackled spots. "Needs a little sanding here," he remarked.

"I'll get it," Buddy said. Ernie turned to leave just as his phone started vibrating.

"Yeah," he said after answering it. "I'm on my way." Without a glance toward Buddy, he was gone.

Buddy felt relieved that he didn't have to engage in a conversation. He kept going until lunch, then sat outside on the steps beside the playground to eat. It was shady there, shielding him from the street. He didn't like to be seen eating at work because he'd heard remarks about lazy custodians and didn't want that to be said about him. He supposed it still was, but he at least could say he didn't get caught eating very often.

He unwrapped his bologna sandwich. Two slices of bologna, with butter and mustard. He also had some chips in a baggie and a few Oreos. Someone was mowing a lawn, and a chipmunk was skittering along the trees, pausing every now and then to investigate something. Buddy tossed a chip toward it, which it eventually picked up. It bit along the edges until the chip was small enough to carry away.

"Hi, Mr. Robertson," someone said, and Buddy turned from watching the chipmunk toward the greeting.

"Hi, Fallon," he answered on seeing who it was. "What's going on?" Fallon was a fifth grade girl who lived by the school. She was a tiny thing, with blonde hair that stuck out behind her ears. She carried a phone and a bag of Doritos.

"I'm walking to a friend's house, but wanted to sit on a swing and eat some of these first," she said, lifting the bag. "If I take them all with me, I won't get hardly any."

"Why's that?" Buddy asked.

"Oh, Bella has a bunch of brothers and they hog everything," Fallon said. "I outsmarted them, though."

Buddy chuckled. "I guess you did."

He chewed on his last bite of lunch. Fallon ate a few chips before folding up the bag. "Why do you have those keys with you all the time?" she asked, nodding toward his belt.

"I have to get into all the classrooms in summer, and into the supply room and the equipment room," Buddy said. "They all use separate keys."

"Wow. How do you know which to use?"

"I have them all marked." Buddy set his baggie beside him, stood, and removed the bundle from his belt, holding it out as the girl came nearer. "See, that goes to room number one, which is Ms. Gray's room. Each key is numbered."

"Good idea," Fallon said. "What are those weird-looking keys for?" She pointed to several with rounded ends.

"Oh, those are for the circuit and fire extinguisher boxes."

"With all those keys, you must have an important job." She moved toward the gate to exit. "Have a good day, Mr. Robertson."

"You too. Watch out for those greedy boys," he said, starting to go back inside. A car made a U-turn along the street just as he went around the corner by the front entrance. He didn't pay any attention to it, throwing out his lunch trash before entering the building.

The next day, he was getting started on another room when Blair Hopkins appeared.

"Miss this place already, eh?" Buddy asked.

Blair seemed preoccupied. Buddy turned back to his task, figuring Blair would pass him by. Suddenly he felt awkward.

"Buddy, I've been asked to look into something that happened yesterday," Blair said.

"What's that?" Buddy tried to appear nonchalant, but he had a sense of foreboding. His grip tightened on the cleaning rag held in his right hand.

"You were observed with a student on the playground yesterday when you should have been inside working."

"Oh, you mean Fallon?"

"Yes. Why were you out there with her when you should have been doing your job?" Blair's expression was friendly but guarded, like a cop asking someone for their license and registration.

"I was on my lunch break," Buddy said, "and Fallon just wanted to know why I carry all these keys." He grasped the ring on his belt. "I showed her how they were numbered."

Blair's expression softened a bit as he ran one hand through his hair. He had nice hair, thick and wavy, not at all like Buddy's. But then, he probably didn't have someone so untrained as Mags taking clippers to him.

"You have to watch yourself these days, Buddy," Blair urged. "You know this. Don't put yourself in a situation with a student where you're the only adult around. People talk."

Buddy felt the blood drain from his face. Who would accuse him of such a thing?

"I would never — I have never," he started, and then felt the emptiness of his words. *Who wouldn't deny it?*, he asked himself.

"I don't believe you ever would," Blair said. "I needed to talk with you, as I promised I would. Just be mindful."

Oh, I will, Buddy thought. He nodded, unable to decide whether he should thank Blair for bringing this up or curse him for his questioning. It made him feel like a scolded child. He needed to take a breath. The cleaning rag was wadded into a tight little ball in his fist, and he forced himself to loosen his grip. Blair exited the room.

Some birds mate for life, and such is the fate of mourning doves. Tending to be monogamous, they are a common bird, members of the pigeon family. Grandpa said their name was confusing because most people, upon hearing them in the morning, assumed they were called morning doves. Grandpa also said their sad coos alone should let people know they were mournful. He said they probably were sad to be related to pigeons, since they were more stately than their cousins.

Buddy finally received the supplies to install the shelves Joyce requested awhile back. He told her he'd do it the day after she asked, but he had to fill out a form for the shelving, and should have known it would take time.

He didn't want to be in the same area as Blair, and could hear him in his office talking on the phone. He decided to install Joyce's shelves now. Buddy loaded them on his cart and headed to central office, getting buzzed in as usual.

"Is now a good time?" he asked Joyce. She stood by her office window facing out, with her back to him. When she turned around Buddy saw she had tears in her eyes. "I can come back," he started.

"Oh, no, now is okay," Joyce said. "I was just watching the saddest thing. A bird hit my window and died, and its mate has been standing here for half an hour, waiting for its partner to wake up. I didn't expect it to be so upset."

Buddy approached the window and looked down. A mourning dove lay on the walk, lifeless. Another sat on the chain link fence edging the parking lot. It let out a coo.

"It's a mourning dove," Buddy said. "They mate for life."

"Oh, that's so sad!" Joyce grabbed a tissue from her desk. "What will it do?"

"Probably sit there for a bit, then leave. It'll be alone for a time, but probably find another dove by next mating season. I'll go out and pick up the dead one."

"Please don't until the partner flies away," Joyce said. "Give it time to grieve."

"Their brains are the size of a peanut," Buddy said. "The mate will forget in a few minutes. It's not a great tragedy, like Romeo and Juliet. Happens every day."

"You're an ass, Buddy," Joyce said, though she also chuckled.

"I'll wrap it in paper towels and give it a proper burial in the dumpster."

"Put my shelves up first, so the living partner can get over it," Joyce said. "I'm going to file while you do that."

Buddy got busy, drilling holes in the wall, leveling the shelves, pausing when Joyce took a brief call.

"You always seem to know little details about stuff," Joyce observed. "I remember the time we were working on a crossword at lunch and you rattled off the answer after we'd all been stumped."

"I'm full of useless information," he said. "Besides, it was an easy clue."

"Not for us," she said. "We just couldn't figure out what an UPA tree was, so we never would have gotten it."

"Cornered prey," Buddy said. "UP a tree."

"That still cracks me up," Joyce said.

"I think I'm done," Buddy stated. "Do these look like what you wanted?"

"Oh, yeah," Joyce answered. "I can put lots of stuff up there."

Buddy looked around at all the clutter. Piles of paper, binders, chintzy figurines, and office supplies filled the room. He took a ceramic angel and stuck it on the bottom shelf.

"Well, there ya go," he said. "Happy to help."

"And the sorrowful dove is gone," Joyce said.

Buddy peered out the window. Sure enough, the living dove was gone, leaving the dead one lying where it was. He left his cart in the hallway outside central office, grabbing a few paper towels. He picked the bird up with the towels, nodded at Joyce (who was watching him), and headed back inside so he could take the bird to the other end of the building, where the dumpsters were.

The bird didn't look hurt. It had probably died instantly from a broken neck. Its little talons were made for perching, with a backward-facing claw. Doves seemed kind of drab to Buddy, but up close he could see the beautiful markings. The feathers were sable and fine. Doves were fat with small heads, but this creature was quite striking.

Buddy was standing at the dumpster, but he found himself unable to toss the bird inside. He looked around. No one was visible. Blair's car was gone. He wrapped the bird gently and held it at his side, taking it back into the school. He'd bury it later, after he got home.

As he made the decision, he cursed himself. *Getting a little weird,* he thought. He wondered what Grandpa would say. He'd tell Buddy nature would take its course, the bird returning to the earth like we all did. He wouldn't belittle Buddy for showing it some grace. The bird would rest in the ground alone, but at least it wasn't in the garbage.

We all die alone. Buddy reflected on this as he smoothed out the sandy soil, again remembering his beloved grandparents. At least Grandma and Grandpa were spared life without one another. They died at the same time, which was how it should have been. Their loss left Buddy feeling like that surviving dove, except he still mourned for them every day. They'd be dead now, anyway, but Buddy sure could have used some more time with them. Yup, he was like that bird, but his brain wasn't the size of a nut. He had way too many things to remember and mourn.

Mags could be heard humming when he entered the house. A generous description, since she was as good at that as she was at making coffee. She was confident, though, he'd give her that. Buddy couldn't identify the song, her voice strong but flat and toneless. He followed it into their bedroom, where she was actually taking a rag to the pile of books on her end table.

"Cleaning?" he asked.

"Nah, just puttering," she said. "I wouldn't know where to start in here."

"I see that." The cobwebs had cobwebs. He was staring at a cluster of them. He reached out for it and it collapsed, wispy and white. Part of it stuck to his fingers, part of it wafted to the floor, and part of it stuck where it was.

"Are we hoarders?" she asked.

Buddy's eyes roamed the room as they had so many times. Was that a rhetorical question? He shrugged. "Maybe you're a hoarder," he said, "but I'm a collector."

"I could clean your crap out in a few hours," Mags said. "It's all junk."

"I could say the same about your stuff."

"There ya go," she said. "Does it bother you?"

"Nope." He stretched and rubbed his stomach. "What's for supper?"

Mags folded her rag and ran it across the dresser this time. Rather, she ran it across the items on the dresser. She coughed. "I dunno," she answered.

"Can we have shit on a shingle?" That was dried beef, milk gravy, and toast. Grandpa used to love it.

"You know I hate that," Mags said. "But I could have a toasted cheese and some tomato soup."

They sat in front of the television while they ate, watching coverage of some local festival. Northern Michigan was famous for its festivals. Asparagus, mushrooms, trout, bass, cherries, alpine living…he and Mags never made it to any of them. Well, they would take the kids to the parades, but that was long ago. And the grandkids never asked, at least to Buddy's knowledge. As he watched someone painting the faces of little tykes, he thought to ask if Mags had heard from her kids lately.

"Oh, yeah, they're goin' camping this weekend," she replied. "They asked about borrowing our sleeping bags."

"You know we'll never see them again," Buddy said.

"Like we'll ever use them."

"True." He offered to find them, though first he was going out to check on the peas. He set his plate on the counter as he went by.

Once outside, Buddy was pleased to see the plants were healthy. The air was still warm and the sun high. He forgot about Blair and his judgmental glare for a few minutes as he stood still, feeling the light on his face.

"What is so rare as a day in June?" Shakespeare again. Blair and all the rest of those asses would be surprised that Buddy knew any of his words at all. Shakespeare sure told it like it was, once Anna had interpreted it for him. Anna, who went on to teach at a university in New York State. She sure made something of herself. He was proud of her, but they left each other's lives decades ago. She advanced herself while Buddy grew up to be a school janitor, a nobody with bad teeth and a house full of junk and dust. It was alright, though. He owned his house, he paid his bills, and he owed no one.

He needed to stake up those gangly tomato feelers over there — soon, before they got overwhelmed and broken, allowing the little green starts to wither and die. He located some cages in the shed and yanked them free from a stack of other debris. As he turned to exit, a muscle caught in his back. He gasped, then stretched backward, trying to work out the kink. It wasn't the first time this happened, and he usually managed to work through it. Buddy set the cages down and rubbed his backside. He'd surrender and take some ibuprofen when he got back to the house.

Well, his project of counting trees might need to be put on the back burner. He barely noticed the thought before dismissing it. He'd still be able to count trees so long as he could lean against them if it came to that.

He clutched the tomato cages close to his body like he'd been taught to do at custodial classes. They weren't heavy at all, but their bulk upset his balance and sent a fresh spasm through his back. He was actually starting to perspire from pain. He set the cages down on the ground and leaned backward once again.

Just then Buddy heard a car coming down the drive. The sun was beginning its decline into the treeline, forcing him to shield his eyes from the glare as he watched Jenna and Carrie approach the house. He tried to wave, and another spasm clutched him.

Jenna jumped out of the car, swigging from a water bottle before setting it into a cup holder on the car door. "You in pain, Buddy?"

He nodded. "Yeah, my back just went out."

"Ooh," she said. "Mags indoors?"

"Oh yeah. Watching educational TV like *Wheel of Fortune*," he said.

"Want some help with your tomatoes?" Jenna gestured toward the cages.

Buddy smiled through a wince. "Nah, I can handle that much." Gingerly, he grasped them once again.

Carrie edged her way out of the car, moving about as slowly as Buddy. She brushed her hair back. There was something about her, the way she consciously attempted to straighten herself, that struck him. *She's drunk,* Buddy realized. She briefly met his gaze, seemed to register that he was aware of her condition, and looked away.

"Hey," she said, almost whispering.

Jenna turned toward Carrie, throwing her palms up in the air. "I thought you were just going to stay in the car." She backtracked, then dismissed her friend with a flick of the hand. "Suit yourself," she said, stomping off toward the house.

Carrie managed to follow her inside. Buddy remained where he was, holding the cages. He considered going in himself, but knew he'd be opening himself up to something he didn't want. So he opted to stay outdoors.

Everything was quiet inside the house, as he knew it would be. Mags would make some food for Carrie to get in her stomach, withholding any tongue-lashing for now. She knew what to do.

He carefully placed one of the cages over a plant, then continued on down the long row, moving at a slow but even pace. Once the sun went down behind the trees, swarms of mosquitoes and black flies began buzzing around his head. Although they didn't bite, Buddy found them annoying this evening.

He left eight unused cages in the garden and entered the house. The woman and the girls were sitting at the kitchen table, Carrie holding a cup of tea and Jenna holding a cat. His plan was to ease by them and start his search for the sleeping bags. He thought they might be rolled up and stuffed in an old suitcase. Since he and Mags never went anywhere, he had to remember where the suitcase ended up. Maybe the bedroom closet? Ned, the cat Jenna was holding, blinked. Ned wasn't one of the friendlier cats, so Buddy was a little surprised to see him cuddling with her.

"Mom made fish for supper, and he must smell it on me," Jenna said, as if she'd read Buddy's mind. "This one's Ned, right?"

"Yup," he said.

Carrie attempted to sip her tea, but it was too hot. "Sorry I showed up here like this," she said. "My wonderful stepfather is going to court tomorrow, and my mom is freaking out. She found out where we're staying and had the nerve to show up today."

Mags shook her head. "She called Ben a liar and told her kids she didn't want them back. Can you imagine?"

"Nope." Buddy attempted to get by them, but the nearest kitchen chair was filled with Mags and he couldn't fit past her.

"They had to call the police before she would leave," Mags said.

Carrie sniffled. "Then it got really ugly, and I just didn't want to think about what she let happen. I stole a bottle of wine from the party store and drank it at the park."

"After she drank most of it, she called me," Jenna said. "I couldn't take her back to foster care like this, so I came here."

"Good thinking," Mags said. "And you are lucky you didn't get caught, young lady." She held Carrie's eyes with her blue stare, then looked at Buddy. "We called her foster parents to let them know she's here and safe. They were worried sick."

"What about Ben?" Buddy asked.

"He was upset, but seems to be okay now," Mags answered.

"He's getting counseling," Carrie said. "I should have stayed with him instead of running off and getting drunk."

"Yeah, you should have," Jenna said.

"Coulda, woulda, shoulda," Mags said. "We've all done things we regret. Good lord, you're only a kid yourself."

"Not old enough to drink," Buddy remarked. "But you're not the first kid to do that, either."

Carrie hung her head. From where he stood, Buddy might have reached over and tucked her hair behind an ear. He could almost see himself doing it, feeling the softness of her hair and skin.

"I don't want to be like them," Carrie suddenly cried. "I don't want to be like that."

Jenna stood, looking for a tissue, and settled for a paper towel. She ripped one from the roll and tossed it across the table. Carrie noisily blew into it, laughing nervously as she wiped away a strand of snot left behind.

"You're such a dork," Jenna said. "I'm still so pissed off at you for getting drunk."

"Like you've never done it?" Carrie protested.

"Well, I've never stolen from a store to get wasted."

"Alrighty, we all know that wasn't the best way to deal," Mags piped in. "Court's gonna happen tomorrow, and the SOB will get what he deserves. If he hurt Ben like he's accused of doin', I hope he's sent away for a long time."

"I hope he's hung up by his…" Buddy stopped himself. "Never mind. Can I get by you, Mags?" He attempted to escape the room without further ado, but the girls were laughing and nodding.

"Good one," Carrie said.

"He comes up with one once in a while." Mags pulled her chair in so he could pass.

Inside the closet he located the old suitcase with the sleeping bags inside, leaving it out on the bedroom floor. Lennie could get it himself when he stopped by.

He had trouble sleeping because of his damn back. Finding a comfortable spot was impossible. A few times he dozed off, but if he moved pain awoke him. Buddy finally got up and went to the freezer for a bag of peas to press against it. Cold was supposed to help.

Mags was still up, slumped on the couch watching some crap

on TV. He sighed and sat down in his recliner. He wasn't going to miss work, so he had to get some relief, and soon.

In a few minutes he was out. Sometimes he slept better in his chair, with the blah-blah-blah of the television. He woke up four hours later, with a blanket over him. Mags had somehow managed to get the peas from behind him because he couldn't find them. He stretched slowly, waiting for the pain to catch in his back. It was a little better. The clock showed 5:42 a.m., light already filtering through the windows, so he figured he'd get up. Limping into the kitchen, he was a little surprised to find Mags sitting at the table.

"Why up so early?"

She gave a shrug and removed a spoon from her coffee cup. "I didn't sleep much at all, Mac," she admitted. "I just can't stop thinking about Ben and Carrie and what chances they have in life."

"Well, your worrying isn't gonna change anything," he said, more gruffly than he intended. "I mean, it's awful, but what can we do?"

"You mean because of who we are?"

Buddy moved toward the coffee. It smelled like it had been sitting on the burner for hours. Probably had.

"Well, we don't know what to do."

"Just poor white trash," Mags answered. "Like those kids."

"I guess." He poured some milk into his coffee and the color didn't change a bit. "How old is this, Mags?"

"Oh, I made it around midnight," she said.

"So it'll be worse than normal." He added more milk.

"Yup." Mags looked around their kitchen, taking in the boxes, cat hair, and piles of junk. "If I had a way, I'd go down to that courthouse today," she announced. "I want to evil eye that piece of shit and get the satisfaction of watching him squirm."

"Aw, Mags, you don't need to be goin' there," Buddy said. "I don't know how those things work, but it'll most likely upset you more." He placed his cup across from her and turned to go to the bathroom. A little crick in his back, but nothing he couldn't live with.

"I haven't done much with my life," she said.

Buddy turned back toward her, raising his eyebrows.

"Well, I haven't. I never had a pot to pee in, and I never had big goals or nothin'. I had those two boys, then you came along and helped me get them raised. Now I mostly sit on the couch and pass the time. I dunno, this whole thing has me thinking about my life. Guess I feel a little useless."

"Well, if you're so useless, why did Jenna bring that girl here yesterday?" Buddy ran a hand through his dirty hair. "I'd say she knew you'd know what to do, and you did. So don't go fretting and stewing about this, because you can't change it. I'm going to make some new coffee, walk down to the creek and see if I can spot a trout or somethin'. You're gonna make a few eggs, and then feed me. After that I'm off to work." He paused. "But first I gotta pee."

"You do that," Mags said. "Run off, will ya?"

He closed the bathroom door. "That's my plan."

Wonder how Carrie feels today. Probably hung over. Buddy never was much of a drinker. When he got to northern Michigan and tried his hand at the oil rigs, he drank with the rest of the crew, though he didn't like it as much as the other guys and was too cheap to spend a lot of money on it. He missed the quiet. Work was noisy, the workers were noisy, and the bars were noisy. He thought it might help him forget what he'd left behind, but when he finally got home the alcohol only made him feel lonelier. He eventually stopped going out, opting to spent time outdoors instead. When the oil industry slowed in the '80s, he lost his job and ended up going to Manpower, a hiring agency, to find work. First the cherry production, then at the school, on a reduced salary until he got permanently hired. The hours suited him, and left time for being outside. The pay was less than what he earned on the rigs, but he didn't need a lot.

"You holed up in there all day?"

Mags. He flushed the toilet and opened the door, three cats skittering away. A man couldn't take a decent crap in this place, and he already had enough trouble with that.

"Why? You got breakfast ready for me or what?" Mags still sat at the table, but she pulled herself up and shuffled to the sink.

"I can throw something together," she offered.

"Give me a half hour so I can walk down to the creek like I planned." He headed outside without making a new pot of coffee, taking Mags's mud with him. He tossed the remains into the sand as he walked.

Dewy webs lined the path. The moss was emerald green and soft, morning air holding hints of the humidity to come. Buddy set his cup in some tree roots and stood on a flat rock, peering into the water. It was clear and clean, and he watched the way the current made patterns on the creek bed. Sunlight was just starting to filter through the forest. He saw a few minnows, but no larger fish. A pair of starlings landed, and one ventured toward the water's edge, leaning in to have a drink. Then it leaned further, taking water on its wings and giving itself a bath. As Buddy watched, a movement caught his attention, and looking closer his eyes met with those of a doe. How long had she been standing there? He noticed spots on a fawn nuzzling at her side. The doe made a little snort, and they moved away. They weren't too alarmed since he couldn't see the whiteness under their tails flagging.

He took in the sustenance of the morning for a few moments before collecting his coffee cup, noting his back felt mercifully better. Then he thought of the ugly world past the serenity of this spot. He thought of Ben, and of Ben's sister.

Chapter 15

Revelations

1974

The enchanted summer stretched on, filled with long days of golden promise. He and Leah were inseparable, though he still helped Grandpa in his gardens. He ran the tractor and the tiller, and they coaxed waxy and fat night crawlers from the black dirt for fishing. Grandpa had the proverbial farmer's tan, his eyes twinkling and his energy strong. Grandma was slowing down some, but she still made plump biscuits for them at night. Anna came home for a week and was happy and healthy, loving her life at the college. She'd changed somehow, though; she had a sophistication about herself that Buddy wasn't sure he liked. She'd always been smart, but now she seemed of a different station than the rest of them, aloof. If he thought about it much, it bothered him.

But there wasn't a lot of time to dwell on it. His hair was blond from the sun, his body lean and quick, and his hands were strong and warm with the feel of Leah's skin. Everything was rich. The earth yielded black, blue, and red berries, and vegetables — every color of the rainbow. Grandpa and he pulled tomatoes from vines and ate them, fruit still holding the sun's heat. They worked hard, and while Anna was home she helped them with canning and preserving. He and Leah didn't have much time during those days to sneak off together, but Leah pitched in, getting her hands stained with the blood of summer's bounty. They got dirty and sweaty and gulped fresh lemonade for relief.

Anna held her glass to her forehead. "My, I haven't worked like this in too long," she said. "Feels good."

"It's hot," Grandma said.

"I could chase you with the hose," Grandpa suggested. He sat beside her and winked.

"The neighbors would talk," she chuckled.

"Let 'em," said Grandpa.

The five of them sat in pleasant silence. Grasshoppers jumped in the yard, a fat bumblebee buzzing among Grandma's holly-hocks. Buddy watched as it almost disappeared into the center of a blossom, emerging a few moments later and moving on to the next. A drop of sweat ran down the side of his face, and he absentmindedly brushed it away.

"Your face is streaked with dirt," Leah said. She took her fingers, wet from her glass, and rubbed them over Buddy's face. They were cool and refreshing. He closed his eyes.

A car pulled into the driveway; he recognized the sound of the motor before opening his lids. It was Mom. They hadn't seen her for weeks. She got out of the car, gave everyone a tentative smile, and started up the knoll toward them.

"Hi, Bonnie, I'll grab you a seat," Grandpa said, but Buddy was already in action. Chair wedged underneath one arm, he met his mom and gave her a hug with the other.

"Buddy, you're so tanned," she said.

"He's brown as a berry," Grandma agreed.

Anna stayed in her chair. She attempted a smile, but Buddy knew she was not excited to see their mother.

Bonnie took her chair and set it next to Anna, then reached over and smoothed her daughter's hair.

"How are you, Anna?"

"Just fine. Busy," Anna said. She managed to look into Bonnie's eyes, though.

"I'll bet. I hear you're doing well at school."

"From whom?" Anna couldn't keep the bite from her voice.

"From Grandpa and Grandma," Bonnie said.

"Oh. I didn't know you spoke regularly." She swatted at a gnat.

"Well, I ran into them at the store," Mom conceded.

"We're glad you stopped by," Grandpa said. "How are things at the shop?"

Mom said they were good; she was doing something new with a big computer system.

"Computers, huh?" Grandma mused. "They're supposed to be the latest thing."

"Well, they are interesting and quite complicated," Mom said. "But I wanted to hear how you all are doing. I miss you kids, and Mom and Dad Robertson." She glanced at Leah. "And who is this young lady?"

"This is Leah," Grandpa said. "She and Buddy are quite the pair, although we all lay claim to her. She's Ross and Peggy's niece. You remember them, from just over the hill?"

"Oh, yes! Don't your folks live in New York State now?" Mom's gaze went from Leah's face to her unruly hair to her feet, covered with canvas slip-on shoes. She then looked up the girl's beautiful long legs, bronzed with summer's light.

"They do," Leah said. "I'm here for the summer."

"How nice," Mom said. She cleared her throat. "It must be different here than in New York."

"Well, we aren't from the city or anything, so it's not too much different. I love it here, though." Leah looked to Buddy and she grinned. He smiled back.

"Oh," Mom said, and Buddy realized she now knew they were a couple. He was a little embarrassed, but proud.

"Want some iced tea?" Grandma asked. Before Mom could protest, she was up and going toward the house.

"I'll help," Leah offered.

Mom watched her walk away. The look on her face was hard for Buddy to decipher, though it almost seemed sad. Maybe she was upset because Buddy found the love of his life and she wasn't around to be a part of it.

"I'm so happy that you and Buddy are doing well," Mom said. She was looking at Anna now. "I miss the two of you so much. You both are welcome to come over, or even stay at our place…" she paused. Anna had shaken with an almost imperceptible shudder, but Mom caught it, and so did Buddy. "Stu likes kids, and we have lots of room."

"I'm going back to school soon," Anna said. "So, thanks, but I have all my stuff unpacked here."

"Well, the offer is open," Mom said. "You always have somewhere to stay."

Buddy sure hoped Mom wasn't going to put him on the spot and ask him to come over, because he didn't want to go, either. He was glad Leah and Grandma were coming back with tea and a plate of cookies.

Mom drank her tea and ate a cookie, and everyone talked about the weather and the news. The war was ending, and Mom said it would be such a relief not to hear the nightly death toll on TV. "All those young people lost," she said.

"Yes, and for what?" Grandpa agreed. Buddy noticed that Grandma was sure quiet.

Mom stood, saying she had to get home and make dinner. Except for Grandma, everyone rose to exchange goodbyes.

Buddy squeezed her tightly, smelling her nice perfume, fruity and clean. Anna returned their mother's hug as well. Mom touched Grandma's shoulder, got a hug from Grandpa, and gave Leah's hand a little tug. Then she was gone.

"Your mom is really pretty," Leah said. "I see her in both of you. From pictures of your dad, I see him, too."

Grandma's tea slipped. She managed to catch it, but a few splashes stained her flowered shirt.

"Oh, look what I've done," she said. She took her hankie from her sleeve and wiped at it.

"At least you managed to save most of it," Buddy said.

"I can't go a day without slopping."

"It was good to see Bonnie," Grandpa said. "Wasn't it." He spoke it like a sentence, not a question. Nobody answered. The silence grew awkward.

"I was happy to see her," Buddy finally asserted. "I miss Mom."

"I miss Mom too," Anna said. "I just wish things were different."

"Bingo," Grandma said. "She's got her life to live."

"And we have ours," Anna replied.

Later, Buddy couldn't get to sleep. He tossed and turned, looked at the new digital clock on his bedside every 15 minutes, and even tried pulling the covers over his head like he used to when he was little. Nothing worked. He watched as sunlight began revealing objects in the old bedroom. First he made out shapes, then a triangle of light appeared on a wall. It faded as the whole room brightened. He finally felt like he could sleep, but it was almost seven o'clock and he needed to help Grandpa again today.

He sat up and rubbed his face. It was still a little chilly. He slipped a T-shirt on, grabbed his jeans, and headed to the bathroom. As he stood on the black and white tile floor, feeling like he would never stop peeing, a memory came to him. In this same little room a long time ago, he'd overheard something that confused him. He remembered Mom saying how she was pregnant with Anna when she and Dad got together. Buddy knew it meant something at the time, only now realizing the significance.

Dad wasn't Anna's father.

Buddy tucked himself into his briefs and then stood at the sink, mindlessly watching water flow from the tap. After a minute he put his fingers into the stream. Without using soap, he flicked his hands halfway dry and grabbed his pants. He knew Anna didn't know, and would never tell her. Yet he really wanted to find out more.

"Ready for your eggs?" Grandma hollered from the kitchen.

"What? Oh, yeah Grandma, be right out."

When he got to the kitchen Grandpa was sitting at the table, looking at the local paper.

"This thing isn't worth the quarter I paid for it," he mumbled. He slurped his coffee.

"Buddy, you look like you slept with an alley cat," Grandma observed. He sat, and she placed two eggs, with hard yolks just the way he liked them, down in front of him. He made a sandwich with the toast. The radio was on, blaring that morning swap show Buddy hated. Farmers called in and asked for used tractors. Housewives called in and wanted to sell couches. The local car salesman phoned and offered "good deals" on Chevys and Oldsmobiles. Buddy found it the most boring thing ever, but it was usually on if Grandpa was inside. Thankfully it only lasted a half hour.

He was still mulling his revelation. He ate slowly.

"You coming down with something?" Grandma stood at the sink, pouring water into the egg pan.

"Couldn't sleep," Buddy said.

"Now, why can't a young man sleep when he's working outside most days and shouldn't have a worry in the world?"

"Dunno," Buddy fibbed. Then he asked after his sister. "Is Anna home?"

"Nah, she went into town, to the library for somethin' or the other," Grandpa said. He folded the paper. "She was up early. The library doesn't open until nine, but she said she was going to walk around town first."

"Why walk around town when we have all these woods?" Buddy asked.

"Anna is of a different make than you and me," Grandpa answered. "And she's got more worldly pursuits. That college education she's getting probably has something to do with it."

Buddy didn't know he was even going to ask anything. It certainly wasn't his intent. He felt just as surprised as his grandparents when the question landed in the kitchen.

"Does Anna have a different dad than I do?"

It was like a string pulled Grandma and Grandpa upright. Their eyes met, and then they looked to Buddy.

"I overheard something just after Dad died," Buddy explained. "I didn't know what it meant, but I remembered it this morning. Mom was pregnant before she and Dad got together. She said he saved her..."

"Jesus," Grandpa said.

Grandma sat at the table across from Buddy, not at the other end where she normally took her place.

"Far as I'm concerned, your dad is Anna's dad just as much as he is yours. Anna never needs to know."

"I won't tell," Buddy promised. "But what happened?"

"You know how trusting your mother is," Grandma began. "She got involved with someone. Who is not important."

"Bonnie is still like a daughter to us," Grandpa interrupted. "She hasn't had it easy in life. Some of it's her own doing, but a lot of it isn't. Your grandmother and I know where she came from. Those kids were dirt-poor and neglected. Naturally, a young girl would be taken in by someone of little character."

The radio guy was giving out the phone number for anyone who might be interested in a stove that still worked. Grandma had a dish rag and was working at some unseen stickiness on the table.

"Your dad was working at the grocery store, bagging people's stuff after school, and Bonnie caught his eye," Grandpa continued.

"She was quiet and shy, and his heart went out to her because he knew the family like we did," Grandma said. "He talked with her when she came into the store to pick up things for her parents. They were on food stamps. She was ashamed, but Butch told her it was nothing to be embarrassed about, that lots of people around here were poor. She was a clean, pretty little thing. He saw something in her, and asked her out for an ice cream. We didn't realize it was getting serious."

"She came here to dinner," Grandpa recalled. "She looked at your dad like he hung the moon."

"I'll never forget how Bonnie's face glowed with him beside her," Grandma added. "That never changed."

"Nope," Grandpa said. He had a wistful smile.

"So how did it happen that she got pregnant?" Buddy interrupted. "I mean, by somebody other than Dad."

"She was pregnant the first time she came here," Grandma said. "She didn't know it yet. Apparently she wasn't very educated about sex. She told us later she thought a guy asked for sex, and if you were a good girl you said no. But he never asked, and the deed was done before she realized it."

"What the —"

"Now, Buddy, kids weren't as knowledgeable as they are these days. All this rock and roll and sex education wasn't around. The boy who got your mother in the family way was just as naïve as her. He only thought he knew everything, the little shit."

"You know him?"

Grandpa nodded. "This is a small town," he said. "He was one of those youngsters that acted up, a little brat, and you knew he was headed for trouble. A likable enough kid, though. Actually stopped by here a few times wanting to help me on the farm."

Grandma said, "Yes, but by then, we'd heard some things about him stealing from other folks. So we turned him down."

"Who was he?" Buddy asked.

"Not important," Grandpa repeated. "A few days after Bonnie came for supper he was out messing around with some other delinquent boys, and they went for a spin on somebody's motorcycle. He took a corner too fast and was killed when he hit a guard rail."

"Wow!"

"Then your mother realized she was in trouble. She tried telling your dad he should stop seeing her, but he was already smitten and asked us what he should do. He said he was in love and wanted to marry that girl."

"While he was still in school?"

"Well, he was about graduated, and so was she. Your dad never gave us a lick of worry, and we saw the way she cared for him, so we gave our blessing. We never regretted it. Anna is our granddaughter, just like you're our grandson. Your dad loved her before she was even born, and no one knows any different — he was her dad, too."

"That's all that matters," Grandma agreed. "He was her dad, and always will be."

"I'll never say anything different," Buddy swore. "Boy, my dad was a hero to my mom, wasn't he?"

"Yes, he was," Grandma said. "Regardless of the choices your mother has made in the past few years, we know she loved your dad. She never had much of a chance, really, to learn about standing up for herself. When your dad died, we tried to fill a hole that won't ever be filled. You just have to remember she's doing the best she can."

The screen door slammed. The radio was back to playing music. Grandpa reached for the off button. Leah stood in the doorway for a second, saw them all at the table and came inside.

"Good morning!" She smiled dreamily, her hair tied back in a ponytail, her feet in flip-flops.

"She looks at you like your mom looked at your dad," Grandma said.

Buddy stood. He felt crummy with the lack of sleep, and was overwhelmed with emotions. He was sad that his mom lost his dad. If Dad had lived, Buddy and Anna never would have suffered at the hands of James Shearing. Moreover, his mom would be taken care of for the rest of her life. He wasn't the only person robbed; Mom had been forsaken many times. One day he should ask about her childhood. He was way luckier than she was, because he had grandparents who helped raise him.

"Buddy!" Leah was chuckling, waving her palm in front of his face. "Is anyone in there?" She looked into his eyes, pulling him out of his thoughts.

"Sorry," he said. "What'd you say?"

Leah threw up her hands.

"I said we need to get outside, because it's too nice for being in and I have to go with my aunt and uncle to some dinner later."

"I'm supposed to help Grandpa," Buddy said, but Grandpa waved them off.

"Go on, we'll work this afternoon after Leah leaves. I can putter along until you get back."

Buddy and Leah headed toward the dirt path behind the farm. She carried her little book. "You were awful distracted a few minutes ago," she said.

It was going to be muggy. Even this early, the air felt thick and heavy. Buddy should have changed from his jeans. He'd do that once he got back.

Leah stopped, took her pencil from her pocket and knelt beside a clump of milkweed. It was flowering, its scent and color similar to lilacs. She quickly sketched its shape onto her paper.

"Monarchs depend on this for food," she stated.

"Yeah, I know," Buddy said. "Have you ever seen a monarch caterpillar?"

"No...have you?"

"Yeah. Let's see if we can find one." They lifted up the leaves and the flowers, and soon Buddy spied a fat caterpillar marked with white, black, and yellow stripes.

"That's gonna be a butterfly?" Leah asked. She examined it closely. She had such intensity in her gaze.

"Kinda ugly now, huh?"

"Well, its form is what it needs right now," she said. "Really cool how this somehow turns into that." She nodded toward a bright monarch floating in the air near them. "It's also pretty neat how the caterpillar finds protection in the milkweed before reaching adult form, and then feeds off it. Makes me think that nature is boundless."

"Is it nature or God?" Buddy asked. "God made all this happen, isn't that what you believe?"

Leah laid her pencil in the binding of her book. She looked

away. "I'm not sure I believe like you do, Buddy," she said. "I find science more real than God, I guess."

Buddy couldn't believe his ears. "How do you think like that? I never questioned if there was a God before; I just thought maybe He wasn't always listening. Or maybe I wasn't supposed to get all I asked for." *Or maybe God can't protect us from everything,* he thought but didn't say.

"What if we're just here? What if we're just a bunch of water and elements like that rock, or this milkweed?" Leah pondered. She was so perfect, Buddy would never believe that was true.

"I can't believe that. You can't, either. You'll go to hell if you don't believe in God."

"Oh, Buddy," she said. "I don't know what I believe. I am questioning, though. I can't make sense of some things, but all this —" she gestured in front of her. "It just makes sense out here. The sun is on us, the sky is blue, things are growing, and I can try to forget what I don't understand."

"I think God made you and you're an angel," he whispered. He took her book and set it down beside them. The conversation with his grandparents this morning sure made him question things. Leah carried her own questions and burdens. She opened her mouth to his, and he tasted her tongue and her sweetness. This made sense. This was the one pure blessing he had. He didn't know how he got so lucky. If it wasn't God who put her in his life, he didn't know who to thank.

When did he stop going to church? Was it during that summer, or when he lost Grandma and Grandpa? Buddy couldn't recall. Was it a conscious decision, or did he stop going because he no longer found comfort there, falling out of the habit? For a time even the quiet of the woods failed to soothe him. Certainly he found nothing but pain whenever walking those paths he and Leah once took together.

"I know it hurts now," Grandma had said. "Your first love, and she was special." She pulled him to her as he sat on the porch steps with his head in his hands, holding him as tightly as her old body could manage. She was wearing her apron and smelled like bread. Buddy allowed himself to fold into her, letting out a long breath.

"Why did she go, Grandma?" His voice broke. "There is no one like her."

"Ah, that may be so. But there will be someone else, different from her but just as special. God puts people in your path when you need them."

"Were you in love before Grandpa?" he asked.

Grandma leaned away from him, grasped his chin and looked into his eyes. "No, I can't say I was," she admitted. "But I've seen quite a bit of life in my long years. I had friends who lost loved ones in war or illness, and somehow they came through it. Might take a long time to recover, but you will. You're so young, Buddy. You've got a lot of living to do yet. So does Leah. You've had to be stronger than you realize, and suffered through some terrible losses. You have your dad's kindness and your mom's trusting nature, and will need to sort those out. But I promise you'll be fine. You'll always remember the sweetness of your first love, but you'll move on."

"What if I don't want to?" Buddy had a big blob of snot in his throat. He turned from Grandma and coughed, then spit it as far as he could. "Sorry, Grandma."

She ignored it. "Life has a way of moving forward," she said. "Now, get up and see how you can help that old man in the garden."

He did as she said. She didn't know the whole story, the guilt he felt over the way he lost Leah.

He noticed it in the dog days of August, when they only had a few weeks before school resumed. At first he thought it was his imagination that she seemed distant and somber, and he attempted to cheer her up. Leah would let him smother her cheeks with kisses and smile. She even took his hand and kissed it.

A few days later, though, she told him that her period was late, and she was never late.

"What's that mean?" he asked, but he knew.

She bit her lip and shook her head. "Maybe it doesn't mean anything." Then, "But I'm scared."

He gathered her into him. "What should we do?"

"Wait a few more days and hope I don't have a reason to be afraid," she whispered.

"Whatever happens, I love you and we'll figure it out —"

"How, Buddy?" she cried. "We're just a couple of kids, and I want to go to college! I have plans for myself!"

"I know!"

"Do you? How did I let this happen?" She sat down in the tall grass and gave him a look so filled with pain that he was afraid too, but in a different way from her.

Buddy sat with her. He'd get help, somehow. He didn't have time to think about anything but her, the way she seemed so helpless. Later, shame would keep him from telling the two people who might have helped. He could never tell them. He couldn't face them.

"I can't be pregnant." A prayer, but he wasn't sure she believed in it. He took her hand.

"We'll figure all this out, Leah," he said. "Like you suggested, let's give it a few days."

"Alright, Buddy," she said. "I do love you, you know. It's just that I have always wanted to be something. I don't want to graduate from high school and get a job I hate, going down that road. I don't want to tell my parents that I've totally messed up. They're messing up their own lives, and here I am, thinking I'm going to do better, and I'm not. I just *can't* be pregnant."

So they let it go for a few days. Leah came to the house, pale and sad, the next day. She said she threw up twice that morning. The next morning she vomited again.

"Maybe I'm just sick." It was windy that afternoon. The leaves on some of the trees hung upside down, sure sign of an approaching storm. Buddy loved days like these, outside in the warm air with the wind a portent of what was to come. Birds chirped about them. A tractor droned in the distance; a farmer was probably taking it to his barn before the rain started. The breeze lifted Leah's hair and blew it away from her face, and Buddy saw the circles under her eyes. Maybe she was just sick. Well, that would be worse, wouldn't it? What if it was something really bad?

"I think we should get you to a doctor," he said.

She huffed. "How?" Then her face brightened a bit. "Wait. I know a place, if we can get a ride there. It's somewhere to get a doctor if you don't have any money, and they give you birth control if you need it. Wish I'd thought of that sooner."

"I'll figure out a way to get us there," Buddy said. "And I have a little bit of money if they need it."

The rain started quickly, pelting them. Leah laughed as they ran toward the house from the woods. It was so good to hear her laughter; in a moment Buddy knew everything would be okay. They waved to Grandma and Grandpa while racing past the garden shed.

He called the bus line while Grandma and Grandpa were outside, finding they could ride a few towns over, where the clinic was located, every day at 7:45, with rides back at 3:50 and 5:50. Buddy looked in the phone book for the clinic and called them next. Not having rehearsed what to say beforehand, he almost hung up at hearing a voice on the other end.

"Women's Clinic," the voice said. He turned from Leah.

"I'm calling to get an appointment for my girlfriend," he stammered. "I — we — are worried about her."

"Can you tell me why, exactly?" the voice asked.

"Well, she's been getting sick, and her period is late —" He felt himself flush. "We don't know if she's pregnant or just sick. Can you tell us there?"

"We can," the voice said. It was a friendly voice. "Is your girlfriend available?"

Buddy turned to Leah. Her arms were crossed over her chest. "Yes," he said, handing her the phone.

Reluctantly, she grasped it. "Yes, I'm 17," she said. "I am about two weeks late." She nodded. "Yes, I have had sex." Her eyes looked away from Buddy's, to what he didn't know.

"As soon as we can," she said. She waited a few moments. "Yes, we will find a way to get there. Thank you." After she hung up Leah held onto the phone for a few seconds, facing away from him. Buddy put his hand on her shoulder. Did she cringe?

"I am supposed to be there day after tomorrow, at 10 in the morning," she said. "So it's going to be answered then. I don't know what I'll do if I'm going to have a —"

"We'll deal with it together," Buddy insisted. "It will be okay." Even as he spoke them he knew how empty the words sounded. He wasn't prepared to be a father! He knew nothing about kids. Grandma and Grandpa would be so disappointed in him. Anna too. Why hadn't he thought about what could happen? All those special times with this girl, who was thinking about consequences? Certainly not him.

Now she stood before him, her mind racing like his. He knew every attempt to calm her was fruitless. He was just as afraid as she was.

"I'm going with you," he said. "I have the bus fare."

"It costs 10 dollars to see the doctor," Leah said.

"I have that, too."

The rain finally let loose in full force. They heard Grandma and Grandpa chattering on their way back to the house. Leah sidestepped around Buddy, heading into the bathroom. Buddy turned from the phone table as his grandparents came inside.

"Some storm, huh?" Grandpa gave a shiver. "It was warm until I got in here with that fan blowing on me." He pointed to the whirring device in the window. "Get that out of there, will ya, Buddy? The rain will warp the window casing."

Buddy made a move and heard water running in the little bathroom off the kitchen, where Leah was. He couldn't tell if she was retching or crying, and hesitated a moment, knowing if he turned off the fan they would be able to hear her, too. He was thankful beyond explanation when she came out, a smile pasted on her face.

The next day he waited for her customary visit, but she didn't come. As soon as he could, he ran the trail they'd made earlier this summer toward her aunt and uncle's house. She answered the door at his knock.

"Where were you?" he asked, a little too desperately.

"Just here," she said. "Thinking." It was almost one in the afternoon, but she had pajamas on. A big T-shirt came down past her knees.

"Are you home alone?"

"Yeah." She moved to let him in. He tried hugging her, but she seemed a little stiff. Buddy searched her eyes for some form of relief, finding none. She was so sad.

"Get dressed and come out," he said. "We need to find some stuff you can draw."

"I can't, Buddy. What good will that do?"

"More good than you sitting in here," he insisted. "I'm not leaving, so you're just gonna have to get dressed and come out."

She threw her arms in the air. "Fine," she muttered, and stomped up the stairs. It wasn't lost on Buddy that she didn't ask him to come with her. They never made love anywhere except in their woods, but he had been in her room before. Normally he'd be invited to follow her, yet now knew he should stay put.

Leah came down a few minutes later wearing shorts and a sleeveless top. Even with her hair unwashed, a worried and strained expression on her face, she was the most beautiful thing he'd ever seen. She grabbed her little book and her pencils, and they left the house.

The day was almost normal. She placed a beech leaf between the papers of her book, then sketched the way some lichen sprawled across a branch. To Buddy, her drawing was as promising as her interest in plants.

"Did you ever think about being an artist?"

She tucked her hair behind one ear, finishing her pencil stroke before looking at him. "No. It's just a means to an end. I like the plants, not drawing them."

"But you make your drawings look just like the real thing," he said.

"Thanks, Buddy. You always say nice things to me."

"That's because I love you, and because you're talented." He smiled and got a trace of a smile reciprocated. She didn't say she loved him back. She closed her book, then her eyes.

"How are we going to get away tomorrow? I mean, what are we going to say?"

He hadn't thought of that. He gave her a blank look.

"I was thinking maybe we could claim I want to do some school shopping," she went on. "I'll pick up a few things and say I didn't find much I liked. I have a little bit of money, maybe enough for a blouse or a skirt." She looked to him for approval.

"That sounds good," he said. "After your appointment, we'll go shopping."

"Okay," she said. "Can we go see your folks?"

"Sure." They walked slowly, and she let him put his arm around her. She even leaned into him a little. The sun was changing its place in the sky, very subtly. Autumn was on its way.

"Only two and a half weeks until school starts," she said, as if reading his mind.

"Yup. Have you thought any more about starting school here?" He hoped against hope.

"Oh, Mom said I can't," she replied. "She said she doesn't want me to spend my senior year away from her."

"When were you going to tell me?"

She stopped in her tracks.

"I've been a little preoccupied, Buddy."

Regret and fear poked his belly. He'd felt this way before, when Dad was dying and when James was around. This life was so hard. He needed help, but had no idea who to ask.

"I know," he said. "I didn't mean to upset you, but I will miss you so much. I'll figure out a way to visit you throughout the school year. I need a job somewhere so I can afford a car."

"Hmmm," was all she said.

Nearing the house, they could smell chicken frying. Grandma stood at the stove, the fan back in the window. Yesterday's rain was long gone. Leah stayed for dinner, picking at her food.

"Leah and I are going to do some school shopping tomorrow," Buddy said as they ate.

"I can take you," Grandpa said. "But we have to get some things done first."

"Oh, no, that's alright, Grandpa. We can head in by ourselves, maybe eat lunch at a restaurant, go wherever we want. You don't need to cart us around."

"How are you getting there?"

"We'll go to the Greyhound station downtown and get a bus ride," Buddy answered.

"It'll be fun," Leah added.

Grandpa shrugged. "Fine, but there's a lot of stuff to get done around here before you go off to school, young man. Promise you'll give me a few whole days of work."

"I'm all yours after tomorrow," Buddy swore. "Maybe Leah can help lessen the load, too."

"I'm always happy to be here," Leah said. "You and Grandma have meant so much to me." Her eyes watered. "I want you to know that."

"Heavens, you mean a lot to us, too," replied Grandma, winking. "Buddy might need a job for covering the phone bill during school."

Buddy forced a smile. "I was just saying that." *Well, not exactly.* Once Leah made it through tomorrow, they would figure something out. After tomorrow.

Chapter 16

Voices in the Hallway

"**R**ats," **Buddy cursed** under his breath as he parked at school.

Blair's car was out front. After their "discussion," Buddy had managed to evade him. The principal didn't visit the school much during summer, so Buddy could usually move about and concentrate on tasks without risk of a chance encounter. Today he entered the building and went straight to the custodial closet, where he set down his lunch and grabbed his trusty cart. He'd almost finished repairing and cleaning the walls, would soon start washing chairs and making sure the desk seats were screwed on and library table legs tightly bolted. Then there were always the wads of gum to be scraped from the undersides of those desks and tables.

Unfortunately, just as he started wheeling his cart down the hall Blair stepped out of his office. Buddy couldn't quite meet his eyes.

"Mornin'," Blair said.

"Mornin'." Buddy kept walking, as did Blair.

Blair was a good principal, interested in the welfare of the kids. He was far better at his job than some of the other administrators Buddy had seen over the years. Maybe that was why his questions and near-accusations got under his skin so much. It wasn't like he and Buddy were peers, but they'd always been friendly, and Buddy assumed they had some sort of mutual respect. He shouldn't have presumed that, and instead stayed mindful of their different stations. He couldn't decide if he was mad or ashamed someone would look at him and suspect him of hurting a child.

Once in the classrooms, he scraped at the walls forcefully. He'd worn this shirt for several days, and was starting to smell himself. Did other people notice? He never got that close to anyone. He'd have to visit the laundromat again soon, and also ask Mags to sew his name patch on better, as its top was loose and starting to curl over. In another few months he'd be able to turn in his old work clothes and get five new uniforms, clean and pressed.

The spot he currently rubbed at was worn down to the plaster. He wiped the wall with his bare hand, finding it dull and rough to the touch. Moving on to another spot, Buddy heard voices coming down the hallway. He stepped into a nearby classroom. It was Blair and the superintendent.

"So are you going back to court tomorrow?" the superintendent asked. Buddy strained to hear.

"Yes, they didn't get the jurors seated until late today," Blair said. "I sure hope that poor kid isn't forced to take the stand. I feel like I need to go. He doesn't have many good male role models."

"Children don't make good witnesses," the super said. "They can't really explain what happened, and they get confused easily."

"Plus it's so hard on them," Blair responded. "I hate to see it."

The two entered Blair's office, and Buddy could hear just well enough to know the subject had changed. He approached his cart and noisily wrung a sponge after pulling it from a bucket of gray water, being loud on purpose. He didn't much want to talk with either of those men, but didn't want to be accused of eavesdropping, either. He would never be involved in a private conversation like that, especially with a school administrator. Out of the question. He was just the custodian.

He continued down the hall, stopping every now and then to use the sponge on spots. He was around the corner by the time the superintendent left, Blair only staying in his office for a few more minutes. Then Buddy was again alone in the building, sponging walls back and forth, his mind dwelling on that kid. *Poor Ben,* he thought, shaking his head in time with his scrubbing. *Poor, poor Ben.*

Chapter 17

The Scorning

1974

No one was smiling at the clinic. Moms were there with daughters, teenagers who sat nervously in stiff-backed chairs. A few girls were there together, Buddy the only guy in the waiting room. Leah fidgeted with her unruly hair, picked up a magazine, then placed it back on the end table beside them. A poster on the wall advised against sex without contraception. A macramé hanger held a huge spider plant beside the poster. On another poster, a question screamed, "Imagine what the world would be like if men were the ones who got pregnant!"

Buddy found himself counting the little offshoots on the spider plant. "Babies," Grandma called them. Thirteen.

After exhaling heavily, Leah took a deep breath. Buddy tried to take her hand, but she pulled it away. She was picking at her nails now. Buddy realized that no one was being called by name, as in a doctor's office; instead a nurse came to each patient directly and beckoned them to follow. After a half hour, a thin woman with penciled-on eyebrows summoned Leah.

"Do you want me to go with you?" he started to ask, but she fiercely shook her head. He watched her disappear behind a door.

He didn't know where to direct his eyes, so he glanced at the titles of the magazines beside him. It turned out *Seventeen* was the only actual magazine; the rest were little brochures for patients. One was about gonorrhea. One was about birth control. One was about teen pregnancy. One was about abortion, which became legal a year ago. Roe vs. Wade, whatever that was. Buddy heard about it on the news, but it never meant anything to him. He wanted to pick up a brochure, but didn't want anyone to see him do so.

His eyes scanned the room. No one was watching him. They were all in obvious but varying levels of distress. One girl, he guessed about Leah's age, had her eyes closed tight. She was moving her lips, like she was praying. She sat by herself.

Buddy took a brochure, folding the cover over so no one could see it. *But why be embarrassed?* he thought. *We're all here for one or another of the reasons spelled out in these pamphlets.*

Scanning the brochure, he read, "Abortion is the termination of a pregnancy. It is not a new procedure, but until recently it was illegal in most cases. The Supreme Court of the United States has allowed it to become legal provided a woman elects to undergo the procedure within certain parameters. This clinic does not perform abortions, but we can direct you to clinics providing those services if you wish. Minors must obtain permission from a parent or legal guardian, and must be accompanied to abortion providers."

Buddy's stomach growled. Sometimes when he got nervous, he had to use the bathroom. This was one of those times. He was debating if he'd have time to go when the same nurse who took Leah behind the door reappeared, coming to stand before him.

"You may come back now," she said. He stood to follow her.

Leah was dressed and sitting on a cot. Her face was flushed, and Buddy knew that she'd heard what she dreaded.

"I'm almost eight weeks pregnant," she said.

"Oh," was all Buddy could think to say. She was farther along than he expected.

"Yes, she is," the doctor said. He was not unkind-looking. "Are you the father?"

"Yeah. Yes."

"Well, you two young people have some decisions to make," the doctor said. "Leah's a perfectly healthy girl, and things are fine medically with the baby. But having a child at your age is not going to make your lives easy."

"I know that," Buddy said. "We have to figure it out, though." He tried to smile. "Right, Leah?"

She shrugged. "Can we go?"

"Of course, but first I want to go over some medical advice with you," the doctor replied. "You need to stay healthy and make an appointment with an obstetrician, and talk with your parents about what your options are."

"Options?" Leah's voice was hesitant, but hopeful.

"Yes. I counsel kids every day who find themselves in this situation, and there are options. You can talk with your parents, but marriage is one option. Adoption is another. If you don't feel ready to get married, lots of families find other ways of working things out."

Leah stood up. "I'm going to college next year," she said.

"Terminating the pregnancy is another option," the doctor said. "It's legal now, and…"

"Thank you," Leah said. "I need to go now." She faltered as she went for the door.

Buddy was at her side, trying to keep up with her. "I need to pay them," he protested as she rushed toward the exit.

"I'll be outside," Leah said.

Buddy placed his 10 dollars on the counter, barely giving the woman at the desk time to ask if he wanted a receipt. He didn't answer, but ran outside, where he found Leah sitting on a curb hugging herself. Her face was pink, and she was trying not to cry.

"How did I let this happen?" she asked. "I know better!"

"Leah, it will be alright," he said. "I just know it." He somehow understood not to touch her, or even get too close to her.

"How?"

"We love each other; we'll make it work. I'll get a job, and we can make do until graduation. I know my grandparents will help us however they can." He paused. They would be disappointed in him. He'd have to talk with them soon. "I'll help you tell your parents," he said. "You won't be alone in any of this."

"But it's not what I want!" she shouted, and the tears came. She angrily used her sleeves to wipe them away. "Don't you get it?" Leah looked at him, and he felt a panic that almost brought him to his knees. He couldn't lose this. He took a chance, sat down beside her and gathered her into him, trying to smooth her hair and calm her.

"You need time to accept it," he said. "That's all."

"No," was all she said. Her body was shaking, almost like shivering, but it was August. The sky shone a defiant blue all around them. "Can we just go back instead of shopping?"

She was so, so quiet all the way back home, her cheeks still flushed from crying. She spent the whole trip staring out the window. Leaves were starting to show signs of autumn's invasion, a red one here, a yellow one there. Buddy felt the betrayal of summer's promise as they traveled.

He couldn't sleep that night. He formulated plans, called himself stupid, felt the desperation to act quickly and help Leah see this was not a disaster. He even imagined what their child would look like. It had her curly hair, her animation, her intelligence and grace.

The next morning Leah called, saying she was going to rest and get up the courage to talk with her parents.

"I don't want you doing that alone," Buddy said. "I told you I'd be there beside you, and I will be."

"Oh, Buddy," she said. Then, "Okay. But give me a day to get ready."

He said he would. He told her he loved her.

"I know," she said. He heard her place the phone back in the cradle. A small *click*, and she was gone.

Following another sleepless night he helped Grandpa like he'd sworn to do a few days ago. He was distracted, and so tired and worried he felt sick. Grandpa gave him a few funny looks, but didn't ask any questions. They harvested some vegetables, and Buddy washed the canning supplies for Grandma so she could put up some spaghetti sauce. It was hot and sticky work. Afterwards, Buddy gulped down a huge glass of water in the kitchen while Grandma watched him, wispy hair stuck to her forehead by the humidity.

"If Leah could, I'd love it if she'd help me with all these tomatoes," Grandma said. "She's quick, and I'd appreciate the company."

Buddy's first thought was how awkward it would be for Leah to stand so close to Grandma, their secret unspoken. Maybe they should tell their news today.

"When Grandpa is finished with me, I'll go get her," Buddy said.

A few hours later he was on his way through the woods. He hadn't bathed before starting to walk, and was still overheated and uncomfortable. The woods were quiet, as if every living thing felt too hot to move. He passed the milkweeds, their flowers now gone, spent specimens he and Leah once cataloged. He passed shady spots where they had been together, underneath the cedars and pines. Flowering burdocks and goldenrod lined his path. The foliage thinned out as he came to the edge of Leah's aunt and uncle's property, and he walked to the front porch. He knocked and waited. The storm door was open, but Buddy stayed on the other side of the screen.

Leah's aunt came to the door, saw Buddy, and stiffened.

"What do you want, Buddy?" She didn't open the door.

"Is Leah home?" He felt it, the disdain. A knot grew in his stomach, like he used to get when he was little.

"No, she's not. My husband is taking her back to her parents. You need to go home."

Buddy couldn't move. "What?"

Glaring at him, Peggy crossed her arms over her chest. She knew.

"I said you need to go home," she repeated in a raised voice. "Leah told us she's expecting. We called her mom and dad, and she's going back. You have no reason to concern yourself with this anymore."

"But I wanted to be with her when she told her parents," he stammered. "I didn't want her to be alone."

"She doesn't want a baby! You two have no idea how to take care of a child. She's a smart, beautiful girl, and she doesn't want you around."

"I love Leah, and she loves me! This is my baby, too, and —"

"You don't get it!" her aunt snapped. "There isn't going to be a baby! She's got an appointment for an abortion, and she never wants to see you again!" Peggy grabbed the doorknob of the storm door. "She's so young. Do you know you could be arrested for statutory rape? The only reason you're not being charged is because she's getting an abortion and we don't want to put her through more grief. She's going to forget about you and carry on with her life. So go home, Buddy, and don't contact her. If you care about her, leave her alone."

The door slammed shut. Then he heard the lock. For a few

seconds, Buddy hesitated. The weight of Peggy's words caused his body to feel heavy beyond belief, though it was the remembered spite in her eyes that drove him off the porch.

He ran. Through their woods, past their summer havens, Buddy ran until he fell. He gasped for air, unable to cry because he couldn't breathe. Prickers and dirt stuck to him, but he didn't notice. Eventually he smelled the earth and the grass and weeds, and tears came. He was shamed beyond imagination, knowing he would never measure up to what Leah deserved. He was just Buddy; why he thought he could have such a precious thing forever he didn't know. Now he didn't care if he ever got up from this spot. They'd find him here with vultures gathered around him, a wake of vultures feasting on his bones.

Down the hill he heard a noise, recognizing it as Grandpa's whistle. Grandpa, working away happily, unaware that a catastrophe was happening.

Poor Grandpa. He already lost his son. How could a man whistle in his garden after such a loss? Life sure wasn't fair. Buddy lifted his head. Grandpa somehow managed to carry on and make the best of things. He was the wisest person Buddy knew. In an instant, Buddy understood he needed to work out a plan of action. He had to convince Leah they could handle this.

"I can't lose her," he said to the thickness of the air. He had to find a way of keeping her with him. He rose, dusted himself off, and walked down the hill toward home.

Chapter 18

Man in the Moon

After all these years Buddy couldn't remember how he went home that day and managed not to tell Grandma and Grandpa what was happening. Maybe they were so busy that they didn't see him sneak in and get cleaned up, or notice him forcing himself to work and act normal. He couldn't recall if he ended up helping Grandma, or what he told her about Leah not coming over.

He learned a lesson that summer. The whole magical season was a cruel trick. He was not meant to share his life with wonderful people like Leah; they came from different places, worlds apart. Buddy would never take a similar chance again, ask for nothing more.

"In here," Mags called out as he entered the house. She was in the bedroom, a pile of old clothing at her feet. He was relieved she wasn't in front of the television. Maybe she wouldn't quiz him about the trial.

"What's going on?"

"Oh, I decided to get some things together for the laundry," she said.

"Those aren't going into the trash?" He nodded toward the pile.

"No, silly. I just gathered them up. Those are the pants I had on yesterday."

"Huh. Guess I didn't notice. They have holes."

She rolled her eyes. "Yeah, I know. But they fit and I don't go anywhere, anyways."

"Well, if we're going to the laundromat I'll get my stuff together, too." He turned to gather some things. His uniforms were overdue for a cleaning, after all. Buddy loaded the truck, thinking she'd be outside by then, but she wasn't. He opened the door and told Mags he was ready, but she remained standing in the middle of the room, her face pale. He saw wetness on her pants.

"Jesus, Mags, did you pee yourself?" he asked. She nodded and winced. "How long has this been going on?"

She shook her head. "Not a word, Mac."

"Mags!"

"Just for a few weeks," she conceded. "Grab me a new pair of underwear and that pair of slacks on the back of the bathroom door."

He started to rummage through her dresser, locating some underpants. The pants on the hook in the bathroom looked just as hairy and pilled as the ones she'd piled up to be cleaned, but he took them to her. Mags was in so much pain he had to help her get her soiled ones off and the new ones on.

"Do you want to rest here while I go do the laundry?"

"Nope," she said. "Get me to the truck."

It was no simple task, but he managed to get her there and into her seat. Mags was obviously miserable. She started sweating and holding her breath as they went down the drive. By the time they got to the laundromat she was gasping, her face even whiter than before.

"Do you want to stay in the truck?" He turned it off, but made no move to get out. He didn't know what to do. Mags had one hand around the grab bar, the other held against her back.

"Don't know," she whispered. Then, "Get me to the hospital, Mac. I can't take it anymore."

"Okay." He was relieved, since he sure didn't know what to do. He started up the truck again and they headed toward Traverse City. Mags tried to be perfectly still, but every few minutes she cried out in pain.

"I hurt so bad," she said.

"I see that."

Buddy hated driving to Traverse City, and he hadn't been by the hospital in years, not since Lennie had stitches when he was a kid. He located the emergency entrance and pulled up to the door. An attendant approached their vehicle with a wheelchair, but he and the kid couldn't get Mags into it. She moaned in pain every time they tried to move her. The kid asked Buddy to go fetch some more help, so Buddy started toward the door, but by that time another attendant was coming toward them. He and the kid put their arms underneath Mags's butt and got her into the chair.

Buddy went and parked. Heading inside, he found Mags in a small room with a nurse who was taking her vitals.

"Can you fill out some paperwork, sir?" she asked.

"Sure." He took a clipboard from her and started answering some questions on a form. After asking Mags a few things, he completed it. Mags didn't have Buddy's insurance because they weren't married, but she got assistance because of her income status. The nurse started hooking her up to a pain med IV, and she calmed down.

"That's some good stuff," she said, soon falling asleep.

"We'll get her into a waiting room and the doctor should see her shortly," the nurse said. "Luckily, we're not too busy today."

They gave him a visitor's pass, and Buddy followed behind the wheeled bed carrying Mags. Once everything was situated, he sat down in the room as she dozed. He counted the barf bags stacked in a plastic container; he studied all the gauges and machines. He watched as Mags got hooked up to a monitor. Noticing a ball of dust underneath a storage cabinet, he cracked a rueful smile. Of course he'd notice that.

After about 45 minutes a man in white entered, washing his hands in the little sink. Mags stirred as he pressed her stomach and attempted to turn her onto her side. She had been put into a gown. Well, her arms were stuck through the gown, but that was about it. Buddy found himself facing her large, naked backside. Mags made a sound and the doctor met her eyes.

"I'm Dr. Mills," he said. "I hear you're in a lot of pain."

"Oh, yeah," Mags said. "But those drugs have been awesome."

He smiled. "That's what they say." He felt along her back and asked her to tell him if it hurt to the touch. She said no; it was more inside. He leaned her back down and asked her to lift one leg and then the other, but she couldn't.

"How long has this been bothering you?" he asked.

"Years," she answered. "I don't much like doctors. No offense."

"None taken," he responded. "But now you've got what I suspect is at least one herniated disk. The pain you say is in your hip is actually from nerve damage. Based on your weight and lack of medical care, I imagine you're diabetic, and you may have heart issues. Your blood pressure is high, so I'm going to order an MRI and get pictures of what's going on. Once we have some answers your overall health will determine our course of action."

"What are my options?" Mags asked.

"Sometimes patients respond well to physical therapy, but your obesity will be a factor. I'm inclined to recommend surgery if your health is good enough to endure it. But let's not get ahead of ourselves. Have you had any incontinence?"

"What's that?" Mags screwed up her nose.

"Any uncontrolled urination or bowel movements?"

"You mean shitting myself? No, but I have peed myself," she said. "Just for the past month or so."

"And you're just coming in?" The doctor put one hand in his pocket. He wore thick glasses, his skin deeply tanned. Buddy hadn't said a word. Mags stiffened, or tried to.

"I want to run some tests and get those MRI results before I let you go," the doctor stated. "You'll probably be here overnight." He then stepped out, pulling a curtain shut behind him.

Mags gave his back the finger. "I'm obese?" she asked Buddy. "When did that happen? You see why I hate going to hospitals. I knew something was wrong, but didn't want a lecture from some snobby son of a bitch."

"I hear ya," Buddy said.

"Shoulda asked that jerk for some more pain meds. It's getting bad again."

"I'll press the buzzer." Buddy reached for it, but as he did a nurse entered.

"How are you doing?" she asked. Buddy could tell Mags liked her right away. She was a chunky lady with gray hair and big boobs, like Mags.

"I could use some of that magic pain medicine," Mags said.

"I'll get an order in for you. Would you like a heated blanket?"

"I knew I liked you." Mags smiled, her teeth yellow under the fluorescent lighting. Her hair was stringy, the dye job she'd given herself months ago dulling to gray.

"How about you?" The nurse nodded at Buddy.

"Me? Oh, I'm fine," he said.

"I'm sure he wouldn't turn down a cup of coffee, and neither would I," Mags said, but the nurse shook her head.

"Nothing for you until after your tests are completed. But do you take anything in your coffee, sir?"

"Nope, he likes it plain," Mags answered for him.

Heading home after Mags was assigned a room and kicked him out, Buddy remembered he had her phone in his shirt pocket. He used it to call the boys upon getting back, then called Jenna. He thought she'd want to know.

"What are you going to do if she needs surgery?" she asked.

"Haven't thought that far ahead yet."

"Well, you're gonna need help. I'll come stay with you guys."

"You'd do that?"

"After everything you and Mags have done for me, yeah, I would. Just let me know."

"Thanks, kiddo."

He got into bed. It was 11:30. The cats were fed, but they were restless. Mags wasn't on the couch watching TV. Three of them sniffed Buddy as he lay there, then they roamed around the house. He heard them thumping and bumping, being mischievous. He hadn't been alone at night since Mags and her boys moved in. Even if they didn't always sleep together, she was in the house. Now he noticed every noise. He also noticed the quiet, the lack of another human heartbeat under his roof. He'd turned off all the lights, and it was strange.

What if something more was wrong with her? What if it was something terrible, like cancer? Why wouldn't it be? She sure didn't take care of herself. About the only thing she'd ever done to help her health was quit smoking many years before. Why'd she let it go for so long? What if something was wrong that could have been fixed before, but now it was too late?

He rolled over. Moonlight shone through the window; the moon was visible, almost full. Since Buddy couldn't sleep anyway, he arose and studied the sky and woods. Long shadows stretched over the ground. Soon the moon would be hidden by trees, but now its orb gleamed brightly. The night was still, undisturbed by any breeze, and a memory came to him of the barn on his grandparents' property, the full moon rising above it.

"See the man in the moon?" Dad asked once. Buddy had studied it and thought he saw a face. Maybe he just wanted to please Dad.

"I see him, Dad," he'd said.

Mags called him bright and early the next morning, complaining that a hospital was no place to be. She hadn't gotten an ounce of sleep, she said, because of her roommate and the nurses coming in and out. The doctor stopped by and told her she was going to be released, but advised that she should see her family doctor to address her high blood pressure and high cholesterol. She also needed physical therapy before the doctor would order surgery. He suggested she lose some weight first, too.

"What about sugar?" Buddy asked.

"Haha, it was normal," she said. "Go figure."

"What time do you want me to come and get you?" Buster jumped onto the table, and Buddy shooed him off. He sipped his coffee.

"A little after noon, they said. I'll have to get some prescriptions filled."

"Awright."

Buddy yawned and stretched. He drained his cup and considered cooking breakfast, but made no move to start anything. He needed to contact work and tell them he wasn't coming in. He had to call the main office because he couldn't remember

Ernie's number and was too lazy to get up and locate his own phone. Joyce answered, and he told her Mags had spent the night in the hospital. She said she'd pass the message on for him.

He knew he had a ton of sick and leave days, but still hated to be gone from work. He worked through his own back pain, and now was taking time off because of Mags. *Darn woman.* He pushed some bread down in the toaster and grabbed a handful of peanuts.

"Breakfast of champions," he muttered to himself.

He hated driving to Traverse City. Years ago, there were times when traffic wasn't bad, but the place had now become so popular with tourists it was always a hassle. He slowed for a backup, and realized there was more to it than the regular pain-in-the-butt slowpokes. Ambulances and police cars blocked the roadway. He sat and sat some more, becoming more anxious by the second. As he progressed he noticed fire trucks, too, and then saw the smoke. Someone's house was damaged by fire. He managed not to look as he made his way by the site. Saliva filled his mouth, and he fought back the urge to be sick. His back was drenched with sweat. He pulled into the hospital lot and gasped for air.

"It wasn't anyone I know," he whispered.

He still said his grandparents' names sometimes, just to remind himself that they had lived and were remembered. Like most of his grief, he kept this to himself. He said their names like a prayer, not just to the darkness of night but sometimes in the middle of the day, at noon, when people were worried about their lunches and the leaves were turning color. His whispers sometimes fell on the weeds in his garden, sometimes on his work mop.

Chapter 19

What Loss

1974

Buddy didn't know where Leah lived with her mom and dad, but it wasn't difficult to find. He'd borrowed Grandpa's good car, the Buick, with the excuse that he wanted to see Leah one more time before she started school. Getting to drive the Buick by himself would have been a great thing under different circumstances.

"Of course you do," Grandpa said. "I can see you're missing your gal."

He remembered her address only because she once mentioned that it suited her, since it was the name of a plant: 101 Oleander Avenue. She lived in a nice house, even nicer than her aunt and uncle's. A white porch wrapped around it, with pretty plants perched all along the railing. *Ferns.* Figured, she loved ferns. Buddy didn't know where to park, so he pulled into a spot on the street. Maybe he should have called first, but he didn't have her number, so he just had to hope Leah was home.

He stood on the bottom step for a few seconds, suddenly

unsure. What if her parents were upset that he came? What if they treated him like her aunt did?

He'd just have to chance it. He couldn't stand being separated from her. They loved each other. They'd work it out somehow, he knew this.

He knocked before seeing the doorbell, which he also rang. A hand pulled a drape aside, and he suddenly found himself face-to-face with her. He couldn't judge her expression. It wasn't happy or sad, it wasn't anything. The drape fell back. Maybe she wouldn't open the door. What could he do then? One thing Buddy knew for sure: he wasn't leaving. They'd have to face this.

Leah pulled the door open. "Buddy."

"Can we talk?"

She motioned him in. The entryway was like none he'd ever seen, with hanging art and a big chandelier and a table with a bouquet of real flowers on it. He registered these observations, but the only thing that mattered was her. He ached to hold her, but felt shy.

"Why are you here?" She asked as if there was nothing left to say. There was so much. She didn't know how far he would go to keep her. Once she did, it would matter.

"Leah, I love you," he started. "I can't let you go, especially now that we're having a baby."

She inhaled, a funny, startled breath. Her eyes went to the floor, and when she looked back up they were full of tears. These spilled down her cheeks, and she didn't brush them aside.

"Not anymore."

"What?"

"My mom took me to this clinic, the doctor there saying it would be a simple procedure. He made it seem like such a small thing, an inconvenience. He said when it was time I would be able to have a baby, that this was what lots of women do these days. Afterward Mom and Dad took me out to eat and acted like I'd gotten my tonsils out. They were even nice to each other. They said they were sorry, but that I'd recover quickly and get back on track. I seem to be the only one not feeling so tidied up and relieved, but maybe I'll catch on to their mood eventually, and…"

"You had an abortion already?"

"Termination of pregnancy is what my paperwork said." How could someone cry so hard and so quietly at the same time? He wanted to shake her or slap her, to do something, but could only stand in silence, absorbing the cost of what they had done.

Too much cost. Too much cost for someone so precious, for something beautiful they'd shared.

"Did it mean anything to you at all?" He mustered up these words at last, even though he could see she was crushed and alone and sad. "And I didn't have any say in this?"

"It's my burden."

"No, it's not! You don't get it! It's not! And what burden, when we love each other? You don't think I'd be there for you through this? You're wrong! I'd have been there through it all, and I'd have married you!"

"I told you, Buddy, I have a life planned! I'm going to college and studying something I love. What we had together wouldn't last because we're two very different people. I want so much more for myself! You think you could support us, but you're wrong. Mom and Dad said it was a bad idea, and I have to believe they're right. Because you come from nothing —" She paused, as if suddenly realizing the insult she'd hurled, but the damage was done.

"And I have nothing to give you," he said. "Nothing at all. I should have known, Leah. Well, guess I know now."

Movement caught his eye as a man came from the back of the house toward them. He must have realized who Buddy was, because he stood straighter and taller on seeing the two of them together.

"It's okay, Dad," Leah said. "It's okay."

"But it's not," Buddy said. "It's not. I can't believe you just went ahead with this, like our time together meant nothing, like that baby was nothing!"

"Young man, you'd better be going," Leah's dad said. He had her eyes, those aqua eyes with flecks of gold. They carried authority and weight and class. Buddy would never have any of those things. He flexed his fingers and thought about fighting on, but defeat landed on him heavily, visibly, and he knew his resolve was useless.

"Just know that I loved your daughter," he declared. "I will always love your daughter."

"Just go, Buddy," Leah pleaded. "Don't come back. Just go."

He should have told her to remember their time together, and to not let what other people said cheapen it. He should have told her to remember those warm days when they were the only people who mattered, because he'd always cherish them. He should have told her what they had was not to be wasted. But he didn't tell her any of these things. Instead, he left. He heard Leah sob, and knew without looking back that her father was comforting her.

Months later, Buddy was up late at night on a weekend when something on television roused him from his drowsiness. Grandma and Grandpa were in bed, and he'd been watching Wolfman Jack. The voice changed from the deejay's growl to a woman pleading, her urgent voice talking about fetuses being real people with heartbeats and limbs, their bodies broken through the cruelty of abortion. He didn't want to watch it and looked around the room, as if someone were there gauging his interest.

Of course he was alone. He'd almost been a father. Would he

have been ready? Buddy wanted to pick up the telephone and call Leah, tell her to watch the TV and see what she'd done. She threw it all away without regard for anyone but herself and her rich family. Well, they could have each other.

Would their baby have been a boy or a girl? Did she ask? What happened to the little thing? Did it go into the garbage, or to a special place where all those unborn babies went? Did it know he was its dad and that he wanted it? When he died would it be up in Heaven, waiting for him? Would he even get there himself now that he had let this happen?

Maybe people like James Shearing ended up in Hell, in fires, but never burned completely. His baby would be safe in Heaven, forever. He hoped the little thing never knew of evil, just went straight there and thought that was what life was, up high where suffering and betrayal didn't exist.

Tiny hands. Green-gold eyes. He remained on the couch until static from the TV woke him up.

He'd missed "The Star-Spangled Banner."

Senior year was both grueling and short, depending on the day. Buddy rode the vocational ed bus with other kids who weren't on the path to college. He usually sat in the middle, sometimes with his old pal Truman, when Truman came to school. Truman missed a lot because he was working at the same factory where Mom worked, sweeping floors and emptying trash at night. His eyes always looked like he needed a warm washrag to take the scum off them.

Buddy thought about getting a job, too, but Grandpa was

moving slower and Grandma had started doing funny stuff, such as putting salt in the sugar bowl. Sometimes she'd be like his old and true Grandma, and sometimes it seemed she was wandering lost around the house. Buddy found mail in the refrigerator one day and teased her about it. She started to cry.

"I couldn't remember where it went," she said, and he made light of it.

"Well, it was all junk anyway, wasn't it?"

Grandpa was concerned and wanted her to see a doctor, but she decided to wait until her next annual checkup. Grandma swore it was no use going to doctors more often than necessary. She probably just had a lot on her mind with chores and whatnot.

"You know, we're not spring chickens anymore," Grandpa muttered, but he didn't press her.

Buddy vowed to help them more, and to keep an eye out for any funny business.

He also made an effort to get involved in school. After all, it was his senior year, and the other kids seemed excited about it, so he tried to feel something. He wondered how Leah was doing, and if she was all signed up for college. He would probably look for a job around town after graduation.

"Have you considered the service?" one of the counselors asked him, but Buddy hadn't. He couldn't leave his grandparents now. Besides, watching the evening news made him not want to go into the service because of how everyone seemed to feel about the Vietnam War. It was finished, no more nightly death tolls, but people still yelled about it on TV when he sat with his grandparents in the living room watching Walter Cronkite. Grandpa even said one night that the war was a wasted effort, and that the kids who gave their lives did so in vain. He said they were used.

"And I'm not a hippie," he added. "I still think Hank Fonda

should take that little girl of his over his knee and give her a good wallop."

"Bad news," Grandma grumbled. "Bad news all around."

As much as Buddy wanted to belong at school, he didn't. He found the girls loud and silly, the boys loud and crude. He was in a different place, like he'd been for so long, though once he belonged to a beauty with bright eyes and unruly hair. But maybe that was just a dream?

Chapter 20

Accusations

Mags started making regular physical therapy appointments. Buddy wasn't sure how these would fly with his work schedule, but she asked for times in the later afternoon. He had to take her by wheelchair to the PT department, as she couldn't walk very far without pain. He passed the time in a small waiting area. After the third session she said it was too painful, that she didn't want to keep going.

"What options do you have?" he protested.

Mags shrugged. "I'm going to get the surgery and hope I can do some of this crap after I'm fixed up."

That won't work, he thought. He shrugged.

"What's that mean?"

"What?" He heard the tone of irritation in her voice.

"This." She imitated his shrug.

"Nothing."

"Nothing is right." She heaved her bulk into the wheelchair. "Take me home."

When Jenna stopped by later, she refused to let her off the hook. "Oh, no," she said, after Mags insisted she wasn't going back to therapy. "You'll be just like my mom. She ignored her diabetes, and now she's on disability and doesn't hardly ever leave the house. Eventually she'll end up losing her feet, the doctors said. You're not getting off easy with me."

Mags was ruffled, Buddy could see, but she agreed to give PT another try. Jenna took her to a few appointments, going in with her so she'd be able to help with exercises following the surgery. Carrie came over, too, and they prodded Mags together.

Buddy came home one day to find Mags in the yard, walking around.

"Looking for something?" he asked.

"Nah, decided I'd try to come down the steps and spend a bit of time outside." She wrinkled her nose. "I guess that therapy is doing some good."

"Well, I'll be." Buddy grinned. "You can help me out here, then."

"Oh, hold your horses," she protested. Yet he could see Mags was pleased with herself. She lumbered over to the porch steps and sat.

Lennie, Luke, and the kids came over a short time later to check on Mags, and she showed the kids some of the exercises she had to do. They tumbled all around her on the floor, and Caleb gasped as Mags lifted her legs to her chest, rolled to one side, and farted.

"Gramma!" he yelled, then collapsed into a fit of giggles, the other kids following suit.

"It was the dog!" Mags exclaimed. One of the kids pointed out they didn't have a dog, and they all rolled around on the floor, making fart sounds with their mouths. Buddy shook his head and Lennie grinned.

"Ma, you're crazy," was all he said.

When they left, everyone was covered in cat hair. Mags kept

swatting at the kids' butts to get some off, and Caleb thought that was funny, too.

"He sure is a happy guy," Buddy said afterward.

"What a blessing," Mags said. "I sure hope he stays that way. Every kid should have that happiness." She sobered, and Buddy knew she was thinking of Ben.

He kept an ear open for news regarding the trial, but days passed and he heard nothing. He knew if Mags heard anything from the girls she'd tell him right away. Jenna had ordered Mags to walk up and down the porch stairs as much as possible, and she was doing it.

At work, Buddy scraped and scrubbed and buffed things. He arranged desks in clean rooms and prepared for the onslaught of teachers anxious to get their classes ready for opening day. If he could stave them off until the waxed floors were dry, he might just make it through another summer.

Blair was in and out more often, and though there was some awkwardness between them, Buddy hoped they could get past it and things go back to normal.

Samantha was back at work, as the secretaries returned a few weeks before the teachers. The copier was collating and stapling, and Sam was bustling about. She nodded at him when he entered the office.

"Another summer gone," she lamented. "Did you do anything special, Buddy?"

"Not really, but I grew some good tomatoes and we canned some."

"I used to can, but now I go to the store," Samantha said. "I would like some little cukes, though. I like homemade pickles."

"I have so many I can't keep up," Buddy said. "I'll bring you some."

"That would be awesome." She pulled her copy project from the trays and moved to her desk. The phone rang.

"I didn't miss that," she muttered. "Oh, and I meant to tell you everything looks very nice around here."

"Thanks," he said, but she was already listening to the caller.

He was tightening the bolts on a teacher's art table when Blair entered the classroom a few hours later. It was hot, and Buddy was already sweating as Blair approached him.

"Need something done?" he asked as the principal drew nearer. Then he saw the expression on Blair's face.

"How well do you know Ben and his sister?" Blair asked, without any pleasantries exchanged.

Buddy tried to stand up straight.

"Well, I guess I know them pretty well now. They've been out to my house a few times. Why?"

Blair's face tightened. "There's been some concern about your relationship with those kids."

Buddy made every effort not to react as he set a wrench on the desk beside him. "What do you mean, 'concern?'"

"Did you purchase items for them at the dollar store a while back? Someone saw you do this, and expressed their concern to the authorities involved with the welfare of these kids. They came to me asking if you had a particular relationship with the children."

"They were in the line, and I bought the few things they had," Buddy said. "It wasn't a big deal. They helped me pick out a puzzle for my, my…" What should he call Mags? His girlfriend? His partner? His common-law wife? None felt appropriate for what she was to him. "I know those kids. Like I said, they've been to my house."

"For what purpose?" Blair interrupted. "Didn't I advise you to keep your distance from the kids at school?"

"What are you saying? That I did something wrong?"

"Did you?"

"No!" Buddy knew he had to set things on the right track, stop this before it got out of hand, but he couldn't put words together. Blair's alarmed look wasn't helping. "Those kids mean a lot to me, and to my, Mags, we…"

"Have you heard of the term 'grooming,' Buddy?" The shades in the classroom were open, and a sudden, useless breeze caused them to clack against the windows. Buddy felt a trickle of perspiration run down his temple, and he fought the urge to rub it.

"No, I haven't."

"It's when an adult looks for a vulnerable child and befriends him or her in an effort to gain trust," Blair started to explain. "The adult wants that trust so they can access the child for sexual purposes."

Blair's gaze was uncompromisingly stern. He was watching Buddy's reaction to this explanation with interest.

"Oh my god," Buddy said. He closed his eyes. "Who would think I'd do that?"

He knew before Blair gave an indication.

"One of our very veteran staff members saw you at the store and felt the need to report this. I don't like it, Buddy. It doesn't look right. It's suspicious."

"So my being at the store and buying those kids a few things is a suspicious activity?"

Blair had started walking away. Now he turned back while looking a little surprised, like he wasn't expecting Buddy to challenge him.

"It is when these children are known to be at risk of abuse.

You're not a relative, and you work for the school one of them attends," he said. "In these times, we can't overlook anything. The only upside for the school is that your action didn't happen here."

"What action? That's what I mean! I didn't take any action!"

"We'll see where this goes." Blair made his exit.

Buddy forced himself to work as if he wasn't being eaten up with anger and resentment. A few hours later, as he was buzzed into central office, he knew that everyone had been informed of his situation. No one stared at him; in fact, no one met his eyes with theirs. He emptied trash, vacuumed, and got out of there, not even attempting to make the usual small talk. At the end of the day he loaded his cart into the maintenance room and grabbed his lunch box and car keys, leaving as quickly as he could.

He felt dirty. Buddy intended to tell Mags all about the accusation when he got home, but turning his truck onto their road saw Jenna and Carrie in a car ahead of him. They pulled into the drive just before he did.

Instead of greeting them and heading inside, Buddy wandered to the garden, which was dry and sandy. He turned on the hose and watched as the sprinklers jerked into action. Finally going into the house, he found the girls in the kitchen. Mags was listening to them, shaking her head.

"Oh, shit," she muttered. "I hoped it wouldn't come to that." She looked at Buddy.

"They're making Ben testify," she said.

"He's really scared," Carrie added. "He doesn't want to talk about it, and feels like what happened is his fault."

"That is so not true," Jenna said.

"Would you talk to him?" Mags asked, and it took a moment for Buddy to realize she meant him. "He really doesn't have anyone to tell him it's not his fault. He needs a good man to help him be brave."

Buddy backed up against the front door. "Jesus, Mags." He saw Jenna and Carrie looking at him, and wanted to be anywhere else. He could not be asked to do this.

"He really likes you, Buddy," Carrie said.

Something stirred in him, a mixture of anxiety and he didn't know what else. "What would I say?" he asked.

The next day Carrie and Jenna brought Ben to the house. "Appearances be damned," Mags had said. After the girls left last night, Buddy told her about his confrontation with Blair. She was pissed off and indignant, vowing she would go to school the next day and give the principal a "talking to."

"Oh, now, don't you go doing anything like that. It would just make things worse," Buddy insisted.

"Ya know what really torques me off?"

"What."

"That if we had a pot to pee in and a window to throw it out of, they'd be thanking us for helping out those kids. Tell me that's not a fact."

"I guess," Buddy said.

Mags shook her fist into the air. "Ya know what else?"

"What."

"Screw him!"

Buddy braced himself for talking with Ben by failing to sleep at all the night before. He thought about saying he didn't want to do it, but he owed the kid — really, any kid who'd been abused.

Lately he'd been thinking too much about James Shearing, and needed to get it behind him. The man was no doubt long gone. Time to forget about his own problems and concentrate on the emotional needs of a young boy. *I can do this.* He pictured Carrie sitting beside her brother, looking at Buddy with admiration and gratitude.

Now they were at his kitchen table, eating Oreo cookies and drinking milk. He sensed they were keeping this light to help Ben feel comfortable. Buddy had been coached to bring things up slowly.

"Pass me a few of those," he asked as he sat down. Carrie removed three cookies from the package, set them on a paper towel and slid them to him.

"Want milk too?"

"Nah." He unscrewed the layers of the cookie.

"You eat those like I do," Ben observed.

Buddy paused. "Do you take the middle off like this?" He raked a wafer against his teeth.

"Nah. I take them apart like you do, but then I do this." Ben put one half of the Oreo in his mouth, whole, and his cheeks puffed out. He broke up the cookie with his tongue, chewed and swallowed.

"Huh," Buddy said. They sat in silence, all of them, the clock ticking on the kitchen wall.

"I wish we could just stay here," Ben whispered.

"Me too," Carrie said.

"You have a big day tomorrow, Ben," Buddy said.

Ben shrugged. He held another cookie, but made no move to eat it.

"Just take big breaths and tell the truth," Buddy offered. "You're not the one who did something wrong."

"But everyone will be looking at me," Ben said.

"They'll be thinking about how brave you are," Mags said.

"That's for sure," Buddy said.

"Where should I look when I talk?"

"Talk right to the judge," Buddy suggested. "That way you don't have to look at everybody else. The judge is there to help you."

"I'll be there too, bro," Carrie said. "So you can look at me, if that's better for you."

"You will?"

"Oh, yeah. I want to be there for you. And I'm bringing Mags."

"What?" Buddy raised his eyebrows and looked at Mags. She lifted her chin as her eyes met his, giving a slight nod.

"Are you coming, Buddy?" Ben asked.

Buddy almost said no, but something inside told him to do otherwise.

"If you want me there, I'll be there," he said. "And I'll get Mags there, too."

"Awesome," Ben said. "I'm really glad you found me in the bathroom the day I took that blade to school. I was going to do something. Something that might have turned out bad."

"Were you going to hurt yourself?" Carrie whispered.

"I'm not sure. First I was going to hurt *him*, stab him for hurting me. I was practicing at school but cut myself by accident. I started crying 'cuz it wasn't going so good. Maybe I wanted to hurt myself, I don't know. That's when Mr. Robertson found me."

He's braver than I ever was, Buddy thought, sick at thinking how an adult could have overtaken a kid with a utility knife.

"Wait. You found him?" Mags said. "When did all this happen?"

"That day at school," Ben answered. "Mr. Robertson came into the bathroom and saw what was going on. Then I got away from Kurt, and Carrie got to come with me."

"Huh." Mags sat back, and Buddy knew they'd need to talk. But Mags, for once, went no further because of the kids at the table.

"Time to come clean," she announced when they finally left.

"Obviously you know more about this whole situation than you've let on."

"Mags, I can't talk about it, and don't ask me to." Buddy looked at her questioning eyes, her decent and honest self, and felt again as if he'd betrayed the one person who'd been with him most of his adult life. She stood and walked away.

Buddy had never been inside a courtroom. It looked like every court he'd seen on TV, in episodes of *Perry Mason* or *Matlock*. Wooden walls, pews like in church, a table for each attorney, and the judge's bench elevated above everything, like where a king would sit. He'd called into work for a personal day, although he wore his custodian slacks. He did find a non-work shirt, even if it felt a little tight across his middle.

Mags wasn't used to long walks, forcing him to match her slow progress as they approached the courthouse. Inside had an air of formality. Buddy didn't realize there would be so much going on; the lobby was crowded. Other people were there for other proceedings. He and Mags finally found the right room, took their seats and faced the front. Mags wore her best polyester pants and a flannel shirt tighter than his. Her hair was freshly washed and combed, though, and she sat upright, with her purse in her lap.

An officer entered the room and stood near the judge's bench, and then a woman with a small computer came in, followed by another woman who took a seat near the witness stand. She had a little machine in front of her. A lawyer and Ben's accused sat at a table, and another well-dressed guy sat at the other table.

Buddy recognized him as the local prosecutor. Buddy had never voted, but during the last election the guy's picture was on his campaign signs.

"All rise," the officer ordered, and Buddy helped Mags to her feet. The judge entered the room. Buddy spotted Carrie and Jenna just a few rows up and to their right. Carrie's hair was braided loosely, draped along the side of her face. She looked like a painting he'd seen somewhere before. Her profile was perfect; her chin was firmly set, and she wore little makeup. He glanced at Mags. Her chin bore whiskers she never noticed or minded. Some were white, fine, and some were dark and thick. She, too, noticed the girls. Just then Carrie turned slightly toward them and gave a nod of acknowledgment. Mags smiled at her and Buddy nodded back.

The judge took her place at the bench, arranging some papers in front of her. She then removed her reading glasses and scanned the room. "You may be seated," she said. Clothing rustled and someone coughed, and the room went silent.

They sat through a series of cases regarding drunk driving and an assault at a local bar, Buddy recognizing some last names of kids at school. He tried to match the accused with their children. Having never been in court before, he was struck by how many people seemed acclimated to the environment. He listened as two individuals were found guilty of driving under the influence, one accepting a plea for a lesser charge. The assault case was dropped. Every case involved someone with a previous offense. The morning passed quickly, his stomach starting to growl. He wasn't sure if he felt hungry or nervous.

"Our next case is a felony charge of child sexual abuse," the judge finally announced. "In the matter of the County versus Kurt A. Fairfield, the jury has been selected and the trial will commence herewith."

The prosecutor stood. "Your Honor, the accused, Kurt

Fairfield, has been charged with two felony counts of sexual penetration of a minor under the age of 13, with the incidents occurring on December 12th of last year and March fourth of the current year."

The judge made a slight movement of her head toward Kurt. The bastard appeared to be smirking.

"Your Honor, I would like to approach the bench," his lawyer said. She beckoned him up, and they whispered for a few minutes.

Then, "Both attorneys approach the bench, please," the judge said. Buddy tried to hear, but he only caught a few words as they seemed to discuss dates and procedures. Mags fidgeted, and Buddy could see she was uncomfortable.

"These pews are hard," she muttered.

Buddy bit his tongue rather than tell her they weren't in a spa. It's not like he didn't know it would feel this way, but the impact of Ben having to tell his story to a jury socked him in the gut. Ben wouldn't get over this quickly; he'd have to relive everything in the coming days. Forever, actually. Buddy looked around, but couldn't locate Ben in the room. *Must be somewhere safe until the trial starts.* Anguish pricked his fingertips like an electrical current.

He'd never told another soul about his own abuse, but here this kid was, forced to tell everyone what happened to him. He'd give anything to keep Ben from having to go through that. Bad enough he was subjected to such things; now he had to talk about them openly. *What kids live with,* Buddy thought. *It's a wonder any of us make it.* He chewed at a hangnail, then flicked it away after biting it off. Again he looked over at Carrie and Jenna, who sat quietly, staring ahead.

"We are going to take a moment and go into chambers," the judge announced. The bailiff again ordered everyone to stand,

and the judge and attorneys left the courtroom. Everyone sat back down.

"Please remain seated," the bailiff said. "You may chat, but I'll call order when the judge returns."

"What's happening?" Mags asked Buddy in a low voice.

"Heck if I know."

Jenna looked back at them and shrugged. It seemed everyone fidgeted at the same time, and then started to whisper. The crowd had thinned with the previous court appearances, but about 50 people remained.

"I need to stand for a second." Mags gripped the back of the row in front of her and pulled herself up. Her blouse rode above her hips, and Buddy pulled it down in an effort to cover her rear end. She gave him a wry look.

"Just helping out," he said, and after a moment she sat back down. They waited silently for several minutes.

"Court will resume. All rise, please." Then back to their seats.

"A development in this matter has come to my attention," the judge said as she pulled her chair closer to her papers and gavel.

"It appears there were some irregularities in the arrest of the defendant, and I am adjourning this case until I have time to investigate. Therefore, the defendant is free on a personal recognizance bond. I will either resume this case or make an announcement in the near future. Let's take a lunch break and resume court proceedings around 1:15."

Mags and Buddy left the building to wait for Jenna and Carrie outside. It was hot, and a breeze did nothing to cool them as they stood. Buddy would have to water those tomatoes again later.

Ten minutes passed, and Carrie and Jenna still hadn't exited the building. Mags had droplets of sweat on her upper lip.

"Do you want to leave?" he asked, but she shook her head.

"I want to see what's happening."

Jenna stepped out and headed toward them.

"Something weird's going on," she said. "They asked Carrie to come back and talk with the attorney who's working for Ben. Their foster mom is in there, too."

"Let's go to the truck so Mags can sit," Buddy suggested.

They waited 25 more minutes before Carrie finally exited the courthouse. She'd been crying. Jenna jumped out of the truck and ran to her, put an arm around her and led her to Buddy and Mags.

"They might have to let the S.O.B. go," Carrie cried. "Something didn't happen the way it was supposed to when they arrested him."

"Oh, I'm sure they'll straighten everything out," Mags said. "Don't jump to conclusions."

"He's — oh!" Carrie exclaimed as a car drove slowly by them. The engine revved, then Kurt put his vehicle in park and leaned out the window. Carrie's mom sat beside him, her face like a stone.

"You stupid bitch," he snarled. "I'll make this right. You'll see. You and your precious little brother better watch your backs."

Buddy was out of his truck, running toward the car, moving Jenna aside. Kurt hit the gas pedal and veered toward Carrie, just as quickly turning away. His tires squealed as he wheeled out of the parking lot.

"He'll kill us," Carrie sobbed. "He'll freaking kill both of us."

Buddy couldn't speak. He felt 50-odd years of fury breaking loose. His fists were clenched, and he was quaking, shivering, seething. He *had* to do something.

Carrie went to her knees, and he knelt down beside her. Pulling her up, Buddy wrapped her with himself, hugging her tight. Her hair smelled like lavender. Dead weight, she hung in his arms as Mags got out of the truck, swearing like a sailor.

An officer came running from under the canopy behind the

courthouse, where he'd been standing to smoke a cigarette. It was the bailiff.

"I saw and heard the whole thing," he said, tossing the cigarette down and crushing it with his boot. "Come back inside and we'll deal with this."

Kurt was re-arrested and locked up within an hour. This time, there was no bail.

"He needs to be put away forever." This from Mags a short time later, after they returned home.

"I'm not disagreeing with you," Buddy said.

"I never seen you so mad." She was watching him over her tea glass.

"I don't think I've been that mad in a long time, if ever," he admitted.

"You care about that girl."

"And her brother," he added.

"I never saw you hug a kid," she stated. "Not like that."

"Kid was a mess."

"Yes, she was."

"My heart is breaking. I hate it when kids lose their childhoods because of the very people who are s'posed to take care of them." Buddy could hear the pain in his own voice.

Mags glanced at him, opened her mouth as if to ask something, and just as quickly closed it.

"I've got to get water on those plants," he muttered, and escaped.

Chapter 21

Alone

1975

Grandpa and Grandma died together, just as Buddy was grieving Leah and the baby they almost had. He'd even admitted what happened to Grandma, on one of her good days when she wasn't so confused. She acted like she already suspected, but then, she and Grandpa were wise people.

"Oh, what sadness," she'd said. "For both of you young folk."

"I guess I wasn't what she wanted in her life, and she didn't want a baby with me," Buddy said.

"Oh, honey, kids your age usually don't know what they want. Someday she'll look back and remember you as the fine young man you are. She'll have to mourn at some point, as you're doing now. I'm so sorry you didn't feel you could come to us."

"I will never understand how she could kill our baby," Buddy whispered. "I never thought she'd do something so awful as that."

"I don't understand it, either, but then I wanted to have a child when I did, and Leah couldn't see beyond her fears. You'll find out that fear can rule a lot of your life. I'm not going to judge that beautiful girl for a decision she made out of desperation and haste. It's so hard to see someone you love make decisions that don't match what you want. Maybe Leah felt like it was her decision and hers alone. And I am so very sorry that you feel so bad. Life is not fair. I've felt that way many times. Like now, I'm forgetting things and doing stupid stuff more often than I'd care to. We can only be responsible for how we react to the trials and tribulations. I've got over 70 years behind me, and there are still so many things I can't answer. I'm nobody to judge anyone. I hope you remember that, Buddy. And remember those who love you, honoring them when they're gone by living a good life."

"Was what she did a terrible sin?"

"It would be a sin for me to judge her," Grandma said. "If I've learned anything, I know that much. I hope you can forgive and try not to judge her either."

"That's a lot to ask."

"I have a lot of faith in you, young man."

Just then, Buddy should have told his grandmother that she and Grandpa were the two biggest blessings he'd ever received in life. Instead he'd settled into her as she put a plump arm around his back.

He'd never know if she shared his confession with Grandpa. Weeks later, he was coming home from school when the bus pulled over to let some fire trucks pass. Then an ambulance, and then another passed. At the yield sign by the farm, as his bus turned the curve, he realized all those vehicles were at his house. He left his books in his seat and ran outside, but someone stopped him.

"You can't go any further, son," the person said. "I'm sorry."

"But that's my house!" Buddy cried. He was almost out of his shirt, twisting away, desperate to reach his grandparents, but the man managed to restrain him. He never knew who it was holding him back, refusing to let him see or do anything. He smelled the smoke; it rose in a huge cloud from where the house should be. One side of the enclosed porch was still standing, but the rest of the structure had fallen into a black and ugly heap. He saw the local firemen attempting to spray the remains, but there was obviously nothing left to save.

"Where are they?" he implored the person holding him, begging for an answer.

"I'm sorry," the man said, yet again.

"What does that mean?" Buddy wasn't sure if he asked it or just collapsed, gasping for air as if he'd inhaled some of the smoke. He finally managed to break away and darted toward the house. A blanket covered something on the ground, and he stepped away from it, hoping to ask the firemen where Grandma and Grandpa were. A stretcher was by the ambulance, with someone lying on it. He felt relieved at first, and getting closer saw the person was Grandma. Body covered with ash, black soot streaked under her nose, she was obviously gone. Her eyes were wide open, but she was dead.

"No!" he shrieked. He leaned into her and saw that her mouth had black around it, too. He reached for one of her hands and drew back. It looked like a piece of burnt meat.

Two firemen and an ambulance man pulled at him and tried to calm him down, but there was no calming, no comfort, no action anyone could take.

He didn't remember anything about the rest of that day. The next morning, Anna was sitting in a chair beside him when he awoke. They were at Mom's boyfriend's house. The siblings quietly wept together, not feeling the need to say anything. Anna had the chair propped against the door so it could only be opened a few inches. After several minutes of silence she stood up, shut the door softly, and returned to her chair. The stillness meant nobody else was up yet.

"I was going to ask you where Leah is," Anna finally said. "I thought she might be here."

"She went back to her parents last summer. I will never see her again."

"How do you know that?"

"She broke up with me…she did something terrible…" He couldn't say more.

Anna looked at him intently. "Was she pregnant?"

He nodded.

She leaned back. "Do you know what causes pregnancy, bro?"

He nodded again.

"Maybe now's not the best time to ask, but did you two talk about it? Did you ever wear a condom?"

He did not want to discuss this with his sister. "No. It just happened, and I thought she loved me. But she didn't. She had our baby aborted, such an awful thing." Fresh tears welled in Buddy's eyes as he spoke.

Anna came and sat beside him. "Oh, Buddy," she said. "I can't see things in black and white and right and wrong like you do. You kinda bear responsibility for the situation too, you know. I think she did love you, though; I saw it. But you can't put this all on her when you didn't think things through either." She touched his cheek, attempting to smile at him. "Got it?"

He couldn't look at her. He was shamed, sorrowful and broken. "I've lost so much," he cried. "I keep asking if Grandma and Grandpa died because of me, too. Maybe what Leah and I did caused them to die and me to be punished."

"Wow. I have a lot of questions about what happens in this world, but I don't think God, or the universe, or whatever you want to call it, works that way. I will miss Grandma and Grandpa forever, but Grandma was getting senile, and you didn't cause that."

"I'm so glad you're here," he whispered.

She hugged him, and he hugged her back. "This is so hard. I know. I'm so sorry, Buddy," she said. "I hate this for you more than I hate it for me. I've got college, where I can be somebody else. That's why I have to go back as soon as possible."

Buddy reached for the sheet and wiped his face. Anna was saying she hoped he'd come visit her at school, but he somehow knew he wouldn't.

He was going to be totally alone from here.

The investigation into the fire showed it started in the kitchen, apparently at the stove, where Grandma must have left something on the burner. The official report was that Grandpa came in while she was trying to put the fire out by herself. He managed to get her to the door before they both collapsed, and then covered her with his body after wrapping a wet towel around her, but smoke inhalation killed them both. His remains were badly burned; the report said he sheltered Grandma as best he could. Their funerals were held together, and most of town turned out for them, everyone telling Buddy and Anna their grandparents were the salt of the earth and genuinely fine folks. Buddy saw Leah's aunt and uncle pass through the line at the viewing, but didn't have the courage or energy to go near them.

"You can still stay with us," Mom told him and Anna after the service. "For as long as either of you need."

"I'm going back to college," Anna replied quickly.

Buddy shrugged. Stu seemed like a nice enough person, but he didn't dare chance it. He had no idea where to go, but would never stay with him and Mom; he'd sleep in Grandpa's truck if he had to.

He walked from Mom's to the property, finding Grandpa's keys underneath the front seat of his truck, where they always were. He then walked to the old barn and went inside, smelling the dirt floor, seeing the old syrup buckets, feeling the loss so

profoundly he almost fell to the ground. Then he heard shuffling.
A man pulled the barn door open more widely, startling him.

"Who are you?" Buddy straightened and recognized the man
from town, a lawyer or something like that.

"I'm Cortland Jessup," the man said. "I took care of your
grandparents' estate."

"They had an estate?" Buddy wasn't sure what that was.

The man nodded. "That they did. A modest one, but I'd like
to discuss it with you and your sister."

Anna agreed to wait around another few days for that meeting, but then she left. She made Buddy stay with her while she
was at Mom's; she said she would never stay there by herself.

Grandpa and Grandma always lived frugally, and they were
simple people. Yet they had wills establishing Anna and Buddy
as their heirs. The property was still worth a sum, and Mr. Jessup
explained that because of careful planning, their grandparents
were able to provide an inheritance. Once insurance was settled,
there would be some money.

It wasn't a lot, but it was enough for Buddy to rent space from
an elderly woman with a sign in her front window that said
"Rooms to Let." It got him through school, and after graduation
he started working at the factory. He hated it. He craved fresh
air and the smells of the woods; the factory smelled like plastic.

He tried staying in Pennsylvania, but he felt empty. Anna
used her money for education. She got her degree, got another
degree, then a job teaching at a college. Anna, always the over-
achiever. Mom moved to Kentucky, and Truman also left the
area. Before going he said Buddy should head to Michigan,
where there were good jobs.

Buddy didn't know anything about Michigan. He pictured
Detroit, and figured that would finish him off. But here, people he ran into from church looked at him with pity, and the
people at work were only people at work. He found nothing

of value anymore where he was. Perhaps he should stay on the property where his beloved grandparents lived, but he couldn't picture himself there, walking the paths he and Leah used to take, living without his family. Maybe he'd go see what Truman was talking about.

He loaded Grandpa's truck with sap buckets, tools, and a few mementos his mom had given him, taking off west and then north. The hills weren't so majestic, but there was water everywhere once he got north of West Branch. The skies seemed so open, and on that first trip the sunset was spectacular. The road ran straight compared to those in Pennsylvania, making it seem like he was driving right into the vivid lavender and red before him.

He was adrift, in uncharted territory. He tried to fit in with the guys who worked the rigs, but only felt more lonely. He saw a "For Sale by Owner" sign at the start of a long driveway one late July day, turned down the two-track and immediately knew he wanted to buy. The house was run down; the yard was a mess, but the place had land with a creek, and he saw plenty of milkweed with monarchs flitting about. He felt something like life in his stomach, went and knocked on the door. Grandma and Grandpa led him to this place, a place of his own.

Buddy moved in, going from one job to another for a while afterwards. Then he met Mags. He knew she wouldn't expect much from him, and he had nothing to give.

Chapter 22

Mags, Too

He felt the bed sag as Mags joined him, surprised at her presence. It had been weeks since she'd slept in their room. Buddy noted the fresh smell of her hair; she had just gotten out of the shower, and the scent comforted him. He found himself glad for her company, knowing cats would be joining them soon. But that was also welcome. He could fall asleep to their purring, though Buster would be the only one on Buddy's side.

"You awake?" she asked. Buddy resisted the urge to laugh. If he didn't answer would she leave him alone, or ask again?

"I am now," he said.

"I was just thinkin'."

"About what?"

"All these years we have," she said. "You and me."

"And?"

"You are a good person, Mac."

"Huh."

"Jenna's taking me to the doc tomorrow to see how I'm comin' along. You can sleep now."

He smoothed out his pillow and closed his eyes.

He was with Leah on the hill behind his grandparents' house. She was drawing in her little book, but her pencils kept falling to the ground, bright blue and red and purple; they got tangled up in weeds so she couldn't grasp them. Buddy wanted to help and started running toward her, but instead of running found himself pulling at roots and flowers to gain traction as he crawled. Finally reaching her, he wondered at her curly hair, her eyes, her lips, even as he started to kiss her. A feeling of great joy surged through him until he backed away and realized he was kissing Carrie. Revolted, Buddy rubbed at his mouth. In his mind he'd claimed her innocence.

He woke with a start, mortified. Mags hadn't stirred, snoring on lightly beside him. He caught his breath while being careful not to move.

She had just told him he was a good man. He felt dirty, unworthy of her assessment. It was only a dream, his mind told him, but he was unsettled. He hadn't left Mags's side, but was a dream cheating? Exactly what did he feel for Carrie? The thought of hurting her was disgusting to him. She was so young. So pretty. Did he envy her that? Could she help the way she moved, the way her skin glowed, the way her eyes held knowledge beyond her years, yet still had light in them? What kind of man was he for noticing? For grieving the fact he would never have that gift of being young again?

Mags stirred. She was hogging the covers, but he didn't pull at them to reclaim his part of the bedding.

In the morning she stripped the sheets off, wondering aloud when they'd last been washed.

"I've lost 27 pounds," Mags announced as she walked from Jenna's car to the porch. "The doc says he's real impressed with me."

"I can see it, can't you, Buddy?" Jenna nodded to him.

"Huh? Oh, yeah!" Buddy appraised Mags. He could indeed see her face was thinner. Her pants still stretched across her middle, but she seemed brighter.

"Jenna is gonna help me color my hair," Mags said. "She does her ma's, so she's practiced."

"Maybe I should do it on the porch?" Jenna asked.

"Ain't gonna hurt anything in the house, and these black flies are awful right now," Mags said. "We can lay some towels on the floor."

"Up to you," Buddy said. "I'm watering the garden, then running into town for a few things if you need anything."

He pulled the sprinkler along, dragging the hose behind, and fiddled with the placement of it, making sure water hit as many areas as possible. It had been fairly dry of late. His dutiful mulching helped, but the sun was blistering. He heard Mags and Jenna laughing in the house.

"Wonder what color her hair's gonna be," he said to no one.

Buddy had to park in the back lot once he got to the hardware store. The place was always busy. He needed some string, light bulbs, and Epsom salt for his tomatoes. He mixed it with water and sprinkled it on the plants, as Grandpa used to do, to make the tomatoes less acidic. He usually wandered around the store a bit, just because hardware stores always had so much to look at.

Cat litter was on sale, so Buddy added that to his cart. At

the corner of aisle eight he collided with Sage Carmichael. She started to say something before realizing who he was, her expression changing from apologetic to hateful. She abruptly turned and walked in the other direction.

"Excuse me," he murmured.

He was not used to outright distaste, although he was no stranger to feeling apart from people. Buddy purchased his items with cash, grabbed everything from the cart, then went and sat in his truck for a few moments, wondering why his stomach hurt like it used to as a kid when he knew things were going wrong.

Back at the house, he mixed the salt with water in his sprayer before going out in the garden. He decided to wait, knowing he shouldn't put the mix on in direct sunlight, but stayed standing in the same spot for some time.

"Buddy, come see your woman!" Jenna hollered.

He tried to seem enthused. Mags's hair was blondish; it hung thin and stringy, but she was grinning, and he managed to grin as well.

"Is it true what they say, that blondes have more fun?"

"Mac, you'll be the first to know," Mags said through a laugh.

"Get a room, people," Jenna said, rolling her eyes.

She took off a short while later. After waving goodbye Mags poured some tea and went out to sit on the porch steps. By then the sun had softened its glare, so Buddy tended the tomatoes. He looked Mags's way, realizing she was watching him.

"What's for supper?"

She shrugged. "How 'bout I make a nice salad and some leftover baked chicken from the other night? That would be healthy."

"You are killin' me," he muttered, then, "Fine."

"Jenna said they charged that asshole for threatening the kids,"

Mags said. "He's in jail waitin' on court. I guess they were glad he acted up so they could keep him this time. No bail."

"Good."

"Maybe there will be justice after all." She sipped her tea and bit at a hangnail. "Let's hope."

He set the sprayer on the bottom porch step, took her glass and drained it.

"Hey!"

"What's yours is mine," he said. "Remember that."

"Like I don't know I don't own a thing in this world."

"Whoa, where did that come from?" He sat next to her, shocked. All these years together, and she'd never said anything like it. Sure, Mags complained about things at times, but this made her sound so lonely. She didn't look at him as he remained seated on the steps.

"Mags?"

"What, Mac." Her face turned, her eyes meeting his.

"Why would you think that?"

"Oh, I dunno. The fact that we've been living here for how many years, never had the energy to get married, I don't even own a car, and you only keep me around 'cause I feed you now and then and don't get in the way much, and so on."

"Ouch," Buddy said. "How long you been feeling this way?"

"Remember when I told you I been thinkin' about things too much? Now what do you think I've been thinkin' about? Did you ever think to ask?" Her blue eyes were not sad; they were angry. The shock of Mags getting angry at him, about anything, was devastating.

"Jesus, I'm sorry, Mags," he muttered. "I guess I always think you're content." A thought slammed into his gut after flashing through his brain. "You are always going to be here, right? You're not getting your hair dyed and losing weight because you're gonna leave, right?"

They stared at each other, Buddy feeling all the earnestness and panic he'd ever felt. Then Mags laughed.

"Get a grip! I'm just talkin' to ya, is all. This is what couples do, ya know. But you gotta admit, I am seein' life go by and I know I only got a few good years left. And I'd like to feel I did somethin' with 'em."

"You have," Buddy said. He took her hand and held it to his face. "You don't know how you saved my life."

"Yeah, right," she said.

"You've been trying to kill me with your coffee, but other than that you're about perfect." They sat and watched the sky turn gold, then pink, then dark, before going inside.

That night, just as he was drifting off Buddy felt Mags's weight shift in bed as she put her arm around him. He pretended to be sleeping, shocked to realize he was actually aroused. The strangeness of it. The wonder of it. He wasn't even sure what to do. Then he heard Mags snore and fell soundly asleep.

She did save his life. She and her boys brought their boisterous selves into his home, and Buddy never bothered to thank them for it. Just another of his shortcomings, not saying thanks when he needed to. If Mags felt as if she'd not accomplished much, how should he feel?

He wrung his mop and made another swipe along the school floors. This building was 75 years old. How many times had it been mopped, and did anyone else ever wonder that? Probably not, because people like him doing jobs like this were invisible.

On 9/11, when terrorists flew planes into the World Trade

Center and other places, he watched as teachers hugged each other, the kids who understood what happened sitting silently at their desks. The world itself stopped as the population gasped and grieved, yet Buddy still felt invisible. People stood in the halls, right here in this spot, and talked about how terrible it was, yes it was. The day was somber, the entire building hushed. Nobody noticed Buddy taking the trash out to the dumpster as usual, running the floor polisher, or pulling up the lunch tables. In fact, no one addressed him that whole day. When he got home from work Mags was watching footage of the horrifying events, and he joined her.

"Why'd they want to hit those buildings, Mac?" she asked. "I get that Pentagon thing, but why those others?"

"They're the World Trade Center buildings," he answered.

"Yeah, but why'd they pick those?"

Buddy had to admit he didn't know, exactly. The buildings must have meant something, but to him and Mags they were as mysterious as the Egyptian pyramids. Wall Street and stock markets and the world economy were just as foreign. It wasn't until the reporters speculated about motives that Buddy realized the significance. Did everyone else get it immediately? Why was he so dumb? Maybe that's why he hadn't been noticed all day. He'd felt this way before, many times, as if he were in some sort of alternate universe looking at other people living lives he didn't understand.

Now that sorrowful day was approaching again, with him none the wiser.

He turned around to see teacher Andrea Wilson walking on his still-wet floor, leaving footprints.

"Sorry," she said, but kept walking. Her apology meant nothing; she was only sorry he'd turned and seen her. She hadn't said one word to him since she took a position with the district. Well, now she'd said one word.

He only had a few weeks until school started, and was going to look for blackberries after work. They had gone from hard nubs to red to black, and he was eager to stand in late summer sun and listen to the bees buzzing as he pulled the juicy nuggets from their briars six at a time. He'd let his fingers get stained, not minding scratches from the thorns. Mags could make a mean crisp from the berries, and he'd pour milk over it like Grandpa used to do.

Luke and Lennie didn't have grandparents like he did. Mags said her dad was out of the picture by the time she had them, with their "sperm donor" disappearing shortly after that. She always pointed out it was for the best both men chose to go someplace else. She seemed to know how to raise her kids by herself, even if she was only eking by when Buddy came along. Her situation was no different than so many in small towns; she never knew anything else. If she only worked a minimum-wage job, so did most everyone. Yet there was always an intelligence about her that Buddy respected. She left school when she was barely a senior, heading south with the guy who would father her kids, and she talked him into coming back to her hometown after his promises went nowhere. She never left again.

Sometimes Buddy wanted Mags to see Pennsylvania, though he'd have nothing left to show her there. He missed hills and good dirt, the way the mist settled in those hills. He wondered sometimes how he ended up here, but it was here that helped him have a life. Maybe it was accident or maybe it was fate, but now he was an old man worried about a boy and his older sister who, due to their circumstances, likely wouldn't have many opportunities in life. They deserved better.

Buddy's mop water was filthy. He needed to drain the bucket, refill it, and start mopping the other wing. Then this day would be done and he could get outside.

Samantha was busy putting the class lists together. A teacher now stood in the office doorway, complaining about the number of high-need kids on her roster.

"How come I get all the kids who need extra help?" Mrs. Olsen, an older member of the staff, waved her copy of the list. It was common knowledge she long ago lost her love for teaching.

"You need to talk with the principal about that," Samantha said. "I only do what he tells me."

"I'll be back after my manicure," the teacher said. "Will he be here?"

"As far as I know."

Her tone of voice implied she didn't really care, and Buddy liked that he recognized it. He kept his stare forward as he passed the doorway.

Leaving his supplies in the closet and starting down the hall toward freedom, Buddy realized he'd left one of the basement doors open, and turned around to go close it. Leaving it open all night would make the hallway smell like the musty lower level the next morning. Once again he had to walk by Sam's office door, hearing voices as he made his way.

Damn, it was Blair and someone else. If he could just turn around and leave he would have, but it was either close that door or get scolded, and Buddy had no taste for that.

"So they don't need to have him in court, then?"

"No. The judge has allowed him to testify via video, so he won't have to go before a jury or the perpetrator."

"Such a relief. They need to start doing that for every case."

"Yeah. I think you'll see it more and more."

They must be talking about Ben. His steps were quiet, but the person talking with Blair turned to look at him. Buddy saw it was the school guidance counselor. He started to nod, but the counselor stepped forward, closing the door in a dismissive way. Buddy had no business knowing what was going on; he was a nobody to those people. Again that knowledge cut into him, like a knife with a dull blade. Still, he felt relief for Ben.

"Are you ever gonna do anything with that yellow tape you've got wrapped around the trees?" Mags asked when he got home. The tree counting project had fallen by the wayside.

"Does it bother you?"

"Looks like a crime scene, but no, why would it?"

She could be such a trying person.

He looked around the kitchen, thinking to say it looked like a crime scene, too, but it was actually pretty clean. The table was clear, although it had that cat puzzle box sitting on it. There were fewer piles on the floor, and it looked like Mags had recently swept.

"So you're turning over a new leaf and expect me to do the same?" He couldn't help but smile. "I've got stuff to do, Mags."

"Yeah, I know. Get outside and fiddlefart around like you always do. I just wondered if you're ever going to finish anything around this place." She picked up the puzzle. "I'm going to start on this today."

"Ben will like that," Buddy said.

"He was the one who mentioned it. It's got a thousand pieces, so I'm gonna set up a card table. I'll put a sheet over the puzzle to keep the cats from messing with it."

"Good idea. Got any tea made?"

She pointed to the porch. "Sun tea out there. I'll bring some glasses with ice."

They sat on the steps, and Buddy took a long sip. Indeed, the tape around the trees near the corner of their property did look like a crime scene, as if marked off to show the vicinity where a body had been buried.

"Speaking of crime scenes…" he started.

"Any news?"

"I heard at school that Ben won't have to testify in person. He can do it by video instead."

"So they're still gonna try that no-good piece of crap for abusing Ben?"

"I believe so."

"Good. Maybe you should leave that tape up until the trial is over, so I can picture where the dirtbag might go if things don't work out."

"Picture a spot farther back in the woods, would ya?" Buddy looked at Mags over his glass. She snorted.

"Could you ever kill somebody? I think I coulda a few times. If anyone ever hurt my boys, I'd be that mom who marches into the courtroom with a gun or somethin."

"I could see that," Buddy said. "I guess everyone has someone who brings out the worst in them." He pictured James Shearing begging for his life, a moment he'd once taken great pleasure in imagining. How would he do it? Of course the killing would need to be a slow, painful one. As a kid that might have brought him some comfort. Hell, even now.

Mags shook her head. "I was watchin' TV the other day and they were talking about sexual abuse of kids. They said people who do that want power and control over someone who can't really fight back. It's not about sex the way healthy people do it. They need to talk about that more, so kids like Ben don't feel they're the ones who did something wrong."

"Uh-huh," Buddy agreed.

"I never told this to nobody, but my uncle did some crap with me, and I always thought it was my own fault. I was a lonesome, fat kid, and he paid attention to me." Mags wasn't looking at Buddy; her eyes were turned away from him on purpose. Her stomach growled, and she absentmindedly put her hand over it.

"It was absolutely not your fault," Buddy murmured. "Your uncle took advantage of you. I hope you know that."

"Yeah, I guess I do, but it made me feel dirty for a lot of years. He forced me to touch him. I still get a sick feelin' when I think about that. It was a time when I shoulda screamed, but I just folded up inside."

"How old were you?"

She squinted. "Let's see. I was living in an apartment with my mom around a year before she died, so I'd have been about 12. I remember brown paneling and a plastic clock on the wall in the room where he made me do it. The clock was an owl with big eyes on it. I felt like it was watching me, doing nothing to help."

The same age as me when I dealt with James Shearing, Buddy thought. *My God.* He should tell her that. She of all people needed to know it happened to him, too. Yet he couldn't say it. The words would not come. He squeezed Mags's knee and stood up.

"I'm sorry," he managed. "I'll get us more tea."

"I never worried about you doing that to my boys," Mags said.

Buddy kept his back turned to her. "I should hope not!" he exclaimed. Then, "But how would you know?"

"I dunno, I just sensed it. Like you can sense someone is bad even when they try to seem nice. That's why it makes me so mad someone could question you at your school. I want to say my Mac wouldn't do anything like that. I just know you."

Could anybody really know a person?

Buddy opened the screen door, let it hit him on his backside, and went into the house. "Going to get more tea," he said. Mags didn't say anything else, but looking back he saw her nod.

As he took their full glasses back out to the porch, Jenna pulled into the driveway. Carrie and Ben were with her.

"Can't stay long," Carrie said as they approached. "We're out for some ice cream, and Joanne wants us back soon so Ben gets to bed. We just wanted to let you know what's happening."

"I don't want to talk about that," Ben whispered.

"I know," Carrie said.

"You don't have to," Mags said. "But we're your friends and we want to be there for ya."

Carrie laid a hand on her brother's shoulder. "They are going ahead with the trial, and now Kurt has additional charges. But Ben doesn't need to testify in court. They're going to record his testimony and play it back."

"That's a great thing," Mags said, withholding how she'd already heard the news. This surprised Buddy; maybe she realized it would upset the kids if they found out others were talking about Ben's case. Mags *could* show some restraint.

"When is anything going to happen?"

Carrie looked at Buddy. She batted some bugs from her face; the evening had summoned them. "Ben's testimony is scheduled for next week, and the trial will start the week after that. They say it should take about two days."

"Can we talk about something else?" Ben complained.

"Like what?"

"Anything else."

"Like school?" Mags asked.

"Well, anything else but that." Ben looked at Mags with his lopsided grin, and her eyes watered.

"You're somethin' else," she said, pulling him to her. He took her hug and returned it.

"Wanna set up that puzzle?" Mags asked.

"Sure!"

Buddy tugged the card table into the living room, where he

managed to fit it among the clutter. Mags dumped out the puzzle pieces, then told the kids to sort them with similar colors, making groups.

"Going outside," Buddy said after watching them for several minutes. They acted as if they hadn't heard him, happily distracted with the puzzle.

He'd been outside for maybe 20 minutes when Ben came alongside him.

"What are you doing now?" he asked.

"Well, when you have a garden you need to take care of it. You have to pull weeds and water regularly and make sure the plants are taken care of. It's a lot of work, but I like it."

"How do you know which are weeds and which are good plants?"

"I've been doing this a long time," Buddy answered. "I guess I learned it from my grandpa when I was even younger than you."

"So, a very long time ago."

"Yeah, back when dinosaurs still roamed the earth."

Ben chuckled. "You're not quite that old."

"I think being outside as much as you can keeps you younger than you look," Buddy commented.

"I don't go out much. One thing I'd like to try is fishing."

"I have a good creek to fish in, but you only take what you can eat. That's an important rule. Although Mags doesn't like fish, so we'd have to clean them outside."

"Does that mean you'll teach me?"

He'd have to find the smaller poles, get new line. The grandkids hadn't asked in some time — too busy with their gadgets, he supposed.

"Well, sure," he answered. "You get permission to come over this weekend and we'll go down there."

"Cool!" Ben was grinning, then he sobered. "I guess it depends on what happens with that other thing."

Buddy fumbled about for words. "Ben, you'll do fine. Mags and I will help any way we can to keep you safe. Whatever else happens, you'll learn how to fish. Now let's get back inside. The bugs are about to carry you away!"

The screen door slammed as they came inside, and the women, young and old, looked up. They'd managed to get part of the puzzle's border done.

"Wow, can I try to find a piece that fits?" Ben asked.

"Just don't mess it up," Carrie said. "And we need to get back! I lost track of the time."

Ben studied the border for a few moments. Then, incredibly, he picked up a puzzle piece and placed it right where it belonged.

"I'll be damned," Buddy muttered.

"Kid's a genius," Mags said, chuckling.

"I know." Ben and that grin! "Mr. Robertson said he'll teach me how to fish."

"Well, isn't that nice?" Mags exclaimed. "Did he tell you the rules?"

"Oh, yeah. He said we can only take what we eat. Also, you don't like fish."

"Yup, and you'll learn all about how to clean the fish, too," Carrie said.

"I'm not afraid of that," Ben said. "Can you bring me here this weekend, sis? I mean, if it's okay with our foster parents."

"Sure, I'll ask them." Carrie looked to Buddy. Were there tears in her eyes?

"Thank you," she said. "I am so glad we have good people like you guys."

"We're the lucky ones," Mags said. Buddy nodded. He couldn't say it any better.

Chapter 23

Confession

The following Saturday, promptly at seven, Joanne and Carrie brought Ben to the house. Joanne said Ben had hardly slept because he was so excited.

"Want a cuppa coffee?" Mags asked Joanne, but she said no, as they were heading back to the house to repaint an old dresser. Buddy was relieved Joanne didn't go inside. He wasn't sure she'd be comfortable with their housekeeping.

"Thanks so much for doing this with Ben," Joanne said to Buddy. "My husband works all hours for the power company, so he doesn't have a lot of time on his hands. That's why we only take a few foster kids at a time."

"I'm looking forward to it." He was, he realized.

"I'm going to finish that puzzle today if it kills me," Mags said. "Then I'll do my exercises." She winked at Carrie.

Carrie laughed and said, "Jenna and I won't let you get away with not doing them." She hugged Mags. "See you later."

Ben was a chatterbox all the way to the fishing spot, proudly carrying the pole Buddy provided him. He talked about what he had for breakfast (a bowl of cinnamon oatmeal), the antics of a dog belonging to his foster parents, the fact that he hated raisins. As they neared the creek he quieted, as if knowing he'd need to concentrate.

"Alright, I'm leaving it up to you if you want to use live bait or artificial," Buddy said.

"What's the difference?"

"Well, I can show you." Buddy opened a container full of soil and poked his finger into it. The worms became alert, squiggling, and Ben laughed. "You'll have to take one of these critters and put it on your hook yourself," Buddy advised. He was pleasantly surprised to see Ben's expression didn't change.

"What's the other way?"

"You can use a lure, or a fly. Like these here." Ben barely glanced at them.

"If I don't catch anything with a worm, I'll try one. But I like the idea of the real thing."

"That's a good thought, I suppose," Buddy said. "I'll show you how to place the worm on the hook before you try it."

Buddy took the pole from Ben and rigged a worm, then removed it, tossing its wriggling form into the water. "Now it's your turn."

Ben pinched another worm from the container and attempted to rig it. "Harder than it looks," he muttered. Yet he kept trying, finally managing to get the creature on the hook, although it was a little battered. He looked at Buddy for approval.

"That's passable, and none of the hook is showing," Buddy said. "Now to cast it." He again showed Ben first. "You have to reel the line in a bit. When you get ready to cast, make sure you hold this little spot on the reel right here, then let it go so your line doesn't keep going out. You want to cast so the worm fools the fish into thinking it got there naturally. Remember, you are invading where they live, and they're a lot smarter about this than we are."

"I never thought about all this stuff," Ben remarked. "Who taught you?" He started to cast, but Buddy warned him away from the trees because the line would become tangled in them.

"Ya gotta go gently into it," he noted. "My father and my grandpa taught me, but I don't do it very often anymore."

"Do they live around here?"

"No, they're both gone now."

"Sorry. Wish I'd had someone to teach me like you did." Ben cast and plunked the worm in the water, where Buddy fervently hoped a hungry fish was waiting. He instructed Ben to reel the line in, slow and steady, but nothing bit.

"Fishing isn't just about catching fish, either," he said. "It's about being out here, I'd say."

Just then a pair of mallards glided down the stream, quacking indignantly upon seeing humans. They lifted and departed.

Ben giggled and nodded. "You get to see things like that!"

"Yup."

"What's the name of this creek?"

"It's part of the Manistee River, one of the best trout streams around," Buddy answered.

"It looks like a picture," Ben commented. Casting several more times, he didn't catch anything, and "drowning worms" began to lose his interest.

"Can we look at your garden now?"

Buddy nodded. "Take that worm off and put it in the creek," he said. "Just be careful of the hook."

Ben disengaged it, wiping his fingers on his pants like a true fisherman. Buddy took the pole.

"Do you want to make up a story about the one that got away?"

Ben looked at Buddy, confused. "Wouldn't that be lying?"

"When it comes to fishing, I don't really know."

"I think I'll catch a big one next time," Ben said. "This was just my practice."

"Right."

When Joanne returned for him, he had a belly full of Mags's bologna sandwiches. Ben told her how he'd learned to pick the mint for her tea. He was dirty and sweaty, and said it was his best day in forever.

Summer continued its decline, Buddy knowing he'd soon be down in the dumps. Out in the garden, tending his plants and listening to the sounds of the woods, he recognized the changing light — just as it changed all those years ago when Leah left. Days were still long, but the shadows fell differently, the late afternoon sun more golden. He loved summertime and fall in the north, but that one stellar summer could never be matched. He felt guilty for thinking so, but there it was.

"Who the hell do I think I am?" Buddy asked aloud of no one.

Dragonflies smacked against each other, and he paused to watch. Such playful things. When they landed on him as they sometimes did, Buddy always took note of how obvious the breathing was in their insect bodies. So confident. They didn't seem to care that, if lucky, they'd only live several weeks. Basking in the sun and skiffing along the creek, they acted just like drunken teenagers. He admired them, since being a carefree kid was a privilege he'd never had.

But I have this, he thought. This little spot on the earth, where the sunflowers from seeds Mags tossed in the dirt now stood as tall as he did, facing the sun and showing off. There were so many zucchini he needed to know and like more people. Or maybe dislike. He could give some to that nasty woman from school, Sage. He should load up her car with giant squash, the kind you can only make bread with. Sweet revenge!

He heard squawking and turned to see a Cooper's hawk clumsily carrying away a sizable bird. Mags would be upset if she saw that, but hawks needed to eat, too.

Always drama in my little corner of the world, he thought. It was the kind of drama he could tolerate. His eyes followed the hawk to an oak branch on the south side of the property, where it pulled its prey apart and ate it.

Buddy again realized, the first day of the trial, that he'd led a simple life without many experiences. He was shocked at the way the courtroom operated, with everyone seeming to know their roles and how things were supposed to proceed. He rather wished he'd been at a trial previously, one where he wasn't so worried about the outcome, because it was fascinating. The defense attorney stood and asked questions of a character witness for Kurt; Buddy recognized the guy from town and knew he wasn't a reliable sort. Yet, the attorney must have worked with him to make him sound believable. He said Kurt was a hard worker and a good family man.

"Bunch of crap," Mags muttered.

The prosecutor had his turn. He tried to bring up the witness's criminal record, but the judge wouldn't allow it after the defense attorney objected.

"He's not the one on trial," the judge said.

"Just trying to establish credibility," the prosecutor argued.

A doctor told the court about the abuse Ben suffered from

Kurt. He said Ben had significant bruising on the lower half of his body, and showed definite signs of forcible sexual penetration.

"Could it have been from a less recent incident?" the defense attorney asked upon cross-examination. "The boy has had other men in his life."

The doctor shook his head. "The bruising was fresh, as were the wounds. The response from the boy was as expected from someone who experienced recent trauma. It was difficult for me to perform the examination, which forced this child to again face the reality of what happened to him."

The defense attorney looked down to the floor. "I have no further questions," he said.

The morning went on like this, with both sides jostling back and forth. Finally, they agreed they'd presented their cases.

"We are now going to adjourn until tomorrow, when the court will present testimony from the alleged victim," the judge announced.

"So soon?" Mags asked. "I didn't expect it yet. I guess the girls did say it would take two days."

After court was adjourned they returned home, where Buddy changed into his boots. Tossing his better shoes toward the kitchen mat, he heard Mags crying in the bathroom. He considered pretending he didn't hear, though in fact his hand was already on the doorknob. Buddy realized he couldn't just leave her. He tapped on the bathroom door, and she cracked it open after blowing her nose loudly.

"Mags? You okay?"

"What do you think?" she sniffled. "This could all be for nothing. What if they don't find that man guilty? What if Ben is forced to go back there, and has no chance to recover?"

"You shouldn't jump ahead and get yourself all riled up, Mags."

She sat on the edge of the tub, so he closed the toilet lid and sat beside her, taking her hand in his. Buddy didn't expect what happened next. Suddenly he found himself sobbing, gasping for air and wiping at his nose and face with his free hand. His shoulders shook. The more he told himself to stop, the more he wept.

Mags stood up. She wrapped her arms around him as he hugged her waist, and Buddy began to talk.

"It happened to me," he cried. "I was a kid like Ben, and I was raped. My sister and I were both abused by a man we lived with. I haven't ever been able to admit this to anybody, Mags. I couldn't. It's been years and years, and I don't know how to get over it."

He continued to talk, telling her how James Shearing hurt him physically, mentally, and permanently. How his mom wasn't equipped to handle it, how Anna left and never came back, how he lost Grandma and Grandpa, how he was sorry he didn't have anything to offer Mags when he finally met her. He didn't get to talking about Leah.

Mags rubbed his back for several moments, then she stopped. Her chin was quivering when he looked up. He reached for her again, but she stepped back. He was preparing himself for her pity, but then she spoke.

"How long we been together?" she asked, and he realized she wasn't sympathetic at the moment; she was angry.

"Long time," was all he could say.

"I'm gonna need a minute," Mags replied. She left the bathroom.

Buddy sat on the toilet seat for some time, feeling as if his whole world had been turned upside down. He was exhausted and tired. He'd just betrayed his own confidence, and for what? The words were out now. Instead of feeling unburdened, it seemed he'd only shed his misery onto the person he valued the most. He only hurt more; he wanted to disappear. All of this heartache. It carried from one generation to the next, one family to the next, and left ruin in its wake. No wonder the world was so messed up.

He heard her footsteps, and she appeared in the bathroom doorway.

"All these years, I've wondered what was wrong with me! You didn't love me enough! I wasn't good enough! My boys weren't good enough! All this time, you carried your shit around and didn't trust me enough to tell me the truth. I'm real mad at you right now, Mac."

"I am so sorry," he said. "More sorry than I can ever tell you. I've cheated you…don't you realize that you're the best thing I have, that your boys are just like my own?"

She was now the one crying. "I am? They are?"

"You have to know that," he whispered.

"Guess I'm mad at the wrong man. I should be mad at the sorry excuse for a person who did that stuff to you, a little boy like Ben. God, what people suffer," she said, head shaking. "I'm real sorry for what we all go through."

"That's why we can't let Ben suffer alone," he said. "And justice has to happen for him."

He stood up and took Mags into his arms. Her snot was getting his neck wet, but he didn't care.

Chapter 24

Brave Boy

Ascreen extended down in front of the court and the video began to play. It didn't show Ben's face, just his hands, on his lap at times and other times fidgeting. Like any normal kid's gestures and movements.

An unseen adult, whom the judge stated was a social worker, questioned Ben. At first he was asked to state how old he was, what grade he was in, what he liked to do. She was making him comfortable. Ben said he liked to play video games, watch funny movies, and hang out. He said he liked quiet time. He lived with his mom and his half-sister, and they moved around a lot. He was glad when they finally got to be in a house with Kurt. He thought things were getting better, since they'd been staying in a cold camper for a long time.

"Did they get better?" the woman asked.

"For a little while."

"Then what?"

"It was good when he was working and wasn't drinking beer all the time. He was gone a lot at his job," Ben said. "Once he lost the job he went back to drinking again. That's when he began hurting my mom. He hurt me, too."

"You have to say who hurt you."

"Kurt."

"Hurting you how?"

"Hitting me, first. I got bruises lots of times, but Mom told me not to show anyone. I tried to be good, to stay out of his way, but I guess I was just around too much. Or he was around too much. Or Mom was around too much. I don't know. We were in a bigger house, but it seemed like we were all in each other's way."

"It's hard to live like that," the woman said.

Ben's hands settled in his lap.

"Yeah."

"When did things get worse?"

The boy's hands gripped his knees. Buddy couldn't take it, and almost got up. But he couldn't tell Ben he wasn't there, so he stayed.

"One night he got real drunk. He came into my room and told me I was stupid, that he wasn't really my dad and had always hated me, even saying I was the reason he got drunk. He called my mom a whore and said he hated all of us, including my sister. I always knew he wasn't really my dad, so I told him I was happy he wasn't."

The woman's hand reached out and touched Ben's hands. She was wearing a wedding ring, and her fingernails were polished.

"Ben, you have to be very brave right now and say what happened," she urged.

"I'll try. First, he told me he was going to make sure I had a miserable life because I made him miserable. Then he forced me to hold onto a private part of him. It was disgusting, and I said I didn't want to, but he made me. After a bit he pulled out this thing he had in one of his pockets, telling me to take my pajama bottoms off. Once I had, he put the thing in. It was like a handle on a hammer but smaller. He stuck it inside my body, making me scream, and Mom came into the room. She started yelling at him, and he slapped her, saying it was what we both deserved."

"How many times did this happen?"

Those hands, clenched. The words, as measured as a young boy could make them.

"I think four times, but he only used that thing once. The other times he touched me in a bad way. Each time I told my mom, but she just said to keep my mouth shut. He warned me that if I told anyone else he'd kill me and my sister and my mom, burying us where we'd never be found."

"So that day at school, why did you have the utility knife in the bathroom?"

At this point Ben's voice broke, as if he'd used up all his energy telling his story. Mags wiped tears away from her cheeks. Carrie was weeping into her hands, and Jenna had her arm around her friend. The courtroom was remarkably still.

"First I was going to use it for stabbing him if he tried again, but the grip was slippery and hard for me to hold. I knew it wouldn't work. So I decided to use the razor on myself and cut my wrists. I saw it on TV and thought, kind of, that I wanted to do that. But Mr. Robertson came in and found me."

"Who's Mr. Robertson?"

"He's the janitor at school, the man with the keys who helps all the kids. He's about the nicest person I know. He and Mags, his partner, help me and my sister all the time. He's teaching me how to fish. They helped me be brave today."

Jesus.

Carrie turned to look at him and Mags. She smiled, yet she was still crying. Mags was openly sobbing.

"Please refrain from any emotional outbursts," the judge ordered.

"How are you doing now?" the woman in the video asked.

"Better. I don't want to be around Kurt anymore. I worry he'll do what he said he'd do, kill us all. I want him to go away. But I'm glad I didn't cut myself."

"I am also, Ben."

"That concludes the alleged victim's testimony," the judge announced. "We will take a break and resume tomorrow with closing arguments. Meanwhile, I am going to remind the jurors they must not discuss this case or watch any news media." She pounded her gavel.

"Court is adjourned."

"All rise," the bailiff announced.

Buddy didn't know how to describe what he felt. He was exhausted, as if he'd testified. But he'd never been that brave; he'd asked a kid to do what he could not.

"So we have at least another day of this," Mags muttered. "Do you think that was enough to have the jury believe Ben?" She worried at a snag on her blouse as they drove home.

"I hope so," Buddy said. "I know it would be enough for me."

"Yeah, but they don't know Ben like we do, and that one guy said the testimony of kids is not always considered dependable."

Buddy recalled the "expert" on the defense who said that. He couldn't pinpoint dates himself, though he remembered how James smelled, how the darkness did nothing to lessen the pain. How he felt at school the day after, how his feet were cold in the car that day Mom caught James with another woman. The day after. Sometime in March? For whatever reason, he thought it happened in late winter.

"You just passed it," Mags scolded.

"What?"

"The damn store! I said we need bread!"

"Oops, I'll turn around," Buddy said.

Mags shook her head. "Sometimes I don't know where your mind is at."

She stayed in the car while he went inside. He searched for the bread Mags liked: "White, cheap, sliced, no seeds or twigs or shit."

Something was different between them. Almost like a shyness, a hesitancy to discuss what Buddy shared. Yet it was there, looming largely, an elephant in the room. He knew she needed time to absorb it, and would give her however much she needed. While they sat on the porch that evening, though, Mags put her hand on his knee, and he felt freed.

Barring unforeseen circumstances, today would be the last day of the trial. Buddy kept telling himself not to count on anything. Mags was nervous as hell, sitting at the table drinking her mud as her foot tapped the floor impatiently.

"Today is a day I could use a cigarette."

"Wow, it's been decades since you smoked."

"I know! If that asshole doesn't get convicted, I'm gonna buy a pack and a bottle of wine."

"I'll help."

The courthouse was filling as they arrived, and Mags wanted to be close to the front. The lobby was again full of people awaiting other proceedings. A few of them nodded at Buddy as they made their way past. There was Tom Wilson, who had been a handful as a kid. Probably owing back child support brought him there, Buddy figured, as he now had seven of his own. And Tom was still a handful. He had a woman with him who wasn't his wife.

There was Gil Bertrand, who still had a scar on his face from the wreck he was in with his inebriated mom. Back then he was a student at Buddy's school; Gil survived, but his little sister didn't. The crowd in the lobby had little chance at much, though including himself in the observation didn't occur to Buddy at that moment.

Then there was Blair Hopkins, in a jacket and tie, the difference between him and the others obvious. He gave Buddy an almost imperceptible nod. Buddy averted his eyes.

What did those like Blair think when they were among the lesser? That's what all these folks were to him. The school district had universal free lunch because the poverty level was so high; most of the adults in this lobby were its product, if they even managed to graduate high school.

Strange as it was, Buddy felt relieved to sit down and stare ahead, awaiting the day's activities. His stomach was rumbling. His jaw was tight.

"All rise," the bailiff called, and Buddy helped Mags stand.

"Yesterday we heard from the alleged victim in this case," the defense attorney for Kurt Fairfield began. He stood with one hand in his pants pocket, like he was posing for a magazine. He carefully regarded the jury members.

"While his statements may seem compelling, they are quite possibly not reliable. Children can be manipulated and coached." The attorney paused. He shook his head. "The child might not realize his words could send an innocent man to prison for some time. Imagine such an injustice. Mr. Fairfield strongly denies any wrongdoing, and thus it's his word against an impressionable child."

Buddy fidgeted, and Mags gave him a sideways glance.

"I ask for the jury to consider this as they deliberate. With that, I close."

The prosecutor stood as if prompted and also addressed the jury. Funny, Buddy didn't know anyone sitting in those seats.

"I beg to differ that the basis of this case is a man's word against a child's," he stated. "The victim in this case was seriously injured with an object that caused medically verified damage to his body and, just as importantly, his childhood."

"Shout that from the rooftop," Mags whispered. A few members of the jury winced. An elderly fellow raised one hand to his mouth and leaned back, as if burnt.

"Let's not sentence the child to a life of believing no one heard him. Let's make the supposed adult pay for his crime. We can allow this boy to grow up with a bit of dignity and acknowledgment that what he said mattered, that what he had the courage to do was more important than anything else in this case. Just imagine it's your kid in the bathroom at school with a razor and the despair of thinking there is no other answer to his pain."

Without another word, the prosecutor returned to his seat.

Quiet for a few seconds. Then the judge sent the panel off to deliberate. Buddy waited with Mags outside the courthouse, where summer's lilies were fading off. He wondered where Ben was waiting, if he was alright, and if someone had washed his glasses that morning.

Different doors, different decades: how odd Buddy never thought of it like that before. How one door opens and scuffs across the carpet to let in evil and abuse, while another door opens to admit fresh air and a cooling breeze.

How a door opens and 12 people enter through it to announce they've found a man guilty of the crime of penetration of a minor under the age of 13, a felony. Somehow they seem to nod at another boy from another time who suffered when a door opened in another state, under another roof, another sky, on another planet.

Buddy was not ashamed of his tears. But he was having a little trouble catching his breath, earning him a stern look from the judge. Hell, he didn't care.

Mags was weeping, too. When the court emptied, she grabbed Jenna and Carrie in a hug so tight they gasped and giggled. Then they drew Buddy into them. For once he felt like a living being, like he was lost but now found.

There's a hymn about that.

Grandma's wedding ring. It was, what, a hundred years old? More?

It was a simple piece. A gold band, tarnished — from the fire? He'd polish it. It had been stuck in a drawer since he'd moved to Michigan. It was in a little box with one picture he'd claimed from the ruins of their property in Pennsylvania. A photo of his father, mother, Anna, and Grandma and Grandpa, with innocent smiles and promise in their faces. Grandpa had his hand on Anna's shoulder.

Had he ever shown the ring to Mags? Surely she'd discovered it at some point, but she'd never said anything. She must have been curious, and most of the time if she was curious about something he'd know it.

Today he would use it to propose. He warmed the ring in his hand and began to put the photo back, but instead propped it next to the bear figurines. He should get a frame. He'd look at the dollar store.

"Mac, I think we should —" Mags stood in the doorway, with her baggy clothes and her half-blonde hair. She was carrying one of the cats and an armload of dirty or clean clothes, he couldn't tell. Buddy tucked the ring into his pocket.

"What's that?" she asked, pointing to the photo.

"My family."

"Lemme see." The cat wriggled, forcing Mags to let him go. Half the clothes tumbled onto the floor, and she stepped over them. He handed her the photo.

"Oh, my." She stared. "You look like your father. So handsome."

"Right."

"Seriously! This is exactly how you looked when I first saw you!"

She *meant* it.

"Just look at your mother! She's very pretty. Your sister is beautiful, too. And your grandparents, well, they look so real." Her eyes watered. "You must have loved them people."

"Yeah."

"How could you have this and never show me?"

"You haven't shown me any pictures of your family, either," he muttered.

"Well, I had shit for family, that's why!" She held the worn picture to her chest. "Thank you, Mac."

"For what?"

"For finally sharing this with me. And we should do some laundry today."

A common thing, laundry. "Okay, sounds good," Buddy said as he wound the ring around his fingers.

At work he still tried to avoid Blair Hopkins. Samantha seemed fine with him, but then she tried to get along with everyone.

He could count the hours until the kids came back, feeling more or less ready as he did every year. Once the halls were filled, it was as if the students never left. A lot of new faces would appear, with Buddy sometimes able to tell the last name of a kid before he even heard it, recognizing the way they smirked or rubbed their noses or carried themselves. It was like there were only so many molds of people in a small northern Michigan town. Mostly white, with a few shades of darker skin now and then. Maybe more often lately.

He stretched. The blinds in the new teacher's room needed changing, so he pulled the old ones from their clips. Maybe he could just use the same clips, as they seemed fine. It would save a little time.

The window was open, and Buddy stood with a foot on the sill and a foot on the ladder, pulling slats one at a time and letting them fall to the floor. The leaves on the big oak across the playground were just beginning to turn red, sunlight slanting longer earlier in the afternoon. He felt the familiar sadness of another summer making its exit, though the atmosphere was sublime and perfect.

Perfect. Like that summer.

Tonight the girls and Ben were coming over for tacos and dessert. Joanne, their foster mom, approached Buddy and Mags after the trial and said she was glad they'd provided comfort to the kids while they went through tough times. Such a thoughtful gesture she'd made. Mags hugged her and thanked her as Buddy awkwardly stood and tried to smile, though he was still getting a grip on his emotions. He hadn't cried in public since becoming an adult. Joanne was also wiping tears away; she said Ben was home with her husband. They were trying to keep him distracted so he didn't get overly anxious about the trial's outcome. He'd be happy, she said.

There. The last of the slats were up, so he could run the old ones to the dumpster. He piled them into a trash container and rolled it outside. As he headed toward the back a vehicle pulled alongside the chain link fence next to him, and Buddy glanced over, realizing after a moment it was Sage Carmichael. He grimaced, trying to act like he didn't notice. She gave him one of her nasty glares and drove away, revving the engine.

He finished putting the slats into the trash, his hands shaking and his palms sweaty.

What could he do? Complain to Blair? Call the police? That would be useless. He managed to get the empty trash bucket inside, but stood in the school lobby and didn't know where to go.

Eventually he trudged to the bathroom and washed his hands, staring at himself in the mirror.

When he got home he thought of telling Mags, but didn't. Instead he stood out in his garden, breathing deeply, and then walked down to the creek.

When the girls and Ben arrived, Buddy tried to act as if nothing was wrong. Maybe they didn't notice. They were eating their tacos, listening to Jenna's idea of putting a hard shell into a soft shell and then spooning the ingredients inside. Grandma's ring was still in his pocket, but he didn't have it in him to give it to Mags tonight.

"I have an even better idea," Carrie said. She smashed some tortilla chips and put them in a soft taco shell, then stuffed it with meat and cheese.

"Yum!" Ben yelled, reaching over to grab the taco from her hand. He held it up triumphantly, smiling, and ate half of it in one bite. Mags giggled as she looked to Buddy. She tried to hide her disappointment in him, that he wasn't present with them, but Buddy saw. A memory came to him of how distracted his mother was after Dad died. How he desperately wanted her to enjoy being with Anna and Grandpa and Grandpa as much as he did. He took it personally then, and could see Mags doing the same now.

"Thought you'd be happier tonight," Mags said after the kids left.

He started to shrug, but decided to honor her observation. He owed her that.

"Remember the woman from school who gave me that dirty look in the ice cream place awhile back?"

"Like I could forget! Why?" Mags ran a dishcloth over the table, scooping taco remnants into her palm as she went. The girls had done dishes, but kids never seemed to clean off the table or the countertops.

"She drove by the school tonight as I was taking out some trash."

"And?"

"Nothing, I guess. She just made a point of giving me another dirty look and driving off."

Mags shook the dishrag over the trash bin vigorously.

"This has got to stop!"

"I know," Buddy agreed. "But what can I do?"

"I'll sure as hell think of something," Mags said. "Damn ignorant scumbag!"

The rest of the night she kept muttering about it. Buddy

wondered if he should have told her, but he kind of liked that she was so pissed off.

"Now that Kurt Fairfield is headed off to jail, maybe we could put that frickin' woman back there with those trees you been meanin' to count."

Mags. God love the woman.

Chapter 25

Blue Sky in September

Sentencing day. Even though school had only been in session for two weeks, Buddy asked for the time off. He'd taken more days in one year than in his entire previous term of employment at the district.

He and Mags got to the courthouse early. Buddy meant to sit in the back so they could leave quickly, but Mags insisted on being close to the front. "I want to look into that jerkwad's eyes," she said. This time Carrie and Jenna sat with them, Joanne joining them as well. They all waited together in silence.

This was the only procedure of the day. Kurt entered with a suit on, his hair trimmed. "Who paid for that?" Mags asked.

The whole thing didn't last very long. Kurt had nothing to say, and was sentenced to 10 years. His ears flushed red as he was cuffed and led away. He found his wife in the crowd, and nodded to her. She was crying.

Buddy took Mags's elbow as they left the courthouse. It was a gorgeous early autumn day, and the sky was void of clouds, a perfect blue. Other people milled about, some vaping or smoking cigarettes, some in small groups.

"We're going back to the house and telling Ben everything is settled," Joanne said. "Would you like to come over?"

A woman passed by them, huddled up as if caught in a March storm. It was Carrie and Ben's mother. Carrie looked at her, but she refused to meet her daughter's eyes and kept walking.

"Sure!" Mags answered Joanne before Buddy could. "But Mac has a day off, so I'm making him take me on a ride later."

"Ride where?"

"I dunno. Maybe over by the bay, up along that road where you found those apples last year?"

He started to say he'd go if she'd make a pie. Her crust was awful, not a bit like Grandma's, but it would do. They were all walking slowly, making their way toward the parking lot.

Buddy noticed Ben's mother leaning into her car, pulling something from it. She stood and turned around, facing him, Mags, and the others leaving the courthouse. She held something in her right hand; at first he thought it was a stick. But it was a gun.

"You!" she shouted, pointing it at Blair Hopkins, who was just behind Buddy. "If you hadn't taken this to those idiots at social services, my husband wouldn't be goin' to prison!"

Blair, stunned, put his hands in the air as if to surrender. He shook his head.

"Tell me how I'm supposed to live now! You've taken my kids from me, everything from me! Those people," — she pointed to the courthouse — "they said I'm going to be charged now! I never had nothin'! I never had nothin'!"

The unkind sun bore down on all standing there, everyone seeming frozen except for the woman holding the weapon. Her breath was coming in gasps. Buddy put Mags behind him.

"It was me," he said, stepping forward. "I found Ben in the bathroom and told Mr. Hopkins. Ben was hurt real bad by your husband."

"No, Mac," Mags whispered. *No, no, no.*

"You're that fucking janitor! You're just as bad! Turning my children against me!"

"Mom, that's not true." Carrie was moving now, nearing her mother, tears streaming down her face. "You know he did it. How could you still be sticking up for him?"

What was their mother's name? Buddy couldn't remember. He watched as Carrie got closer, reaching forward while attempting to hold her mom's eyes. She tried going for the gun, but the woman wrenched away from her, wildly flailing the weapon. Buddy moved forward, grabbing Carrie's arm just as he heard a loud *pop!* He felt something warm in his side — not exactly pain, but pressure — and saw the gun skitter across the concrete walkway. Falling to the ground, dimly he made out Carrie's beautiful golden hair above him, her eyes looking down wide and wet with tears. Then the sunlight faded.

Golden hair, hazel eyes. Flecks of gold in those eyes.

No. Blue eyes, gray hair with streaks of blonde, a beloved face. Mags.

"Mac?"

"Where am I?"

"In the hospital, asshole. What were you thinking?"

"Apparently not a lot. Is Carrie okay?"

"Thanks to you, yes. You saved that girl's life." Mags pressed his cheeks tightly with her hands, kissed his lips and began to cry.

"Don't do that, sweetheart," he begged. He tried to sit up, but couldn't. "Tell me no one else got hurt."

"Nah, but that sad, mixed-up woman was arrested," Mags said through a sniffle.

"How are the kids?"

"Doing better than expected, considering what they've been through."

"Thank God."

"Mac, you were damn lucky, too. You coulda been a goner."

"So what am I looking at?"

"The doc got the bullet out and they had to fix up your insides a bit, but they said you're gonna be fine."

"How long do I have to be here?"

"Maybe a week or so," Mags said.

"Am I in Traverse City?"

"Yeah."

"Damn. How'd you get here?"

"Just you never mind. I got my ways."

Buddy drifted off, dreaming of nothing. He didn't know how long he was out, but when he woke up Mags was still there. He was surprised to see Blair Hopkins beside her.

"Hey, Buddy," Blair said.

"Hey."

The principal nodded, an earnest look on his face. "I wanted to see how you were doing."

"I dunno," Buddy said, looking to Mags.

"I apologized to Mags, and now I need to apologize to you," Blair continued. "I was wrong for accusing you of anything."

"Yes, you were," Mags said.

"I was influenced by a bad source of information, and I should know better."

"Sage Carmichael?"

"I won't say. The bottom line is you didn't deserve it. I let hysteria get the better of me. You were so brave at the court-house, a better man than I was. I already realized how wrong

I'd been about you, but then you stepped up when I didn't. I can't explain why I was so quick to judge you —"

"You judged me by how I look," Buddy said. He held Blair's eyes.

"Maybe we both did that," Blair agreed.

"What's gonna happen now?" Mags interrupted. "That teacher at school needs to stop harassing him, and you need to make it clear that my Mac didn't hurt anybody."

"It's being handled," Blair said. He smiled. "She calls you Mac?"

"Long story," Buddy said.

Blair stood. "I'll get going. Have to catch up on some rest myself; I couldn't sleep these past few nights. I needed to make this right, and I hope you can forgive me."

"Thank you," Mags said.

Blair exited, leaving just the two of them.

"I love you, woman. Had to tell you that." Buddy paused and blinked slowly. "There are some other things I never told you."

"I know."

He went back to sleep.

Chapter 26

A Poem

In the morning, he smelled bacon. An aide placed a tray table over his legs. Buddy saw Jenna first. Then he made out Carrie standing beside her, and there was Ben.

"Mornin," Mags said from the other side of the bed.

"Well, what a sight to wake up to."

"Eat," Jenna ordered.

"Are you missing school again?"

"It's Saturday, silly," Ben answered.

He managed to swallow a few bites, but was extremely sleepy.

"The boys and the kids are coming over later," Mags said.

"Did you warn the nurses?" Buddy muttered. But he was grinning. They all shared a laugh.

Carrie fished around in her pocket, pulling out a wrinkled paper. Her face looked so young, her eyes alive and shining; Buddy realized she was going to be alright. He didn't know how, but she reminded him of Anna. Funny, she used to remind him of Leah. Strong. Beautiful. Smart. He drifted off, but she nudged him.

"Can I read you something?" she asked. "We're doing poetry in

English, and I thought I'd hate it, but I found this old book and one of the poems reminds me of you. It's by a Michigan poet."

"Poetry?"

"Just listen. It's by Max Ellison. It goes like this. It's called "I Saw the Bridge."

My friend traveled a thousand miles to see a bridge.

I spent an hour looking for an oriole's nest,

And found the ribbon black skin that a snake had shed,

A vixen's pup dead from a punctured throat,

And, in the summer dust, a weasel track.

My friend came back and said,

"I saw the bridge."

"Why does that remind you of me?" Buddy asked, as if he weren't moved beyond words, trying to ignore the nuisance of a lump in his throat.

"Because you don't need to go anywhere or be anything other than what you are," Carrie said.

"Yeah, you're just Buddy," Ben said. "And that's pretty good."

Tears escaped his eyes and ran down the sides of his face. He thought of his grandparents, how he always wanted to be like them. He thought of his father, the good man who married his mother because he loved her, and of Anna, who made her way. He would try to find her, have the girls look for her on the darn Internet. He thought of the girl with the golden hair, the lost baby, the boys he'd been privileged to have, their children who considered him their grandpa, and the mother who didn't have a chance to grow old with her husband. His mother. He thought of these beautiful kids beside his bed. Last but not least, he thought of the woman who had been part of his life all these years, past so many summers when he'd mourned a girl long gone.

Her blue eyes, her cats. Her bad coffee. Buddy owed Mags more than he could ever repay. He thought of Grandma's wedding band, how he'd recently dug it out and put it someplace. Then he recalled where, just as he heard his grandkids in the hall.

"Hey, where are my pants?" he asked.

Acknowledgments

Everybody has a story. It's a cliché, but it's true.

When I see an unknown, aged couple shopping for groceries, I see them as they are now. I don't know them as people who have earned each wrinkle and slow step.

I try to remind myself people judge me the same way. It is human nature. It is a joy to find people who know your story and love you anyway.

It's impossible to list all of those who have encouraged me to tell a story. My mom and grandmother urged me to write when I was young, but I told them I hadn't lived enough yet. They are gone now, and somehow I'm old enough for Social Security. I've lost a spouse, raised a beautiful son, and had the privilege of learning how to live and love again. With less time ahead of me than behind me, it's finally time to tell a story. Buddy, my fictional character, has been in my mind and heart for years. I hope I honor him and Mags by creating a world for them.

My siblings have traveled with me throughout this journey; somehow, we've weathered this great adventure. This novel is dedicated to them.

Made in United States
North Haven, CT
14 December 2024

62511167R00174